The Wrong Envelope

Liz Treacher

First published 2018 by Liz Treacher
Tollich, Skelbo, Dornoch, IV25 3QQ.

ISBN: 978-0-9955877-3-1

Cover design and typesetting by Raspberry Creative Type, Edinburgh

Contents

The Mole

It was the most magnificent mole. Bernard couldn't take his eyes off it. It nestled in the nape of a long pale neck, which emerged elegantly out of a prim blouse and disappeared into a tight blonde bun. But whose neck? The young lady who owned the mole was facing away from him, talking to a friend on the other side of her. She must have boarded the train at Salisbury without him noticing – and now she was deep in conversation and he still hadn't seen her face. He looked out of the window, but there was the mole again, reflected in the glass of the railway carriage. Ravishing. So ravishing that he suddenly wanted to touch it. Bernard shoved his hands deep into the pockets of his trousers and looked around for a distraction.

The only other passenger in the compartment was an elderly woman dressed from head to toe in black. She sat opposite Bernard, engrossed in a book, although she looked up occasionally as if weighing him up. The long black skirt, the lacy black bodice and the large hat with its ink-black feathers all conspired to give the impression of an enormous crow, or perhaps a dark cloud threatening rain. Bernard focused instead on an advertisement on the wall, for a French wine called Moseloro. Just looking at the picture of the tall, elegant bottle made him thirsty. He looked away then back again. Moseloro. He shifted in his seat, inadvertently catching sight of the mole again as he did so. Moseloro, or was it

Moleloro? The old lady looked up and glared at him. Had she seen him eyeing the wine, or the mole? He seized the opportunity.

'Do you drink it?' he asked her pleasantly.

'I beg your pardon?' she took off her spectacles and stared at him.

'Moseloro,' he continued cheerfully, squinting at the advertisement, 'does not create flatulence, or bile.'

'Well, really!' she exclaimed, looking to the two chatterboxes to support her in her consternation. But they hadn't heard him and carried on talking. The old lady returned to her book, using it to shield her face from any further eye contact.

Bernard decided to go to the lavatory. That way he could hopefully have a good look at the mole lady on the way back to his seat. He jumped up, almost hitting his head on the luggage rack, and bounded out of the compartment into the swaying corridor. En route he passed the advertisement for Moseloro; close up the wine looked even more inviting. In the WC, he glanced in the mirror above the wash-basin, inspecting his bushy red hair and round, weather-beaten face. His eyes were a bit puffy – too many late nights probably. He grinned, revealing a pink tongue and large, creamy teeth. Then he admired his outfit – a blue cotton shirt mostly hidden by a beige knitted gilet and a brown linen jacket thrown over his shoulders. At his neck, a blue and beige cotton scarf was tied in a chaotic knot. He looked quite the 'artiste'.

He sprang out of the lavatory and walked back down the corridor to the compartment. He hoped the two girls would now be facing him, but they were huddled together talking and their faces were still hidden. The one without the mole wearing a fashionable cloche hat with a curl of hair peeping out of it. The only visible facial feature was a rather large nose but her white dress was very up-to-date: four apron tunics, dotted with cherries, drooping like petals over a straight skirt.

The one with the mole had no hat, but her face was concealed from view because she had put a pretty hand up in front of it and appeared to be whispering. Perhaps she was talking about him? Bernard started humming as he passed, but the girls didn't seem to notice – surely they had registered him by now? He reached his seat, swung himself into it and carried on assessing the mole lady. She was definitely the more old-fashioned of the two, in a black-and-white plaid skirt and a crisp white blouse with a lacy collar. The outfit was more 1915 than 1920, but it suited her somehow. He glanced down – the skirt was too long to reveal much more than her slim ankles, but he had the feeling that, further up, her legs were sturdy, muscly even. Perhaps she had been a land-girl in the war? If only he could engage her in conversation.

'Ho-hum!' he said loudly, but she didn't hear him and the only result was that the black widow raised her book higher and closer to her face.

Bernard sighed and looked out of the window. The mole moved slowly over the landscape, disappearing into tunnels and reappearing again. His eyes followed its progress but his thoughts returned to earlier that day when, over lunch at Claridges, Mr Carruthers had explained, for the hundredth time, why he was sending Bernard to Devon.

'You need to buckle down and concentrate,' he said, tapping the ash of his cigar on the side of his cheese plate. 'London is too distracting for you. You'll never be ready in time if you stay here. Hollybrook is charming and the house delightful – and quiet. Nothing to do but paint.'

'I can't paint if I'm not inspired,' Bernard mumbled.

'Yes you can,' his agent insisted. 'Anyway, you will be inspired – the messy hedgerows, the rugged coastline, the sea tumbling in.' He caught a waiter's eye and gestured for the bill.

'And no girls,' Bernard added sourly.

'And absolutely no girls, Bernard.'

The door of the compartment opened.

'Tickets please!' A small, bearded man in his late forties limped in, one leg splaying awkwardly. The ladies stopped their chatter and started looking in their bags. The mystery girl fished for her ticket at the bottom of a small velvet purse. How old was she? Twenty-two? Twenty-three? While she was too busy to notice, Bernard took the opportunity to stare. Her neck was bent right over; the mole was tantalisingly close and its owner preoccupied. Surely she wouldn't feel it? A quick touch. A brush of skin on skin. A touch so light it would be like a tiny fly landing on her neck. Perhaps he could be a butterfly? His hand slid out of his trouser pocket and across the aisle. His middle finger stretched out, anticipating the firm knob of flesh, darker in the centre and possibly softer too. Bernard's hand shook slightly and in this moment of hesitation he was undone.

'What do you think you're playing at?' The other girl had spotted him and she nudged her friend sharply. 'I say, Evie, watch out – that chap is trying to touch your neck.'

The mole owner swung round and clapped her hand to her neck, covering her mole completely. 'What on earth were you doing?' she demanded, her pale face blushing to the roots of her blonde hair, her blue eyes wide with indignation, her small mouth open.

Evie. As he jumped up to apologise, he silently turned the name over on his tongue.

'I'm so sorry,' he smiled at her. 'It's just, it's just,' he searched desperately for a plausible explanation. 'I thought you had a spider on your neck and I wanted to brush it off.'

It was a ridiculous excuse and no sooner had he said it than the old lady opposite started warbling: 'A spider, a spider!' and holding a handkerchief up to her face.

Evie went redder and her friend, who was far less attractive, bit her lip. The ticket inspector spluttered.

'It was just a small one,' Bernard tried to reassure the wailing woman.

'How dare you!' hissed Evie. She looked furious.

Bernard felt the situation slipping away from him. May as well be hung for a sheep. 'Don't worry,' he said, nodding mischievously at the old lady, 'it wasn't a black widow!'

The octogenarian sobbed into her handkerchief.

Bernard was a tall man and the ticket collector pulled himself up to his full height in order to confront him. 'Sir, I'm afraid we cannot tolerate this sort of behaviour on the London and South Western Railway. I must ask you to leave the train at the next station. You have caused quite enough trouble.'

Bernard felt almost relieved. He reached up to the luggage rack, pulled down his tatty leather suitcase, bowed to the three ladies and started to follow the limping inspector towards the door of the carriage. A glance back saw the two young ladies comforting the older one. Evie looked up and her eyes flashed; Bernard turned and hurried away.

A few minutes later he was put off on an empty platform at Crewkerne.

'You may need another ticket,' said the inspector darkly. He started to pull the heavy train door closed and then stopped. 'Were you in the war?' he asked.

'Yes, and no,' said Bernard, truly apologetic this time. 'I didn't actually see any action. I was still—' but the train door had shut.

Yes, Bernard was in the war, but no, he didn't make it to France. He was at a training camp outside Saffron Walden on Armistice Day. Fortunately for him – or not. As the train pulled away from the station, and with a two-hour wait for the next one, Bernard wished, and not for the first time, that he had contributed something of note to the conflict. There seemed to be an endless number of wounded men who somehow sniffed out his lack of actual war service. He would have fought. But he didn't. He couldn't. He was, as usual, too late. He had fallen off the roof of the Slade just weeks before war started and fractured his pelvis in three places. This student dare had led to months in hospital and a prolonged recuperation. He was only passed fit for service in the August of 1918 and it was all over before he was due to leave for the trenches.

His plunge from the top of the Slade had led to his expulsion from Art School, but it hadn't stopped him painting. All those years laid up allowed him to hone his natural talents and he was now an up-and-coming artist. Yes, people bought his pictures, he had an agent and a gallery and an exhibition in five weeks' time. But the critics didn't take him seriously. They always praised him politely, but never sounded excited. Perhaps they saw through him like the war veterans did.

'Ho-hum,' sighed Bernard. He carried his suitcase over to one of the benches and heaved it up onto the peeling wooden seat. Then he straightened up and looked around. The few passengers who alighted from the train had scattered, like midges on the wind, and the platform was deserted. He popped his head into the waiting room. Empty. He wandered along the platform, right to the end, where the stone slabs of the platform edge sloped away into a patch of waving willowherb. He looked down the track, back towards London, his eyes following the slow convergence of the two rails, trying to pinpoint the spot where they merged into a single dot on the horizon. As soon as he had located the point, the two rails seemed to spring out of it again and hurtle back towards him – two lines from the past, racing into the present. Bernard turned and looked the other way, towards his future destination, but as it left the station the railway bent sharply to the left, concealing from view the journey to come.

Colyton

After her assailant was put off the train at Crewkerne, Evie stared moodily out of the window. She had always hated her mole and the fact that a stranger on a train had reached out to touch it was mortifying. That he had reclassified it as a spider was intolerable. On the journey from Crewkerne to Seaton Junction, while she pretended to watch the landscape, Evie felt the mole come to life. It started creeping backwards and forwards across her neck then, as if exhausted by its efforts, it began throbbing in the most painful way. Was it growing now? Would it soon be bigger than her neck? She inwardly cursed the man, whoever he was, who had been so cruel in such a light-hearted manner.

Her friend, Cassie, was still engaged in small talk with the elderly lady who had been so upset at the mention of a spider, but from time to time she looked over at Evie and tried to give her little smirks. Cassie loved a joke, especially when it was at someone else's expense. Evie decided to ignore her friend's sparkling eyes and concentrate on the view. But in the window, she kept seeing the reflection of Cassie's sleek brown bob and long neck and the long neck kept turning towards the window, trying to catch her attention. Cassie and Evie had been good friends for years but, shortly before the war, Cassie's father inherited a large house and a small fortune from a distant uncle, so the family moved to London. Almost every time they met up, Evie noticed something different about

Cassie; her shorter dresses, the way she cut her hair. She seemed awash with money, spending her days browsing round the London shops, whereas Evie had to work. For four years now, she had worked as a post lady. When the two friends wanted to see each other, it was usually Cassie that made the pilgrimage back to Devon as Evie had very little time off. Today they had met in Salisbury and looked at hats and now they were heading home.

As soon as they got off the train at Seaton Junction to catch the branch line to Colyton, Cassie started giggling and she was still giggling when they walked up the drive to North Lodge, where Evie lived. Evie had tried to join in and laugh off the incident but she just couldn't see the funny side. Cassie was the sort of girl who didn't let things lie and Evie was almost regretting inviting her to stay.

'Wait till we tell your parents!' Cassie gasped.

'I'd rather we didn't,' said Evie firmly.

'Didn't tell them what?' Evie's father emerged from his potting shed, a trowel in one hand, an uprooted geranium in the other. Mr Brunton was a keen gardener, but if he was pleased to see two young flowers appear in his garden he didn't show it. He rarely looked pleased to see anyone. A tall man with a pronounced stoop, Mr Brunton was a retired solicitor. He had spent thirty-five years hunched over his clients' papers and now he intended to spend the rest of his life in his garden hunched over the asparagus.

'So, what did you not want to tell me?' With a slight nod to Cassie, Mr Brunton turned his full attention to his daughter.

Evie blushed. 'Oh, it's nothing, just a silly thing that happened on the train.'

'And what exactly happened on the train?'

Cassie breathlessly repeated the story and Mr Brunton listened impassively. When she had finished he pronounced his verdict: 'A conscientious objector no doubt, I've met the type before.' Then he waved his trowel, causing a few soily roots to fall on his gardening trousers. 'Well, Mother and tea await you inside.' He glanced at the homeless geranium: 'I'll be in shortly.'

Evie turned towards the kitchen, followed by Cassie, who hoped for a better reception indoors. She always found Mr Brunton's lukewarm welcome rather disheartening, but Evie's mother would surely be pleased to see her.

'Goodness! You're here already!' Mrs Brunton looked almost alarmed when the two girls trooped in. 'You've caught me red-handed,' she confessed, pulling off her apron to reveal a flowery dress; nervously touching her grey bun and tucking loose strands of hair behind her ears. 'It's funny how everything takes longer than you think. I nipped into town to get some cream for the scones, but then I met Mrs Brown and we started chatting—' she broke off and glanced at Evie. 'And here I am again, rabbiting on, instead of welcoming you. Cassandra! It's lovely to see you again!' She offered a plump rosy cheek to Cassie who gave it a little peck. 'I wondered if we should have tea outside. It's a lovely day but Mr Brunton hates finding wasps in the jam.'

Cassie started to laugh and then realised it wasn't a joke.

'Inside or out, what do you think, girls, I can't decide.'

'In,' said Evie with a definite tone in her voice.

'If you think in is better, then in it will be!' Evie's mother gave a little giggle. 'You girls go through to the parlour. I'll fill the teapot. I think you like Earl Grey, is that right Cassandra?'

'I prefer Lapsang, but if you don't have any—'

'Lapsang, of course! And I was so sure it was Earl Grey.' A cloud of disappointment seemed to descend on Mrs Brunton.

'I like Earl Grey too.'

'Do you? Do you really?' Mrs Brunton looked at Cassie with worried eyes.

'We'll go through,' said Evie, steering her friend out of the kitchen.

Cassie had forgotten how pokey the Brunton's parlour was. A faded sofa and lampshade were crammed in beside the window, while two armchairs, recently re-covered in a loud flowery material, loomed menacingly over a coffee table. She made for an armchair, hoping it would be better sprung than she remembered the sofa to be.

'That's Daddy's chair,' said Evie, apologetically.

'You've had it re-covered,' observed Cassie, wondering if re-covered was the right word for the florid effect. 'The material looks rather—'

'—Reasonably priced?' Mr Brunton finished the sentence for her as he came into the room. He slid into the chair, folded his long legs under the coffee table and picked up the newspaper.

'Bright,' said Cassie, but she said it quietly. She sat down on the sofa, feeling the seat cushion, already flat, deflate further.

'I expect it'll fade, eventually,' said Evie, doubtfully. She plonked herself down on the sofa beside her friend, causing a small cloud of dust to rise into the air. Cassie instinctively put her hand to her nose to catch a sneeze.

Mr Brunton's face appeared round the side of his newspaper. 'I hope you don't suffer from hay fever, Cassandra, because if so you've come at the wrong time of year.' The emphasis was on *the wrong time*.

'No, I don't,' said Cassie quickly, but his words hung in the air, beside the dancing dust.

Mrs Brunton bumbled in with the tea tray, bumping into the furniture like a disorientated moth. Mr Brunton seemed distracted by something in his newspaper, but Evie jumped up and took the tray from her mother.

'There's never enough room to put anything down,' sighed Mrs Brunton, as her daughter distributed the cups and saucers between the coffee table and the windowsill. Mr Brunton continued reading.

'It all looks lovely,' said Cassie, determined to combat Mr Brunton's disinterest with an enthusiasm she didn't usually feel for scones.

'I only hope it will be,' said Mrs Brunton, passing her a plate.

'I always look forward to your blackcurrant jam,' Cassie smiled, graciously accepting the plate, avoiding Mrs Brunton's anxious eyes.

'A particularly good year for blackcurrants,' announced Mr Brunton, putting down his newspaper to open the jam pot, 'but otherwise the garden has rather suffered from the unseasonably hot weather.'

Cassie recognised this as his one and only conversational gambit, but she had absolutely no interest in gardening.

'Am I sleeping in the piano room again?' she asked instead.

'I'm afraid so,' said Evie. 'We've made a bed up for you. I hope it'll be all right.'

'It'll be fine,' said Cassie, with a magnanimous smile. She glanced at Mr Brunton, who had picked up the paper again and was busy turning the pages.

'You are a brick for putting up with our eccentric guest-room!' said Mrs Brunton.

'Talking of eccentrics, we met one on the train,' Cassie ventured mischievously.

'Oh?'

Mr Brunton ruffled his newspaper and Evie winced as Cassie took the opportunity of repeating the mole story, this time with one or two embellishments. Cassie thought Evie's mother would be horrified, but as she listened a ray of hope seemed to flash across her face. She picked up the teapot and sat quietly, gazing out of the window, lost in thought.

'Is there any more tea, dear?' asked Mr Brunton.

'I'll refill the pot.' Mrs Brunton got up and, like a feather in a stream, drifted out of the room.

The others sat quietly, chewing on their scones. A few moments later, the silence was broken by someone playing a short hesitant scale in the room across the hallway. This was followed by a more confident arpeggio, then the opening bars of 'Für Elise' could be heard wafting out of the piano room.

Mr Brunton sighed and put down his newspaper. 'Tea?' he called.

'Just waiting for the kettle,' said a small voice. The music stopped.

Mrs Brunton reappeared with the teapot but Mr Brunton had disappeared back behind his newspaper. Cassie caught Evie's eye and gave her a conspiratorial smile. Evie smiled back, but it wasn't the wide, carefree smile she had used on the train when they had gossiped and giggled all the way from Salisbury to Crewkerne. It was the tense, furtive smile she had used after Crewkerne – after their encounter with that peculiar chap.

Later that evening, after Mr and Mrs Brunton had turned in for the night and Evie, exhausted from her adventure on the train, had followed them upstairs, Cassie retired to the piano room. But she didn't go straight to bed. Instead she turned the tiny key in the lock of the French window and slipped out into the garden. She walked quietly along the path that skirted the flint and red-bricked house and out of the back gate into the dusky lanes of Colyton. It was still light but the sky was a heavy blue, and an occasional bat swooped silently overhead.

It was strange how she still knew the place like the back of her hand. She had lived in London for six years now, but she could have found her way around town with her eyes shut. It was nice to stroll along the empty streets with their old houses squashed together, higgledy-piggledy, like too many teeth. During the day, she shied away from walking through the town; there were just too many people who knew her and who asked after her parents. But a night-time promenade was solitary and exciting. Meandering along the narrow lanes was like turning the clock back to an earlier period of her life.

Cassie passed St Andrew's Church, with its octagonal tower of honey-coloured stone, and wandered along to the post office where Evie worked. She normally feigned indifference to Evie's job so Evie didn't talk about it much. But tonight, while no one was watching, Cassie peered into the dark windows of the sorting office and played the 'what if' game.

What if her father hadn't inherited and she had stayed in Devon? What if she had had to work when she left school? What would she have done? With so many men away at the war she would have had plenty of opportunity to find a vacancy and earn her living. Perhaps she would have been a post lady too. Perhaps she would have got the job and not Evie.

Not that she was envious of Evie's position; she had no desire to give up her life of leisure for a meagre salary. She was just curious, that was all. Nor was she jealous of Evie's looks. But it was irritating how Evie had a knack of attracting attention. The incident on the train was just another example of the way she could turn a man's head without trying and, even more infuriatingly, without noticing. Cassie had been aware of the young man from the outset. She had watched him gazing at her friend's neck for quite some time before his thwarted attempt to touch it. Evie had been furious. Would she have been as cross, if it had been her – if she was the one with blonde hair, blue eyes and a mole?

She turned for home. Flinty cottages with thatched fringes flanked the quiet road. Cassie reached out and ran her hands along their walls as she walked, feeling the changing textures of the stones, some smooth, others rough and knobbly. She could never roam the streets like this in London. Returning to Devon gave her the opportunity to float through the lanes of her past, like a ghost. She stood for a few moments on the bridge over the Coly, listening to the river. Then she quietly opened the back gate and tiptoed across the lawn towards the piano room.

Hollybrook

When Bernard eventually arrived at his destination it was nearly nine o'clock. He had waited an age at Crewkerne and then he missed his connection at Seaton Junction and had to hang about for the next one. When he finally reached Hollybrook, the sun had set. He fished around in his pocket for Carruthers' scribbled map before setting off up the narrow Devon lanes. The air was heady with the scent of flowers and he felt slightly giddy with hunger after his long journey. How stupid he had been to get himself thrown off the train. He could have been here hours ago. Still, he was here now and the place seemed charming. Tall trees and hedges lined the lanes and ivy scrambled all over them, covering trunks and branches. The evening breeze lifted the leaves and they rustled like the wings of a thousand insects.

A sudden bend in the road and there was High View. It towered above the other thatched cottages in the village, its slate roof and tall chimneys piercing the blue dusk. The house's whitewashed exterior was broken up by small-paned windows: downstairs they winked in the last of the light; upstairs they snuggled cosily under the low eaves like roosting birds. A short curving drive led to a small porch. The front door had been left open for him and he went into a dark hallway. A flight of stairs led off from the hall and Bernard dashed up, plonked his suitcase on the bed of the first bedroom and rushed to French windows. The handle was stiff but he forced it open and walked out onto a balcony, breathing in the cool air. He could see the driveway curling back round the corner towards the road and beyond it the thatched roofs of other houses in the village.

He ran downstairs again, along a narrow corridor and into a large drawing room with more French windows looking onto a darkening garden. A sofa, chaise longue and two armchairs were covered with sheets and more sheets were lying on the wooden floor. Leaning against the wall by the fireplace were twenty blank canvases, two easels, a box of brushes and his paints. Carruthers must have sent them down earlier in the week. Bernard grimaced at the sight of them. 'Rumpelstiltskin,' he muttered, banging the door shut and heading for the kitchen.

On the way, another door caught his eye. He turned the handle and peeped inside to find a small room housing an upright piano and a bookcase of music. Hoorah – a piano. He continued towards the kitchen. There on the side was a loaf of homemade bread, a pat of butter, a jar of jam, a pail of milk and a note: *Welcome to High View. I hope this will do you tonight. Back in the morning. Mrs Wilson.*

The sight of the food made Bernard feel ravenous and he set to work straight away, cutting great chunks of bread, smearing them with jam, gobbling them down. He sprawled at the table, amused that his previous meal had been lunch at Claridges. Then hunger gave way to exhaustion and he headed back up the stairs and threw himself on the bed. He would unpack tomorrow.

Or perhaps the day after, because the morning brought sun streaming in at the many paned windows, bathing everything in a heavenly light and Bernard couldn't wait to start painting. He ran down to the kitchen to find Mrs Wilson had been and gone. The remains of his supper had been washed up and there was fresh bread and milk on the table, plus a saucepan of some sort of soup. The range had been lit, and he opened the oven door to find a chicken casserole slowly simmering inside. Wonderful: Breakfast, lunch and supper all provided. He snatched up a tray, plonked the new loaf on it with some butter and repaired to the drawing room. He pushed open the door with his elbow and put the tray down on the fireplace, then he opened the French windows and went out into the garden.

Before him lay a lawn, punctuated with flower beds, all bursting with colour. To the left, a vegetable patch and then a gentle hill covered with lush green grass stretching upwards towards blue sky. To the right was a garden wall and beyond it an open view of soft undulating fields bordered with dark hedgerows. Bernard beamed. This was the place. His breakfast quite forgotten, he hurriedly unpacked two canvases and set one up on one easel and one on the other. They balanced precariously on the stones of the patio while he darted between them, daubing paint here and there, standing back to admire, daubing again, mixing, diluting, all the while humming with the intensity of an oversized bumblebee.

This humming was an important part of Bernard's creative process. He hummed to summon his daemons. And once he had started humming, once his pursed lips were vibrating ten to the dozen, the daemons always came. Today they were disguised as faeries, hidden in the roses and the gladioli. They heard Bernard and they flew to him, landing in his hair, still ruffled from sleep, whispering in his ear. The daemons told him exactly what to do and how to do it. Sometimes they dictated instructions with a raspy whisper, sometimes they sent a clear image of the finished work straight to his mind where it sat gleaming in his inner eye. Then he just had to copy it onto the canvas. It was all astonishingly easy, almost too easy. He never bothered to work on the image his daemons presented; he just copied it. Some critics said this gave his paintings a rather two-dimensional effect, but no matter. He couldn't spend long on anything – there was always another idea buzzing in his head and the next painting awaited.

A bicycle bell. Bernard wiped his hands on his trousers and trotted round to the front of the house. There, standing in the driveway, looking in her postbag, was the lady from the train, the one with the marvellous mole. Gone was the flared plaid skirt and lacy blouse, instead she wore a Post Office uniform: blue serge skirt, dark blue coat, blue straw hat and sturdy black boots. She looked up, saw Bernard and gave a start.

Bernard sensed her discomfort and acted quickly. 'Evie,' he said, coming forward to greet her, smiling, holding his hand out.

'Miss Brunton,' she corrected.

'Miss Brunton, how lovely to see you again! Allow me to introduce myself! I am—'

'Bernard Cavalier,' said Evie drily, glancing at the letter she was holding, avoiding his handshake.

She had pronounced cavalier like the adjective.

'It's actually a French name,' Bernard was quick to point out. 'E – A. Pronounced Caval E – A, like the French knight.'

'I thought that was *Chevalier*.'

'So you are my post lady,' Bernard said, ignoring her riposte, continuing to smile at her.

'Not your personal post lady, but I am the local post lady. I will bring any mail for you and take anything you want posted, providing it has a stamp on it.'

'How many posts a day?'

'Three – the first is around seven o'clock.'

'What? In the morning! I won't be up for that!' he laughed.

'Then there's a midday and afternoon post,' continued Evie, ignoring his joke. 'Post from outside the area is usually delivered at midday.'

'So, I'll see you tomorrow lunchtime,' he beamed.

'Only if you have mail,' said Evie and with that she handed over the letter, turned her bicycle round and cycled off down the drive without looking back.

'Well I never,' said Bernard, half to himself and half to the garden. He stood and watched her pedalling up the hill, all the while flicking the letter with his finger. He was in no hurry to open it. He knew it would be from Phoebe.

Bernard tended to live life the way he painted. When embarked on a new painting he would excitedly splash on colour, totally absorbed in his canvas. Then he would turn away, forget all about it and move swiftly on to something else. He was apt to do the same with people. This exuberant attentiveness, followed by forgetfulness, was considered by some as a lack of sensitivity, but Bernard was not really an unkind man. And this was why he was still writing to Phoebe. He had met her during his time at the Saffron Walden training camp. The local girls were encouraged to write to one of the soldiers and Phoebe was allotted to him. She was the daughter of a vicar and very witty. Her entertaining missives helped him endure the dull weeks of training in the cold Essex mud. They met a few times, went for walks around Saffron Walden and consumed crumpets in the town's tea rooms.

It was an innocent friendship, particularly as Phoebe, though tall and thin, was not especially pretty. But Bernard liked her jokes and grew quite fond of her. When the war ended and the camp dispersed, they agreed to stay friends. Bernard liked Phoebe, but not in a romantic way. Their meetings were like the buttery crumpets – pleasant enough at the time but not worth dwelling on afterwards. This letter, like the many before it, stirred a vague guilt that she might feel differently. He sighed and went inside to open it.

82, Summerhill Road, Saffron Walden, Essex
Monday 26th July 1920

Dear Bernard,

Well, here you are in Devon! I imagine it seems very quiet after London. You must make sure you settle down and paint. Don't be distracted by the startling scenery and wander, lonely as a cloud, among the fields and hedgerows for which Devon is famous. You are hereby forbidden from: fishing, swimming, mushroom picking, loitering along lanes and absolutely barred from local tea shops. In fact, the only leisure you are allowed is writing to me – reporting back with a list of paintings finished (yes finished, not started and abandoned!)

I will reward your efforts with gossip from Saffron Walden – if there is any, which I very much doubt, but I mustn't undermine my own incentive. I shall reward you with a pleasant reply if you work hard and an unpleasant one if you don't (think wailing banshee at a writing desk!) I would draw you a picture of a carrot and a stick but firstly I can't draw and secondly you are, although stubborn, not a mule.

However, I sense you are wasting time reading this letter, so stop immediately and return to your studio.

I wish you luck and fortitude and remain,

Your sincere friend,

Phoebe

As he read Phoebe's letter, Bernard's mind drifted back to his meeting with Evie. She was cross; there was no doubt about that. Possibly crosser than cross. How could he win her over?

Spilling the Beans

If Bernard was pleasantly surprised to see Evie again, Evie was horrified to see Bernard. She cycled away cursing. It was as if he had followed her to continue his gloating and staring. She hoped he was only a very temporary resident in the area. High View was often let for short periods. Perhaps he would be gone in a few days? And such a rude man would have few friends and little mail; she might never have to see him again.

These thoughts occupied Evie as she cycled the mile uphill back to Colyton. The sorting office, post office and telephone exchange all shared the same building in Market Square, straight across the road from Colyton Grammar. She parked her bicycle outside and glanced over to the Tudor building where she had been at school. Funny how she hadn't gone far in life. Her job was based just a few yards from where she was educated and yet she felt like an intrepid adventurer when she set out with the post. Although there were three deliveries a day, she was only responsible for the midday and four o'clock rounds, so she could lie in and have a leisurely breakfast before putting on her uniform and heading for work on her bicycle. Home was dull but work was exciting and Evie was happy with her lot and with her nest egg, slowly growing in her Post Office savings account.

She went into the sorting office and handed in the letters she had been given by people on her round. These were sorted and franked and the ones for further afield were taken in a van down the narrow Devon lanes to meet the mail train at Axminster. Then she had a sandwich and a cup of tea while she waited for the four o'clock postbag.

As she slung the bag on her back, Evie wondered gloomily if there would be another letter for that unpleasant character. She glanced inside. Luckily there was very little post at all. She stirred the letters around with her hand. They all seemed to have local postmarks. Thank heavens. It didn't take long to deliver the post, return any letters to be posted to the sorting office and drop off her bag. Then she jumped back on her bicycle and headed for home.

As soon as she lifted the latch of the back gate of North Lodge, Cassie rushed round to greet her. She had endured a whole day of scones and geraniums and was very relieved her friend was back from work. She looked so pleased to see her that Evie suddenly wanted to spill the beans and share the secret.

'You'll never guess who's staying in Hollybrook!'

'Oh let me try, I love a game.' Cassie thought for a minute. 'Someone I know from London?'

'No.'

'Someone we haven't seen for years?'

'No.'

'Let me see.' Suddenly a cloud crossed Cassie's face. 'Not the mole toucher?'

Evie couldn't help laughing. 'Spot on! Bernard Cavalier, also known as the mole toucher! He's staying in High View. I think he's an artist – he was covered in paint.'

Cassie looked rather dumbfounded by the news. 'And did he try again?' There was a strange tension in her voice.

'Certainly not,' said Evie, colouring slightly. 'Anyway, I barely acknowledged him.'

Cassie huffed. She was clearly niggled by something and Evie assumed it was concern for her.

'Please don't tell my parents,' she begged.

Cassie shrugged. 'Well, if you insist, I'll keep quiet.'

* * *

Cassie was staying with the Bruntons for two whole days. Halfway through day two she found herself at the kitchen table shelling peas with Mrs Brunton. The kitchen was quiet, just the tick of a clock and the pop, pop of the pea pods followed by the rattle of peas in the bowl. Mind numbing. Cassie glanced at the clock. Only two o'clock. Evie wouldn't be home till five.

'You're quiet today, dear.' Mrs Brunton's voice roused Cassie from her reverie.

'Am I? Sorry.'

'I know it's a bit dull staying here with the old folks while Evie's at work.'

'Actually, I'm a bit worried about Evie.'

'Oh?' Mrs Brunton put the pea pod she was holding back down on the table and looked at Cassie.

'It's nothing really.'

Mrs Brunton looked quite alarmed. 'But you must tell me if you're worried, it's important that we know.'

'Do you really think so? It's just she said I shouldn't mention it.'

'Do tell me,' said Mrs Brunton. 'It won't go any further, I promise.'

Cassie turned her own pea pod over and over in her hands.

'Well in that case I think it's more important to protect Evie than keep my word to her,' she began. 'On this occasion,' she added quickly.

'Good heavens!' gasped Mrs Brunton. 'What is this terrible secret?'

Cassie's cheeks flushed and her eyes sparkled with excitement. She let go of the pea pod, which bounced off the table top onto the floor, and moved closer to Evie's mother.

'The mole toucher is living in Hollybrook,' she whispered.

'The who?'

'The man on the train. He's on Evie's round.'

Cassie waited for guilt to descend on her, but it didn't. So, she had obviously been right to spill the beans. A problem shared was a problem halved. She sat back and watched the effect her comment had on Mrs Brunton.

'Well, I never,' said Mrs Brunton. 'Oh my goodness.'

But she didn't look dismayed. If anything, she looked almost hopeful.

'He's an artist.' Cassie played her trump card but Mrs Brunton didn't gasp.

'An artist,' she repeated, half to herself. She picked up the bowl of peas and went to the sink to rinse them under the tap. She had her back to Cassie but Cassie could see her face reflected in the window. It was a face full of thought. There was a trace of anxiety, but only a trace.

'I'd rather you didn't let on to Evie that I've told you,' Cassie said.

'Of course I won't, dear. Thank you for telling me.' Mrs Brunton turned and smiled at Cassie. 'I don't know what Mr Brunton will say,' she added in a voice that suggested she wasn't planning to mention it.

What a strange family, Cassie thought: an unsociable father who was completely detached from family life and a mother with no sense of responsibility. It was fortunate they lived in Devon; they wouldn't survive a day in London. Cassie sighed. Only one more day and she would be back in the capital.

Mrs Brunton had no desire to tell her husband about the mole toucher but, as the day wore on, she became increasingly uneasy. After all the man might not have honourable intentions and he was living on Evie's round.

'Do you think,' she began, as she sat up in bed that night, brushing her hair, 'do you think that someone who has a penchant for moles could be dangerous in any way?'

'So he's staying locally,' surmised Mr Brunton, not looking up from his book.

'Who?' asked his wife, playing dumb, amazed that he had so quickly grasped the nub of it.

He didn't bother to answer. Instead he closed his book and asked: 'Did Cassie tell you?'

'Yes.'

'Oh dear.'

'Why oh dear?'

'Because if it didn't matter, Evie would have told us.'

Mrs Brunton realised her husband was right. 'He's an artist,' she said.

'So he's posing as an artist,' said Mr Brunton. 'Oh dear,' he said again. He put down his book and turned off the bedside light, leaving Mrs Brunton to lie worrying in the dark.

Breaking the Ice

The very next day, Evie found another letter for Bernard Cavalier in her postbag. It had a London postmark. She hoped it brought bad news, and as she cycled towards Hollybrook she amused herself by imagining what this might be. Perhaps it was an unpaid bill, one that had gathered an enormous amount of interest. Or a poor return from his stockbroker, except he wasn't the type to have a stockbroker. Perhaps it was from his family doctor, warning he had caught a nasty bug for which there was no cure.

The darkness of this last fantasy shocked her. She wasn't in the habit of wishing unhappy endings on people. Clearly the man had got under her skin. No, she wouldn't let him. As she turned into the drive of High View, she decided that the best course of action would be to avoid him completely. Perhaps she could pop the letter through the letterbox and escape unnoticed. She quietly leaned her bicycle against the porch and crept to the front door. She silently opened the letterbox and slipped the letter in, holding on to one edge of it till the last possible moment so it would fall noiselessly to the floor. She waited for a soft swish as the letter hit the ground and gently shut the letterbox again. Then she turned, jumped on her bicycle and shot back down the drive.

'Ah, Miss Brunton!' Bernard Cavalier suddenly emerged from behind a bush near the entrance to the driveway.

He must have been standing there the whole time. What on earth had he been doing in the shrubbery?

'I was just admiring the view,' he explained, 'and watering the plants!'

Evie glanced around. There was no sign of a watering can. He was teasing her; how she hated him.

'You have a letter. Inside.'

'Terrific. And I have one for you.' Bernard fumbled around in the pocket of his painting trousers.

'Only if it has a stamp.'

'No need for that,' said Bernard cheerily and gave her a small cream envelope with *Miss Brunton* written on the front.

'Oh.' Evie swallowed her surprise and casually took the envelope from him, shoving it in her postbag with the others.

'I hope you will overlook my impudence,' said Bernard. Then with a slight bow he turned and disappeared into the house.

Once he had gone, Evie rescued the cream envelope and put it in the pocket of her jacket. Thank goodness Cassie was on her way back to London. She could quietly read the letter and then destroy it without anyone knowing. She could of course destroy it now, without reading it, but it would be useful to know what the enemy was thinking.

Evie decided to wait until she had delivered the four o'clock post before she opened the envelope. She had a suspicion the contents might throw her off her stride, and there was no way she was going to allow such an annoying man to affect her job.

The afternoon postbag was lighter than usual and she soon finished her deliveries and returned to the sorting office. She handed in the stamped letters to be franked, hung up her postbag, got back on her bicycle and cycled home. The house looked quiet. Mrs Brunton appeared to be out and Mr Brunton was in the garden, weeding.

Evie let herself in through the back door. The late afternoon sun shone through the window, illuminating a vase of flowers, casting blue shadows on the scrubbed kitchen table. She picked up an apple from the fruit bowl and went upstairs to her bedroom. It was small but comfortable with a large sash window overlooking the garden. There were two pictures: a watercolour of the cliffs at Beer and another of a small child playing with a dog. On one wall was a chest of drawers and a matching wardrobe, the dark wooden handles decorated with carvings of flowers. On the chest of drawers, an old mirror caught and reflected the sun-lit garden. Opposite was a single bed with a white iron bedstead and a patchwork eiderdown. The mattress was a bit saggy and squeaked when she flopped onto it. She fished the letter out of her jacket pocket and opened the cream envelope.

High View, Hollybrook, Devon
Wednesday 28th July 1920

Dear Miss Brunton,

Please forgive the formality of this letter but I feel it is the most tactful way to approach a rather delicate matter. I am writing to apologise for my appalling behaviour on the train. I don't know what came over me. Perhaps I was just nervous about the journey to a strange place. London men are very set in their ways and unused to change. Your lovely mole somehow offered a beacon of hope, like a lighthouse beckoning to my tiny barque, tossed on a choppy sea.

I realise this explanation may not help and may instead lead you to despise me more than ever. However, I think we both know that I would never have behaved in such a way if I had imagined we were ever to meet again. What I mean to say is, you are entitled to punish me for my crime but not for living in Hollybrook. That was my agent's doing and I am only obeying orders. I have an agent – a Mr Carruthers – because I am a rudderless artist. I need direction or I never get round to doing any work. He has sent me to Devon so I can paint undistracted.

And now for the good news: the house is not mine – only rented. In fact, I will be here for just five weeks, preparing for an art exhibition and I will be far too busy to ever annoy you again. However, you are my post lady and I will see no one else but my housekeeper and I haven't seen her yet. It would be so nice if we could exchange the odd pleasantry – or at the very least, have no awkwardness between us. I hope you will consider it possible to forgive a silly prank and make a foolish artist happy.

Yours sincerely,

Bernard Cavalier

Evie finished the letter, screwed it up into a tight ball and tossed it under the bed. How could a man have been born so annoying and how could she have been so unfortunate as to meet him? So, he was staying five weeks – she could hardly bear it. She slumped on her counterpane and sighed with exasperation. The mole was throbbing again.

* * *

While Evie was getting over her letter from Bernard, he was stretched out on a chaise longue in his make-shift studio, reading the letter she had delivered to him.

19, The Mansions, Berkeley Square, Mayfair, London, SW.
Wednesday 28th July 1920

Hello Old Chap,

Well, how is it? Are you still alive in one of the most dismally distant corners of our glorious isle? Are you lying weeping in a darkened room, wishing you were back in the fair capital, or are you out meeting the natives? Or, heaven forbid, are you actually painting? Be careful how you reply, Carruthers will be asking me. I'll see him on Saturday at the Summer Show and he will be inquiring, of that there is no doubt.

What a pity you are so ill-disciplined and have to be sent away from the fun in order to get anything done. I miss your sweet little face at the RAC club and no one can hold their champagne like you can. I drank Miles under the table last night. It was a pathetic performance and then he was sick in the cab on the way home and it cost me two bob to pay off the driver.

Other news from London – Milly and Dorothy have both cut their hair. Milly gets away with it, but Dorothy looks even more like a horse now. Poor girl, it's the teeth I think. I told them both they looked marvellous. Dorothy's mother has designs on me – she's asked me to dinner again – that's twice in as many months. I said I was planning to come and see you so I wasn't free. I'm not coming of course, we both know I'm allergic to fresh air and I detest clotted cream. Anyway, you need to get on with preparing for your show.

Now for some gossip – Benedict, as in your adopted father, has been seen in public with Penelope Armstrong on more than one occasion. I thought he was keen on Molly Grayling but he seems to have switched allegiance. I saw them together at the opera last Tuesday and then lunching at Brown's yesterday. I don't suppose he's written? Do let me know if you hear in the affirmative. I might have a stab at Molly myself.

Well old chum, I must go and meet Mother, she's been moaning she never sees me and has reeled me in with the promise of a weekend in Brighton. I hope to catch up with young Philip while I'm there – if I can escape her clutches for an evening. If I do, we will toast you and any Devon milk-maids you encounter.

Do write soon!

Your dear pal, who you are no doubt missing dreadfully,

Toby

Bernard smiled and, without getting up off his chair, he fished around on the floor for a piece of watercolour paper and a pencil.

High View, Hollybrook, Devon
Thursday 29th July 1920

Dearest Tobe old bean,

Many thanks for your letter. Life in Devon is top-notch. Everything is charming – the house, the garden, the locals – all definitely up to London standards. The weather is delightful with plenty of sun and the views here are splendid. I'm sure I'll find lots to paint once I get going. For now I'm settling in and acclimatising to the Devon lifestyle.

Funny to think I was dreading this enforced exile. In fact, as soon as I boarded the train I felt the excitement of a really good adventure. The wildlife here is beautiful and there is one delightful mole which I will tell you about on my return.

What a pity about Milly, I can't abide a girl with short hair. Regarding Molly – my advice is don't touch her. If Benedict has had a good swipe at her, there'll be nothing left.

Well old chum, I must return to thinking about my show (so don't forget to tell Carruthers when you see him on Saturday).

Be good!

Bernard

Bernard folded the letter and let it drop to the floor beside him. He fumbled in his waistcoat for his pipe and matches and relit some half-smoked tobacco. Then he put his head back, inhaled deeply and blew smoke rings into the room. They floated over his easel, with its half-finished canvas, filling the air with the pleasant smell of pipe tobacco. It could have been the RAC club, except it wasn't. Not a bit of it. Instead of leather chairs and dark wall-paper, flowery sofas and French windows. Instead of the murmur of male voices, the buzz of insects, bird song and the distant sound of cattle. He wasn't missing London as much as he thought he would; he would return to the social whirl soon enough. This stay was turning into a respite – a reprieve. London girls were exhausting, so hard to please. Here he could be a hermit – a hermit with a charming post lady.

The Shed

Bernard was not altogether confident that his letter to his charming post lady would receive a positive response. When he woke the next morning, he found himself regretting the lighthouse metaphor. It had been unnecessary and might be wrongly interpreted. It was just possible Evie would be crosser with him now. After breakfast, he found himself lurking in the garden again, hoping to see her and apologise for his letter of apology. It was no good waiting in the house, he had seen how furtively she put his post through the box – he would never hear her from the drawing room. It was difficult to know when she would appear and Bernard decided to explore the garden while he was waiting. He examined the flower beds and an extensive raspberry patch and then he came across a little shed. It was set against the garden wall and was made of bricks, with a low wooden door painted a charming blue.

Curious as ever, he lifted the latch and, stooping down, squeezed into a small dark space with an earth floor and brick walls. He could see the shapes of gardening tools in the gloom. As he looked around he heard the wooden door swing shut with a click behind him. The shed went pitch black except for a thin beam of light shining through a hole in the wood. Feeling suddenly claustrophobic, Bernard tried to push the door open again. It was stuck. He looked for a latch, but there wasn't one on the inside. He was trapped.

Bernard was not a slight man and, squashed between a rake and a roller, he felt like Alice in Wonderland. He could feel himself growing ever larger in a space that was getting smaller. One thing was certain: he wouldn't survive in here for long. He pushed against the door with all his might but it refused to budge.

'Help!' he called, 'Help!' But there was no one to hear his cries. The housekeeper wouldn't be back till tomorrow and the gardener was apparently on holiday. He realised he was totally dependent on his post lady coming to his rescue. He would have to stay very calm and very quiet and listen for the tick-tick of her bicycle wheel and then holler like mad and hope she heard him. But Evie would only come if he had post.

Bernard started to sweat and his breathing grew quick and shallow. Was he expecting a letter? He racked his brains; Toby had written yesterday and Carruthers wasn't much of a letter writer. He couldn't think of anyone else who might write to him except Phoebe. Bernard knelt in the dark and prayed inwardly to his correspondent in Saffron Walden: 'Please Phoebe, please have written me a letter.' It was a ridiculously conditional prayer. He was praying that yesterday it was dull and wet in Saffron Walden and Phoebe, short of any other occupation, was reduced to staying indoors and writing to him, even though he still hadn't replied to her. Bernard let out an involuntary sob. This was too awful; how could he have got himself in such a pickle?

Ten minutes later, he was planning his own funeral. There would doubtless be quite a turnout – he had many acquaintances. Toby would give the eulogy, or Mr Carruthers. Bernard imagined Phoebe sniffing into a handkerchief and leaving before the tea afterwards. He could picture her on the train back to Saffron Walden, gazing out of a window lashed with rain. He wondered mournfully whether his paintings would increase or decrease in value once he was gone. Before he could decide, he heard the tick-tick of a bicycle on the gravel.

'Miss Brunton!' he shouted with all his might. 'Help me! Miss Brunton! Please help!'

After Bernard's sudden appearance from the shrubbery the day before, Evie had approached the house with caution; his disembodied shouts merely increased her suspicions. He was up to some trick again. She would ignore him, post the letter through the box and take off. But the shouting grew more desperate and Evie felt compelled to investigate. She pushed her bicycle over the lawn and followed the sound of his cries, until she reached the shed. As she stopped outside, there was a banging from the inside which made the wooden door shake.

'Is that you, Miss Brunton? Please help me!' Bernard moaned.

When she had inwardly cursed him the previous day, Evie could not have hoped for a quicker result. Here was misery indeed. How delicious. How delightful. She lay her bicycle on the grass and stood in front of the heaving shed, grinning from ear to ear. If Bernard was Alice, Evie was the Cheshire cat. She felt on fire with the power his predicament gave her. There were so many choices. She could turn around and leave him to suffer. She could sit silently all day and watch the shuddering door and ignore his pleas for help. Or she could humiliate him and then rescue him, which would humiliate him further.

'I will let you out if you correctly answer three questions,' called Evie.

'Anything, anything,' said the voice inside.

'Were you extraordinarily rude to me on the train?'

'Yes!' cried Bernard, eagerly.

'Was your letter merely a chance to insult me again?'

'No!' he said indignantly, despite his dark prison. 'I can't admit that.'

'Goodbye, Mr Cavalier!'

'Wait!'

There was no reply.

'Yes!' he shouted. 'Yes, Miss Brunton!'

'And are you an ill-bred, arrogant oaf with no manners?'

Her voice was very close to the door. She hadn't planned to go anywhere. She had tricked him. He didn't answer.

'I beg your pardon?'

'Yes,' he said sulkily.

'What are you?'

'An ill-bred, arrogant oaf with no manners!' He banged on the door.

'That's all very well, but you still haven't actually said you're sorry.'

'I'm sorry Miss Brunton. I'm so sorry. Really I am. Please, please let me out!' He was practically sobbing.

Evie took her time. She fiddled with the latch for a while before she lifted it and slowly pulled the door open. Bernard fell out, almost on top of her. His hands and arms were black from trying to force the door and there were streaks of dirt around his eyes. Evie gave a little start when she saw him: there was something so vulnerable about his bent body and filthy face.

Bernard was not a man to hold grudges. Some men might have been resentful that a lady had taken advantage of their predicament; if Bernard thought this, it was only for a second. Any bitter humiliation he felt passed quickly over his countenance, like a cloud racing across the sun, leaving him beaming. He was free from the dingy shed. He had been rescued by his valiant post lady. He was alive. The garden seemed to burst with life and colour and he wanted to hold everything close and breathe it in.

'How can I thank you?' he cried joyously.

'There's no need, it was nothing,' said his rescuer modestly.

'If you hadn't come—'

'With the noise you were making they would have heard you in Seaton!' she laughed.

Before he could stop himself, Bernard had grabbed Evie's small white hand in his large sooty one and was pumping it up and down. 'I do believe we have patched things up,' he grinned. 'Now you have rescued me you will have to accept my friendship.'

'Will I?' Evie said archly, but she was laughing.

'And you will call me Bernard and I will call you Evie,' said Bernard, quick to capitalise on the advancement in his fortune. 'Friends?'

'Friends,' agreed Evie as she withdrew her hand, wiped it on her skirt and picked up her bicycle.

'Come back soon!' called Bernard, as she rode back over the edge of the lawn.

'Only when you have post!'

She was gone. Bernard hastened into the kitchen. It was high time he replied to Phoebe.

Bernard's housekeeper always came early in the morning, long before he was awake. Mrs – whatever was her name again – was a good cook. Safely back in the kitchen after his adventure to the centre of the earth, Bernard tucked into today's lunch offering – carrot soup. Then he cleared a space on his kitchen table, rolled up his sleeves and got down to the serious business of writing to Phoebe. He carefully spread out her two letters. He felt enormous gratitude towards them. The first had brought Evie to him; the second, received this morning, had saved his life. His eyes darted between them, as if they were two canvases he was working on at once. He would ingest them, digest them and trot out a cheery reply – one that would ensure Phoebe wrote back promptly, without committing himself to always doing the same.

High View, Hollybrook, Devon
Friday 30th July 1920

Dear Phoebe,

I was delighted to receive your second letter this morning, but also embarrassed as I hadn't had a chance to reply to your first. Things have been a little hectic down here in Devon. As instructed, I have been working full pelt on my paintings and have had little leisure time to explore my surroundings or meet the locals.

Your letters, as always, both charmed and entertained me. Do keep them coming! I won't be able to reply to them all, but I will reply when I can – that is, when my work allows me. I'm sure that Saffron Walden is not as dull as you think. I hereby appoint you the town's chief correspondent, charged with updating far-flung individuals, like myself, with the goings on there. Please sniff out any bits of gossip and dispatch them to me, daily if possible! I have no newspaper and your letters will keep a hermetic artist in touch with reality. The price of tea, the results from the flower show, anything and everything will keep me in contact with the outside world beyond this dull backwater. And now I must return to the studio.

Do write soon! I know I am a rotten correspondent but I love getting your letters.

Your sincere friend,

Bernard

Bernard sat back and admired his handiwork. Then he folded the letter and slid it into an envelope. *Miss Phoebe Carson, 82, Summerhill Road, Saffron Walden, Essex*, he wrote on the front of it. He noticed a blob of carrot soup had smudged itself on the back. Drat. It would probably have seeped through to the letter itself. He couldn't be bothered to start again, so how to explain it? He drew an arrow from the blob and wrote *a blob of my burnt ochre paint*. But he couldn't bring himself to deceive to this degree. Above it he added *I wish I could say that it was* and below he wrote *but in fact it's carrot soup!* There, he was an honest man. An honest man who, after the morning's excitement, was much too tired to paint. He would wander into Hollybrook to find a postbox. Then he would lie in the garden, contemplating his next creation.

The Art Critic

Phoebe was not as prompt to reply as Bernard had hoped. The next day, from his bedroom window, he caught a glimpse of Evie cycling further up the hill. Nothing for him. The following day was a Sunday – no post. On the Monday, there was another sighting: Evie had dismounted from the saddle and was pushing her bicycle up a steep incline to a farmhouse on the hill opposite. Nothing for him again. So near and yet so far. Bernard watched her from the garden; from this distance she looked as small as a Lilliputian. He stretched out his hand and cupped it under her bicycle, like a giant. The difference in perspective pleased him. Perhaps there was a picture here? Perhaps not. He sighed and went back inside. He began to hope for a great disaster in Saffron Walden – fire, flood, pestilence, anything that would induce his correspondent to write to him. These dark thoughts bore fruit. The very next day, a letter arrived with Phoebe's handwriting on the envelope; the lovely Evie delivered it.

'Evie!' Bernard bounded out of the house to greet her. 'Lovely to see you! I hope you're not in a rush. Mrs – what's her name, made some buns this morning. Allow me to make you a cup of tea.'

'I shouldn't really stop. I have to be back in time for the mail train and then I've got another round starting at four.'

'Heavens, how hard you work! No peace for the wicked, but the buns must be tasted.' He gently but firmly took her bicycle from her (what slim arms she had for a post lady) and guided her inside.

The kitchen was in disarray with the remains of breakfast still on the table. Evie sat down carefully, keeping her elbows off the wooden surface, sticky with jam. Bernard felt delighted to see her and buzzed around, filling the kettle, chatting, sweeping the dirty dishes into the sink with a clatter. The buns were good but the tea was too strong and Evie seemed to be gulping down the scalding liquid as quickly as possible. How could he keep her longer?

'I say, would you like to see what I'm up to?'

'I beg your pardon?'

'What I'm painting. Only, it's in my studio.'

To his delight, Evie put down her cup and followed him along the corridor. As they passed the piano room, Bernard briefly considered a detour – he could impress her with some musical improvisations. But perhaps not today; one thing at a time. He opened the door of the drawing room. 'Voilà!'

Over by the window was an easel with a half-finished canvas on it. Around it, on a floor covered with bits of old sheets, lay a dried-up pallet and dozens of half-squeezed tubes of paints, like bright fat worms. Evie hesitated in the doorway.

'Come in, come in and tell me what you think.' Bernard gestured towards the easel.

Evie gingerly approached the canvas and looked at the painting. It was an interior – a drawing room with a large fireplace and a glimpse of window. The flames of the fire were more like a design than real flames and they were painted unusual colours – greens and pinks mixing in with the more usual orange tones.

'Well?' Bernard was waiting.

'Lovely colours,' she ventured.

Bernard smiled. 'Thank you.'

'Charming composition.'

'Thank you again.'

He stood back and admired her admiring his work. Evie cocked her head on one side and grew serious.

'But what does it actually mean? What's it trying to say?' She looked at Bernard as innocently and quizzically as a child. 'I mean, when it's finished – will it have a point?'

Like a man who has embarked on a fencing match for fun and suddenly realises his life is at stake, Bernard gave a start, but managed to dodge the blade.

'I don't think you can quite read the work,' he said, or you would understand its significance.'

'Of course,' she hurried to agree with him. 'I have no idea about these things. I don't really understand art at all. I'm sorry to be so ignorant.'

Bernard nodded, accepting her apology gracefully, determined to keep the upper hand. He didn't want to lose his grip on the situation again and guided her firmly back into the kitchen. It had been a mistake to show her his painting: she wasn't up to it. She had no training, no education, he should have realised. He remained charming but aloof; he couldn't wait for her to go.

Evie must have sensed his disappointment. She quickly downed the last of her tea, thanked him and got back on her bicycle. He waved to her from the porch, but as soon as she was round the corner Bernard gave a sigh of relief. What a pity she wasn't more receptive to art; still, he had tried.

He wandered back to his makeshift studio and picked up his paintbrush, but his heart wasn't in it and he decided to call it a day. He lit his pipe and wandered out into the garden. It was glorious weather but he couldn't seem to enjoy it. Something was irking him. 'What does it actually mean?' She might as well have said: 'It doesn't mean anything.' He had taken her into the Holy of Holies, shown her a Cavalier painting in progress, and look how she had rewarded him. She was a pretty little thing, but she wasn't helpful to his art. He needed someone who would support him. He was looking for a muse who would admire and adore, not question his work. He puffed crossly on his pipe and decided that he wouldn't encourage his post lady any further. Instead he would read his letter from Phoebe – she at least was nice to him. He went inside to find it.

82, Summerhill Road, Saffron Walden, Essex
Monday 2nd August 1920

Dear Bernard,

So sorry for the silence! I will explain why in a minute, but first let me say how pleased I am that you are knuckling down and getting on with the serious business of painting! Very well done! I'm proud of you and am sending you a small reward. Look out for it! It should arrive in the next few days.

Now, you are wondering, why was Phoebe Carson so slow replying to your last letter? I expect you thought that my nose was, as usual, stuck in a book. But no, the excitement of your challenge has distracted me from my current novel (Three Men in a Boat – again – well, you must admit, it's hilarious). Anyway, I have put my book to one side and taken my promotion to Saffron Walden correspondent very seriously (by the way, what is the salary? – do you know roughly?) I have tried very hard to uncover some really interesting news for you. Over the past few days I have skulked around town like a regular sleuth but I haven't been able to unearth a single thing of interest! How Sherlock Holmes managed to discover mysteries around every corner and almost stumble over dead bodies is beyond me. Baker Street must be much more exciting than where I live; I couldn't sniff out even a petty crime. I trudged around for a couple of days with my notebook, and then on day three, as I trod wearily homewards, I saw it – a trail of ants, walking purposefully down

Summerhill Road. They were going my way so I followed them with interest.

Imagine my horror and astonishment when I saw the line disappearing under my own gate, up the garden path, round the house and into the scullery! While I looked for news elsewhere my own home was being invaded by foreign troops – it was under siege and it still is! The little blighters are determined to conquer and then colonise, but I will get them all in the end. Rest assured, they will be annihilated!

Well, I must return to the front line and see how things are going in the scullery.

Your favourite war correspondent,

Phoebe

Bernard grimaced as he tossed the letter aside. He didn't appreciate Phoebe's metaphors at all. They reminded him of his own lack of war service and made him feel guilty that he hadn't done his bit. Phoebe wasn't to know – he couldn't blame her for his feelings of inadequacy, but it was irritating. And another thing, he felt sorry for the ants, marching purposefully to certain death. There was a darker metaphor there, one he didn't want to think about. He wandered into the garden, muttering to himself. It was just too bad: the war, the suffering and his inability to help in any way. It had been an awful day. Evie had insulted his painting and Phoebe had opened a can of worms with her ant story. Perhaps tomorrow would be better.

He walked through the garden, past the vegetable patch and on up the hill. He reached the top and surveyed the landscape. Behind him soft green fields were folding in on themselves like lightly whipped cream. Before him the countryside flattened out like a colourful tablecloth. In the distance, the sea shone silver in the afternoon sunshine. Wonderful. His mind cleared immediately. He lay on the grass and gazed up at the sky. Clouds drifted slowly past and he lay and watched them: a lion's head, a slightly deformed dog, a bicycle. He closed his eyes and a picture appeared. He chased it away. Not now. He kicked off his shoes and socks and tugged at the long grass with his toes, feeling the soft blades, enjoying their squeak. This was the life. He would work again tomorrow. What had Phoebe called it – knuckling down? Well, he would knuckle down in the morning.

Jam

As Bernard lay on his back on the warm Devon hillside, in Saffron Walden Phoebe was crouching uncomfortably among her gooseberry bushes. There was definitely an art, she decided, to picking this particular fruit and not one she was conversant in. Every time she reached out to pluck one of the hairy green berries, she got stabbed or scratched by a thorn. She sat back on her heels and looked at the swollen green globes, tight as rugger balls.

'I will get you!' she warned them. Then she laughed out loud. 'First ants, now berries! Phoebe Carson, is nothing safe from your murderous hands?'

She wiped her brow with the sleeve of her blouse. The berries were eluding her, just like the ants had. It was frustrating when things were elusive. Take Bernard, for example. He was elusive, replying to only one in every two of her letters. And if he only wrote half as much as she did, perhaps he only cared half as much? Silly girl, she chided herself. You don't know if he cares at all.

She made another grab at a gooseberry but, in her eagerness to get hold of it, she squashed it slightly between her fingers. The green skin ripped and a splodge of the soft centre came to the surface. Phoebe squeezed it with interest. Why had the gooseberry been invented? Was it some sort of divine joke – giving France the grape and Britain the gooseberry? She sniffed the insides with her long nose: they smelled deliciously tart. Gooseberry fool, that was what it reminded her of. But was she a fool? 'This great stage of fools' – who wrote that? It must have been Shakespeare – but which play? She was getting rusty; it was time to read the bard again. Anyway, the question was this: did Bernard really like her or did he take her for granted?

Phoebe tentatively put out her hand and picked another berry. She wished she had gardening gloves; it would make the job so much easier. She pulled down her jumper, stretching it over her blouse until it covered half of her hands, then she went back into the fray. It was a risky business, picking fruit for Bernard. Phoebe knew that, just as she was risking her hands in this enterprise, she was also risking her heart. Still, she had promised him a present and she would keep her word.

A few more jabs and she decided to call it a day. She picked up the basket and peered inside. She had enough for half a dozen pots and her father didn't like jam anyway. Bernard only needed one pot. She would give two to the Women's Institute, to make up for the fact that she had turned down their invitation to serve on the committee – again. That left three pots for her to enjoy or perhaps share with friends. Phoebe made her way back through the garden towards the kitchen, her long skirt swishing against the flower beds. She glanced over at the study window. The Reverend Carson was gazing out distracted. She gave him a little wave but he looked away. She shouldn't have disturbed him; he was no doubt working on his sermon.

Phoebe gave a little sigh. Her father was not unlike a gooseberry, round and hairy on the outside with plenty of barbed comments for those that got too close. And on the inside quite tart, not unpleasantly tart, but it needed someone with a sweet disposition to cope with him. She smiled. How clever she was and how Bernard would have laughed at her comparison, though she wouldn't put it in a letter: it would look too mean written down. It was a joke to be shared on a walk, perhaps when Bernard was next in Saffron Walden, if she hadn't forgotten it by then.

In the kitchen, she washed and trimmed the gooseberries, then found her jam saucepan and tipped them in. She added water and simmered them on the stove while she carefully measured the sugar. What a relief to be able to get hold of the stuff again. She slowly tipped the shiny white granules into her brass scales, stopping to add weights on the other side then pouring more sugar in. It had been a wretched war, but it had brought her Bernard. If he hadn't signed up he wouldn't have come to the training camp in Saffron Walden.

She slid the sugar into the saucepan where the gooseberries were now boiling angrily. It sat momentarily on the surface, like virgin snow, before turning green and disappearing into the bubbling potion. War had brought Bernard to Saffron Walden and war had kept him there. And there had been nothing else for him to do. If he had been in London or another smart place, she would never have had the chance to get to know him. There would have been too many other distractions. In Saffron Walden, she was a big fish: clever and witty, even a little daring in her comments. And she made him laugh. That was important in a girl, not the most important quality, but one of the most important.

Phoebe found her glasses on the draining board – what were they doing there? – and rechecked her recipe book: How to test for a set. Remove pan from heat – put a teaspoon of the jam onto a saucer – wait a moment – then test for a skin.

She carefully picked up the saucepan and put it on a mat. Then she dipped a teaspoon into the jam and placed it on a saucer. A test. And how did one test for feelings? Remove the man from the lady in question, place a letter in a box, wait, then test the reply. And how could she test the reply? She shook her head. What had got into her? She couldn't expect Bernard to start gushing about her when he had an important exhibition to work on. She tried to chase all thoughts of him from her head. He was a fly, an annoying fly, but what sort?

Of course, a blue-bottle, a big one; now, that joke she would share with him.

Back to the test. She would play a little game, use the test as a sign. If the jam was already set, then that would mean that she and Bernard would last; if not, well, then they wouldn't. It wasn't a real test, just a bit of fun, nothing serious. Phoebe peered anxiously at the teaspoon cooling in the saucer. She slowly stretched out her hand and touched it tentatively with a finger. A wrinkly skin had formed on the surface. Her finger trembled. Ha ha! A surge of delight rushed through her, then she laughed.

'You're soft in the head, Phoebe Carson,' she said and went into the scullery to find six clean jam jars and check on the ants.

Jekyll and Hyde

North Lodge, Key Lane, Colyton, Devon
Tuesday 3rd August 1920

Dear Cassie,

I hope you got back to London all right. I imagine the return journey was dull compared to the adventure of the outward leg! All is well here. Mother continues to bake and father garden. Meanwhile, I am now on first-name terms with the mole toucher! The story is almost too bizarre. I arrive at High View to find its sole occupant, a certain Mr Cavalier (pronounced Caval E-A) locked in the garden shed! Imagine! Seizing the opportunity for revenge, I refuse to let him out until he apologises for his despicable behaviour on the train. When he does so, I condescend to lift the latch on his dingy prison cell. The captive emerges as one reborn, newly baptised as 'Bernard', covered in cobwebs but radiant with joy! How you would have laughed if you'd been there. I wanted to laugh too and yet there was something so pathetic about him – I just couldn't. Anyway, now I'd got my own back I felt more charitably towards him. Having been released from purgatory he certainly felt charitably towards me, so we decided to shake hands and call a cease-fire.

As this strange eccentric has few correspondents I then got a few days' reprieve. But today I had to deliver another letter. Bernard, as he insists I call him now we are friends, rushed from the house and more or less forced me to stop for a cup of tea and a bun. What a mess his kitchen was in – I pity his housekeeper. (He couldn't even remember her name, poor woman.) Anyway, we drank tea and talked quite pleasantly until he asked if I would like to see one of his paintings. He took me into his 'studio' – really a drawing room, covered with sheets and full of blank canvases, stood me in front of 'something I am working on' and expected me to come up with comments that were both flattering and intelligent.

The colours in the painting were nice enough but the picture lacked any sort of depth. Typical me – I couldn't resist asking what it meant! His face suddenly flashed with thunder, but he remained the new 'charming' Bernard. He whisked me out of the room before I could dent his ego further and, as soon as he could, shooed me out of his house.

The question is – will the 'Post-shed Bernard' remain as polite as promised, or will the rude, inappropriate 'Before Shed Bernard' take a hold again? I had quite a few deliveries further up the valley and when I cycled back past his house again I could hear him pacing in the garden, muttering to himself. He really is a Jekyll and Hyde character – all beaming and buoyant one minute, irritated and impulsive the next. Anyway, I will keep you 'posted'! Ha ha! Meanwhile, let's hope my next visit is some way off.

Do write soon with news of London.

Your loving friend,

Evie

Cassie was not over the moon with Evie's letter. There seemed to be a worrying trace of a classic love plot emerging in Evie's encounters with the mole toucher. Delightful heroine meets tricky hero who insults her but she gets her own back and he promptly falls for her. It was only a trace, but it was definitely there, like a vein threading its way through a piece of marble: sometimes darker, sometimes lighter, but always present in the cold stone. Cassie felt a twinge of jealousy, just a twinge of course. She wanted her friend to be happy; it's just that she wanted to be happy too. And, if possible, she wanted to be happy first.

Still it sounded like Bernard was a) not a good artist and b) not pleased that Evie had suspected this. But was he really as bad as Evie suggested? Cassie couldn't rely on her friend's opinion. Evie lived in Devon and rarely had the opportunity to attend exhibitions in the capital, while she was a regular at art openings all over London. Cassie wished she had seen Bernard's work for herself. So why hadn't she come across this man before? It was worrying that she didn't know him. A successful artist wouldn't be drawn to a girl like Evie who lacked sophistication and mature ideas; however, an up-and-coming artist, one who hadn't yet burst onto the art scene, might be interested in a young post lady. And what if that up-and-coming artist suddenly did very well and dragged Evie into the limelight with him? She would do some research and unearth something that would put Evie off. Yes, that would be the perfect solution. She was due to meet some friends at Fortnum's for tea. She would make some discreet enquiries about Mr Cavalier. Someone would know him. And if she could squash this relationship with some unsavoury information, she would also be protecting Evie.

Cassie went upstairs to dress. She chose carefully. She knew her line of questioning would be more nonchalant and therefore more effective if she felt more attractive than usual. She didn't want to sound peevish when she asked about Bernard; she wanted to sound mildly curious. She needed a dress that oozed sophistication and flattered her. She chose a long red tunic with white pearl petals sewn along the hem. A long necklace of pearls, which fell down to her waist, complemented the pearl border and a small white flower added a very feminine touch to her dark brown bob. She surveyed herself in the mirror. It was too grand a look for teatime but at Fortnum's she would get away with it. Perhaps someone would notice her as well? She pictured herself and Evie getting married together. But no, they had different friends and their fathers had very different incomes. Cassie smiled at herself in the mirror and hurried downstairs to summon a cab.

When she reached Fortnum's, Lavinia and Daisy had already ordered.

'We've plumped for the full afternoon tea,' said Lavinia. 'I hope that's all right?'

'Of course,' smiled Cassie, kissing them in turn. 'Did you order me Lapsang?'

'Yes darling, now sit down and tell us your news.'

Cassie slid gracefully into her seat, taking the opportunity to check her friends' outfits. Daisy was wearing a dress coat in a powder blue. Two large buttons at the waist gave it a modern air and a tiny peep of lacy chemise slip at the neck gave it a playful touch. A light blue scarf made her eyes, usually green, look almost blue in colour. Lavinia wore a similar dress, but in a very pale pink which complemented her grey eyes and blonde curls. The two girls looked cool and elegant in their pastel shades and Cassie felt as if she clashed in red. *Tant pis*.

'So how was Devon?' asked Daisy.

'Oh, rather dull. There wasn't much going on.' A pause. 'And my friend has to work.'

There was a moment's silence during which the three friends pitied those who were not as fortunate. During this pensive interlude two waiters arrived, one with a silver tray rattling with bone-china cups, the other with silver cake towers piled with dainty sandwiches, scones and cakes. The mood lightened as they passed round plates and poured tea. They chatted away, exchanging gossip. Cassie bided her time; she would pick the right moment to ask about Bernard.

'Has anyone heard of an artist called Cavalier?' she said eventually, leaning over and plucking a tiny eclair off the cake tray.

'Who?' Lavinia knitted her eyebrows together. 'Cavalier? No I can't say I have.'

'Yes you have,' Daisy interjected, 'except you know him as Mr cavalier.'

'Oh, you mean Bernard,' laughed Lavinia. 'Yes, we know him a little. Why do you ask?'

'Oh no real reason. I met him the other day, on a train.'

'Did he try to engage you in conversation?' asked Lavinia, grinning.

'Oh, not really, well a little.' Cassie flushed.

'So he's keen on you!' laughed Daisy. 'Funny, he usually goes for—' she changed tack mid-sentence, '—for fair-haired ladies.'

Cassie knew what she meant. The conversation wasn't going the way she had hoped.

'He's not keen on me. We talked a little, that's all.'

'You're lucky then,' said Daisy, 'because he is a real pursuer of ladies.'

'Until he tires of them,' added Lavinia. 'That's why we call him Mr cavalier.'

'He sounds like a dreadful man,' said Cassie.

'He's very loud,' agreed Daisy.

'But rather sweet,' added Lavinia. 'Even when he tires of a girl he stays friends with her. He's unreliable, but he's not mean.'

Cassie soaked up all this information as she picked up the teapot and topped up her friend's cups.

'So, what's his art like?'

The girls shrugged.

'I mean, does he sell well?'

'Some people buy his pictures,' said Daisy, 'but actually I'm struggling to remember a single painting.'

'Doesn't your mother have one of his still-lifes?' asked Lavinia.

'Does she?' Daisy looked blank. 'I can't picture it.'

After that the conversation moved on to other things, but Cassie had more than enough ammunition. As soon as the tea-party was over she rushed home to reply to Evie.

72, Fairholme Road, Kensington, London, SW.

Wednesday 4th August 1920

Dear Evie,

Many thanks for your amusing letter. Mr Cavalier is obviously a very interesting creature. I was intrigued by your story, so much so that I have done a little research on your behalf.

It turns out that your critique of the mole toucher's work is spot on. No one I have spoken to can remember a single one of his paintings! He is obviously highly forgettable! However, some girlfriends of mine did consider his approach to women to be more memorable. They were very polite and delicate about him but I got the strong impression that he's very fickle. Apparently, he's always smitten in the beginning but then he quickly loses interest. He sounds like a real cad. I hope you won't get keen on him, I'd hate to see you hurt. Leave him in the shed next time – the art world won't miss him!

My regards to your parents and my love to you.

Do keep me posted.

Your best friend,

Cassie

Cassie was confident that Evie would appreciate her prudent warning, and when she received Cassie's letter, Evie felt grateful to her friend. It all made sense: the unremarkable paintings, the short attention span, the erratic behaviour when it came to women. Cassie's letter validated what Evie had instinctively guessed at. She was pleased her gut feeling had been proved correct and she was amused that Bernard didn't know he had been investigated. How fortunate Cassie was in London with her ear to the ground. Evie remembered her father's maxim – forewarned was forearmed.

The Downpour

After her unfavourable comments on his masterpiece, Bernard stopped looking out for his post lady. He lurked in his studio, thinking up lots of painting ideas and then dismissing them again. The week flew by; the weekend came and went. Bernard sat in the drawing room, smoking pipe after pipe, contemplating his blank canvases with the serenity of a philosopher. On the Monday, he woke mid-morning to the sound of heavy rain drumming on the roof. It seemed to be speaking to him, awakening some deep call of the wild. He jumped out of bed, threw on a shirt and some trousers and ran downstairs to the piano.

Meanwhile, Evie was cycling into the weather. The rain seemed to be throwing itself at her, stinging her face, running down her collar, and the postbag slung over her shoulder was getting wetter and heavier. Luckily there wasn't as much post as usual and Mr Thornber, the Post Master, had told her there was no need to get back to the sorting office in time for the mail train.

'Just do what you can,' he had said kindly. 'If you are given any post, explain it won't go till tomorrow morning.'

'And the four o'clock delivery?'

'This will be the last delivery today,' said Mr Thornber. 'You can finish early, go home and dry off.'

Tired of battling against the elements, Evie stopped and looked back. A sheet of rain was moving along the road like a curtain, bouncing off the surface, billowing up again like smoke. The sight of it made her feel even colder and wetter and she quickly turned around again and continued up the hill. Water from her hat dribbled down into her eyes and her boots were squeaking. Her long skirt was so wet that it started to flap about like a bit of cardboard; she turned a corner too quickly and the end of it got caught in her bicycle chain. She had to very carefully get off the bicycle and slowly unwind it, crouching on the sodden grass at the roadside, blinking water out of her eyes.

In the music room, Bernard was lost in a reverie. He gazed out on the sopping garden, watching the rain streak past the windows, allowing it to enter his body, his mind, his soul. There was no need to go out in it when he could feel it metaphorically. Debussy had written *La Mer*; now he, Cavalier, had been chosen to interpret this incessant rain. *La Deluge*, he thought, yes, that would do – apologies to Rimbaud. He smiled, slid onto the piano stool and lifted the lid. First his fingers tinkled gently over the ivories then, as his inspiration intensified, notes came pouring out of him – in fistfuls. The thunder crashed, lightning flashed and that was just in the music room.

Evie was not conversant with the latest musical trends. As she cycled up the gravel driveway to High View, avoiding the puddles, trying to keep under the shelter of the trees, she wondered what on earth was happening inside. It sounded like a piano was being dropped from a great height – repeatedly. With this din going on it would have been the perfect opportunity to slip the post discretely through the letterbox and disappear. Unfortunately, Bernard had a parcel and it wouldn't fit. She rang the doorbell and waited, trying to avoid the large drops of water dripping off the roof of the porch.

Inside the house, *La Deluge* was reaching its climax. Bernard was playing his heart out, leaning back on the piano stool, eyes closed, perspiration running down his face. The sound of the doorbell was a most unwelcome interruption; he decided to ignore it and carry on. There it was again. He stood up, slammed down the piano lid, stomped to the front door and flung it open.

Evie stood on the doormat, absolutely sopping. Bernard was quite taken aback: the rain seemed to be running through her, starting from her hair, which was plastered to her face, and working its way through her soaking coat and sodden skirt, down to her squelching boots.

'Evie, is that you? You look like a drowned rat. You must come inside – at least till the rain stops.'

The warm dry hall behind him was just too inviting; Evie went in without a murmur. She took her hat and boots off and followed Bernard into the kitchen, leaving wet footprints on the wooden floor. He peeled off her coat and hung it on the clothes-pulley above the range. From here it dripped great drops of water onto the hot-plate with a hiss. Divested of her coat, Evie was still far from being dry – her blouse and skirt were fit for the wringer. Bernard couldn't help with the skirt but he did have a shirt she could borrow; Evie was too wet to refuse. He raced upstairs, rifled through his wardrobe to find something clean-ish and ran downstairs again.

Evie disappeared into the pantry, took off her blouse and re-emerged in Bernard's shirt. Her face was flushed from the rain; her hair, which had caught on one of the shirt buttons, had slipped out of its bun and was now sticking out in all directions. The shirt was much too big for her and this seemed to accentuate her slight shoulders and thin waist. It was almost like a night shirt and Evie, with her hair askew, looked like a small child who had just clambered out of bed. Bernard fussed around, filling the kettle, making a cup of tea.

'Sit by the stove,' he commanded. 'I'll light the fire in the drawing room.'

Evie sneezed.

'What about your stockings?'

'They're fine, thank you.' She sneezed again.

'Look Evie, I don't want to sound dismissive of your pins, but I have seen legs before you know. I have done hundreds of life-drawing classes and discovered that legs, particularly from the calf down, are really no big deal. Besides, we all have them. I really think you should take off your stockings and let them dry.'

'Actually, I think I should probably get going.'

'Not in this weather. Not in the middle of a storm.'

Bernard went into the drawing room to get a fire started. How funny that he suddenly felt brotherly towards her. He wanted to make her warm and dry and that was all. How nice he wasn't overwhelmed with other thoughts. He screwed up some newspaper, hid it in a huge pile of kindling, laid bigger sticks round it and then set it alight. The fire blazed into life. He nodded at it and returned to the kitchen. Evie's stockings were hanging from the bar of the range. A small pool of water was collecting on the floor underneath them. Forgetting all brotherly thoughts, Bernard glanced over at her; the bare skin of her calves was marbled pink and white from the cold rain. Beautiful. He wanted to paint them. He needed a distraction.

'Soup?'

'Yes please.'

They sat side by side at the kitchen table while he cut slices of bread and ladled Mrs Whatsit's soup into bowls. Considering they hardly knew each other, considering Evie's mottled calves were present, albeit safely under the table, it all felt very normal. They chatted about his impressions of Devon and how it compared to life in London. He told her about his studio in Pimlico; she told him about some of the other people on her round. And then she remembered.

'Your parcel!'

She went back to the hall to find it and brought it into the kitchen. The brown paper covering was sodden from the rain and opened easily revealing a jar of jam. *Phoebe's Gooseberry Conserve* said the label.

'My maiden aunt,' said Bernard, quickly.

'She writes to you a lot,' said Evie, noticing the Saffron Walden postmark.

'She's lonely,' said Bernard, truthfully this time. 'I'm all she's got.' He flushed with guilt.

'Let's try it,' said Evie and she sat the jam pot between them. They smeared it on the last of the bread. It was delicious, but Bernard felt increasingly uneasy.

'Come and sit by the fire,' he said. 'Leave all this, Mrs Thingy—'

'—Mrs Wilson, I happen to know her.'

They went through to the drawing room. Evie noticed that the painting she had questioned a few days earlier had been worked on considerably: the green and pink flames were deeper and bolder now and they shone like jewels. The sky was clearing and although rain was still falling, a watery sun was emerging. The whole room danced with light and colour. Bernard instructed Evie to sit by the fire, put her head back and relax. Evie, exhausted by her morning in the storm, was only too glad to sit quietly for a few minutes. She sank into a large armchair, tucked her legs up under her skirt to hide her bare calves and closed her eyes.

Bernard wasn't sure what he should do. He couldn't work on his painting, not with its critic sitting opposite. Instead he quietly lit his pipe, picked up a notebook and pretended he was sketching something in the garden. He hummed to himself as he doodled on the paper. How different everything felt with Evie here. The drawing room was softer, lighter and there was a new feeling in the air, a whiff of something altogether exciting and delicious.

As she pretended to doze, Evie desperately tried to focus on Cassie's letter. What had she said? That he was fickle, that he quickly lost interest. He was a cad, she mustn't forget that. Through half-closed eyelids she could see the blaze of the fire and a bright light dancing in the garden. She could hear the scratch of a pencil on paper, a gentle humming, the last of the rain sliding down the windows. She could smell the wood fire and Bernard's pipe. What would she normally be doing now? An errand for her mother in town; a visit to the library looking for a book she hadn't read. Dull. Indescribably dull.

Evie hadn't met an artist before. She peeped through her eyelids – he was busy with the sketchbook, bending over it, absorbed in drawing something. She watched him at work, noticing the way he held his pencil, the quick movements of his hands, the darting eyes. How different everything felt here, among the canvases and oil paints. She could have sat for hours and just enjoyed the creativity of it all. At home, the only creations were her mother's scones; here, there were a thousand possibilities flying off the pages of Bernard's sketch-book. She could almost feel them whizzing past her, brushing her cheek like faeries. She glanced again at the latest painting, drinking in the vivid colours. There was something so edifying about them: looking at the picture was like taking a long gulp of something warm and energising. The greens and pinks seemed to whirl off the canvas. There was a strength in them that swept through her. She wouldn't fall for Bernard; she would just be his friend. She would enjoy his artistic energy without getting her heart broken.

She shifted slightly in her seat and had another peep at him. She could see the top of his head moving to and fro as he bent over his sketch-book, working away with his pencil. His hair was auburn in colour and as he sketched he ran his left hand through it. The hand was large and slightly tanned, long fingers, nails flecked with paint. The humming stopped. Sensing she was watching, Bernard looked up and caught her eye. Evie blushed. The energy in the room was rising. Feeling slightly panicked she put her hand to her neck and remembered she was still wearing his shirt. She was slipping into a dangerous place; how could she stop herself? Grabbing hold of the chair-arms, she smiled at him and desperately searched for something to say.

'Would you like to come for dinner?' She hadn't planned to say this and she was surprised at the way her invitation slipped out.

'Sorry?'

'I mean you've looked after me so well – I should really repay your hospitality.'

'Do you live at home?' Suddenly remembering Phoebe's vicarage, Bernard felt wary.

'Yes, I do.'

'The thing is,' Bernard smiled awkwardly, 'some parents don't like me.'

But before Evie had a chance to digest this confession, he had an idea.

'I will come for dinner, on one condition – you allow me to paint your portrait.'

Evie was startled. Her offer of dinner had been mangled. She thought she was doing him a favour, but it turned out he was doing her one, and the price for that was – well – she wasn't sure about a portrait. This was new territory.

'I don't think—'

Her mind whirled with thoughts, but when the whirling stopped she realised it was highly unlikely that any artist anywhere would offer to paint her ever again. She might regret refusing this opportunity more than she might regret taking it.

'Agreed! Dinner on Saturday and yes, you can paint me.'

As if she had just given him permission, Bernard got up and came over to her. He crouched down by her chair and started studying her face closely, scanning her features, looking into her eyes. Evie was not used to this sort of scrutiny, especially from a man.

'But not today!' she said and, jumping up quickly, headed towards the door. After that everything speeded up, like a black-and-white film in reverse. She disappeared back into the pantry and reappeared wearing her blouse and stockings. She left Bernard's shirt lying discreetly over a kitchen chair and reached up to the pulley for her coat.

'Well, thank you for looking after me,' she said, smiling but brusque as she pulled it on.

'A pleasure,' he bowed stiffly.

'Perhaps you really are a chevalier!' she laughed.

He waved politely from the porch.

It was a clever pun, she thought, as she cycled away. But not one she would be sharing with anyone else, least of all Cassie. She flew home along the narrow, tree-lined lanes. Everything was covered in a film of water which caught and reflected the late-afternoon sun. The ivy climbing the trees was lit up – every leaf, every root outlined in silver, a net of light cast over the countryside.

A Blank Canvas

After Evie disappeared, Bernard went straight back to his studio. He wanted to start on her portrait right away, while her face was still fresh in his mind. He decided to make a quick study of her in his sketchbook, while he could still remember. He found a clean page and picked up his pencil.

He shouldn't have stared at her like that: she was obviously very shy. The trouble was that he always looked at a model in an intense way in order to really understand her. London ladies loved being pored over and he could quickly capture their essence. Like the net of a butterfly collector, his eyes would skim, scan then swoop to catch a beauty and pin her to a canvas. His adopted father, Benedict, worked in exactly the same way. Benedict was a sculptor, but he had the same gift – an ability to devour a model with his eyes, then spit her out again. With only a few sketches the two artists could recreate someone with extraordinary accuracy – Bernard in paint, Benedict in clay and then bronze. Of the two, Bernard was the more honest artist; he always portrayed the sitter as they were, warts and all. Benedict was happy to make artistic corrections, but these were always subtle, hardly noticeable, or, if noticed, silently and gratefully so. And Benedict was thanked in all sorts of ways. One thank you gift was a baby, left in a basket outside his Chelsea studio. The baby's name was printed on a little label tied to the handle – Bernard.

As he hurriedly sketched the outline of Evie's head and shoulders, Bernard realised that he and his adopted father were not just alike in their approach to art; they were similar in many other ways. They shared the same loud voice, the same way of filling a room with a natural charisma that rubbed some people up the wrong way, the same smile in the company of ladies. But perhaps he had learnt, rather than inherited, these mannerisms. Physically they looked very different. Benedict was dark and short, while he was tall and ginger haired; and Benedict's eyes were brown, whereas his were blue in colour.

Bernard frowned: the sketch didn't look right. He should have started with her nose and worked upwards and outwards. He stopped to sharpen his pencil. As the curls of pencil shavings dropped onto the carpet, he wondered for the thousandth time about his mysterious arrival on Benedict's doorstep. He cast his mind back to all Benedict's different ladies who had played games with him as a child, all smiling, all temporary. But the first lady, the one who had placed him in the basket and left him outside Benedict's, he couldn't remember at all. It was rather unnerving having an uncertain start in life. His beginning was blank, like a blank canvas.

Bernard suddenly realised he was still sharpening the pencil. He stopped abruptly and pulled it out of the sharpener. Too late, the lead had grown long and wobbly. As soon as he tried to use it, the point broke off with a snap, leaving a large grey dent on the paper. Bother. And his vision of Evie was fading fast. Funny how she always distracted him from his art. Muses were supposed to encourage and inspire, not produce feelings of restlessness.

That night, Bernard's muse had a most delightful dream. She was in a white room with white curtains billowing in at an open window. The whole place was flooded with light. On the walls were the most beautiful paintings. As she looked at them, her feet started lifting up off the ground; she floated higher and higher and then out of the window.

A few miles down the road, Bernard couldn't sleep at all. The house was still full of Evie. He wandered around, trying to drink in the last of her. Then he put on her shirt and lay on his bed, imagining the softness of her skin against the cotton fabric, trying to recreate the image of her bare legs.

A Fly in the Ointment

The next day, Bernard rose earlier than usual. A picture had formed in his mind during his fitful sleep and straight after breakfast he went along to his studio. He found his paper, prepared it with an initial wash and, while it was still wet, taped it to a board, tacked it to an easel and put it outside to dry. Then he opened his watercolour paints, rather dried out through lack of use, and located a brand-new squirrel brush. He lit his pipe and sat smoking in the sunshine, waiting for the paper to dry. A few pipes later, he took his paints and sketched in the hills that formed his charming valley, filled them in with colour and painted a road winding up them. Then he added dark blues and greys to his pallet and obscured everything with a heavy wash of rain which swept down the valley towards the front of the picture. Finally, he took a fine sable brush and painted in a tiny bicycle, struggling up the road, moving out of view. The rider was leaning into the rain, flattened by the weather.

As he painted, he thought of his post lady: her courage, her resilience, her wet footprints in his hallway. He thought too of the woman whose jar of jam had led to their most recent encounter. Now he had established a friendship with Evie, he no longer needed Phoebe to write to him with the same regularity. In fact, it would be better if Phoebe stopped writing altogether. He felt guilty about their correspondence. And it was dangerous. If Evie happened to find out that

Phoebe was not really his maiden aunt – if one of her letters should drop in a puddle, and Evie happened to notice that the writing was too modern and the content too jovial for an old lady, he was in trouble. He would have to do something about Phoebe. But what?

While Bernard was reconsidering his relationship with Phoebe, Evie was rejigging her impressions of Bernard. She had thought him a self-obsessed man with unpredictable mood swings. Cassie had strongly hinted that he had a capricious approach to women. But during the rainy afternoon she spent with him, she had glimpsed a different man: a caring Bernard – almost brotherly in his concern for her. He had looked after her beautifully, almost tenderly. Most importantly, he hadn't tried to take advantage of her. Perhaps Cassie's friends were wrong. Perhaps the Bernard she was discovering was decent and true, not inconstant and vacillating. He always looked pleased to see her and he was always respectful of her person. Even when her calves were exposed, he had remained calm and composed, thoughtful and friendly.

Apart from one unnerving stare, Bernard's attitude towards her had been predominantly platonic. She found this display of innocence and valour extremely attractive; in fact, she couldn't stop thinking about it. He had taken care of her, found her dry clothes, poured her soup, made tea. Added to this, he was an artist – such a refreshing occupation compared to the mundane professions of the local boys. The 'mole day' must have been a strange, never to be repeated aberration, one that she should expunge from her memory. It was important to give him a clean slate, not dwell on past mistakes. Perhaps he was only fickle in London. She felt optimistic, hopeful even. There was just one fly in the ointment – his candid comment: 'Some parents don't like me.'

Evie had heard the remark at the time, but the confusion caused by a possible portrait had distracted her from its full implications. However, when she had more time to consider it, she realised it was a shot across the bows and one that she had not heeded. Her parents were very middle-class. They admired young men with proper professions and impeccable manners. Evie was aware that her mother was keen for her daughter to meet a nice young man. Bernard was young, but was he 'nice'? What did 'nice' mean? If it meant strict adherence to the conventions of Colyton, if it meant always saying the right thing about scones and geraniums, Evie was almost certain that Bernard was not 'nice.' Still, it was possible that he would pull out the stops and charm his way through dinner. Thank goodness she had sworn Cassie to secrecy; her parents would never make the connection. She would tell them that she was inviting an artist who was visiting the area and who she had met through work. Her parents liked culture, her mother loved the Impressionists – and none of the Impressionists lived dull lives. They would be interested in Bernard's art and overlook any small faux pas like refusing second helpings or not writing thank-you letters.

'I'm inviting an artist to dinner,' Evie announced the next day, as they were finishing a particularly good plum duff.

'An artist?' Her mother, who was delicately extracting a plum stone from her mouth, suddenly looked hopeful.

'He's visiting the area,' Evie said nonchalantly.

'Does he live on your round?' Mr Brunton's sharp legal mind cut to the chase.

Evie sensed this was a leading question and one to which she was about to give the wrong answer. She inwardly cursed Cassie.

'He's staying in Hollybrook,' she said, trying to dodge its significance.

'I see,' said Mr Brunton.

'I invited him for Saturday.'

Mrs Brunton immediately began to ponder out loud what the butcher might have on Saturday in the way of joints – a joint was always nice. During this soliloquy, Mr Brunton stood up and, with a nod to his wife and daughter, left the table. He trotted up the stairs to his study, two steps at a time, went inside and shut the door. He sat at his desk and stared out over the fields. Cassandra was rather irritating, but her indiscretion had its uses. Forewarned was forearmed.

After she had helped her mother with the washing up, Evie went out into the garden. She chose a rectangle of lawn which was not visible from her father's study and there she paced up and down, pulling the tops off Mr Brunton's long grasses. So, Cassie had told them. Both of them. Either that or Cassie had told her mother and she had passed it on. But how could she? How could Cassie betray her confidence like that? She had asked Cassie not to mention the fact that the mole toucher was in the vicinity, but she had mentioned it and she hadn't told Evie she had mentioned it. It was an act of betrayal, a small betrayal but an extremely inconvenient one. Now Bernard was coming to dinner, Cassie's lapse of loyalty put Evie at a disadvantage. She would forgive her of course, but it might take a few days. One thing was certain, she wouldn't be writing to tell Cassie about it. And she would be much more careful in future.

Upstairs in his study, Mr Brunton couldn't settle to anything. He picked up the newspaper, but there was nothing of interest; he opened his latest Dickens novel, but he couldn't concentrate. He glanced outside. It was a lovely evening. Perhaps a cycle ride would clear his head. He reached for his green tweed jacket, draped over his chair, slipped it on and went out. Soon he was cycling slowly down the Devon lanes on his large, lumbering bicycle. Dusk was falling and the air was heavy with honeysuckle. He turned a corner and there was Mr Franklin, the greengrocer, busy digging in his allotment.

'Lovely evening!' Mr Franklin called.

'Lovely.' Mr Brunton pushed the pedals of his bicycle a little harder, a subtle acceleration that might just propel him past the fence of the allotment before Mr Franklin could engage him in conversation.

'How's the family?'

Mr Brunton applied his brakes. This was the worst sort of question. The greengrocer saw Mrs Brunton every day. He knew how she was already.

'Evie is well, thank you.'

'She certainly seems to be blooming,' said Mr Franklin, with a knowing smile. Then, before Mr Brunton could cycle on, he tossed his spade on the ground and ambled over to the fence.

'She's a lovely girl, your Evie. She'll be a catch for someone.'

'A catch? My daughter is not a fish, Mr Franklin, she's a hardworking post lady.'

'But perhaps not for ever, Mr Brunton.'

'No, not for ever. She'll be promoted to a position at the sorting office eventually.'

'Unless she loses her job.'

'I beg your pardon?'

'You must have seen the unemployment figures in the papers, Mr Brunton.'

'I'm sure the Post Office will hold on to Evie.'

'Well, times are hard, Mr Brunton. Drastic measures may be called for. The war, you know—'

'Yes, I'm aware there's been a war, Mr Franklin.'

'And now the soldiers are home.' A pause. 'And looking for work.' Mr Franklin leaned over the fence, 'Anyway, like I say, you don't have to worry. Evie will be a catch for *someone*.'

The Bandit

The day of the dinner dawned bright and sunny. Bernard lay watching the light playing above his bed. Trees danced and waved in the breeze, silhouetted against the ceiling like a magic lantern. Despite this beautiful light show, a terrible feeling was growing in the pit of his stomach. Dinner with Evie's parents would ruin everything. There must be a way out. If only he was ill, inconvenienced, indisposed, then he could bow out gracefully without hurting Evie's feelings. But he didn't feel the slightest bit indisposed. He felt full of beans.

When Evie came up the drive to deliver the latest letter from Bernard's maiden aunt, she was met by a strange apparition. Bernard appeared at the door wearing a large spotted handkerchief folded over his face in a triangle. He looked like a cowboy, or perhaps a bandit. His nose and mouth were covered completely, only his eyes were showing.

'It's not fancy dress this evening,' she smiled, handing him the letter.

'Don't come too near, Evie. I've come down with something dreadful.' Bernard's voice sounded low and muffled.

'What on earth have you got?'

'Some sort of wretched flu – such bad timing.'

Or good timing, thought Evie. He looked comical in his rig out, but she felt furious. She smelled a rat: he wasn't ill at all, just trying to avoid his dinner invitation. Although she had been considering making up an excuse to cancel it herself, now he had pipped her to the post she was determined that he wouldn't escape.

'Oh, that flu, my parents had it last week. No chance of giving it to them. I do hope you're still coming tonight?'

'Or perhaps it's not flu,' he mumbled, 'perhaps it's something more sinister.'

Evie took a step nearer to the cowboy-bandit, who took a step backwards. 'Mr Cavalier,' she said, half mocking, half serious, 'whatever has assailed you, I hope you recover from it quickly, because I can assure you of one thing – no dinner, no portrait.' And with that she turned, left the porch, jumped on her bicycle and left, without a backwards glance.

'Bother,' said Bernard, pulling off his hanky and staring after her.

Bernard loved to socialise with a crowd: he could recount a story to a group and make them laugh out loud, but having a deep and meaningful conversation with one or two people was more of a challenge. If those one or two people happened to be parents, he felt even less sure of himself. He was terrified of being asked what he wanted from life; whether he had any long-term plans; if he would ever settle down. He was terrified because he didn't know the answer. Perhaps because he didn't know where he had come from, it was hard for him to know exactly where he was going. When girlfriends' mothers asked him how he envisaged his future, he would quickly try to change the subject. When the going got really tough he was known to jump up, race to a piano and compose and sing a ditty about them – something fun and complimentary, to distract them from their questions. The Bloomsbury appreciated his songs, but would the Colyton set?

Still, Evie's parents were surely not made of stone; he could charm them with his good looks and talent. Bernard rushed upstairs to his bedroom and threw all the clothes that were lying higgledy-piggledy at the bottom of his wardrobe on the bed. The jumble of white shirts, variously coloured woollen socks, hankies and other sundries made an interesting picture.

The first job was to pair the hand-knitted socks. Then he subjected each pair to a rigorous examination using his nose. Only one pair passed and the rest were consigned to the laundry basket for Mrs Wilson to take home and wash. Some of the more pungent socks had contaminated the shirts. Why had he not sorted them earlier? Why had he not hung up the shirts? The truth was he hadn't been expecting to be social in Devon and so he hadn't bothered with things that mattered in London – things like ironed shirts and fragrant feet.

He had at least hung up his jackets and trousers in the wardrobe. He took out his tweed jacket. The right-hand pocket was full of pipe tobacco and loose flecks were crawling out onto the Harris Tweed like hundreds of tiny worms. He gave it a good brush and hung it by a window to air, glad he had started his preparation early. He found a clean red spotted handkerchief and put it in the breast pocket, just a small tip peeping coyly out of the top. The handkerchief suggested he was well-organised, and the spots against the herringbone pattern of the tweed injected a bit of sophistication.

Now he had perfected his look, it was time to show off his talent – but how? Perhaps a small picture for Mrs Brunton: a watercolour he could dash off in a morning but which would woo Evie's mother and show her father he was a promising artist. What could he paint? Something innocuous but attractive. He wandered out into the lane and started hunting for some wild flowers to copy. When he had picked a large bunch, he took them into the kitchen and plonked them in a jam jar. Then he fetched his watercolour paints and a small piece of card and set to work.

The morning light shafted through the kitchen window and reflected in the glass of the jam jar, creating a patchwork of colours. Bernard became quickly absorbed in the beauty of the effect – the flecks of coloured light in the jar emphasising the thin fragility of the flowers. He worked hard and the time ticked by. When he had finished it was nearly five o'clock. Crumbs, how had that happened? The afternoon had flown and Evie had asked him for six. He sped upstairs to shave and change.

Twenty minutes later, he was admiring himself in the mirror: brown shoes and trousers, a white shirt, mustard coloured tie and brown Harris Tweed jacket. The *pièce de résistance* was the red spotted handkerchief which added a certain *je ne sais quoi*. Or did it? He was an artist, after all; he didn't want to look too ordinary. He pulled the handkerchief a little, so it splayed out in a more enthusiastic manner. There, that was better. Then he went back down to the kitchen to pick up the picture which was leaning against the jam jar of flowers. He hesitated. Perhaps he was trying too hard; he didn't want to appear a show-off, or desperate to please. He left the picture where it was and instead grabbed the flowers themselves and made for the door.

A Ballad and a Quarrel

Mr Brunton looked pointedly at his watch.

'I'm sure he'll be here any minute—' Evie began.

'I hope so dear, or the chicken will be overdone,' said Mrs Brunton, hurrying out to have another look at it.

'I can't abide lateness in a young man,' said Mr Brunton.

The doorbell rang and Evie rushed to get it. Bernard was well turned out in a jacket and tie. But in the pocket of his jacket, an enormous spotted hanky, possibly the one that had earlier acted as a germ barrier, fanned out in an over-exuberant way. It seemed so out of place in their dingy porch that she couldn't bear to look at it. It also made her dress look shabby somehow. She had chosen a light blue dress with tiny mauve dots. It had a scooped neck and a high waist and she was hopeful it would flatter her. Now, next to Bernard's bright spotted handkerchief, it looked faded, tired and rather 'last year'.

'Do come in,' she said.

'Thank you.' He was holding a bunch of flowers and they hadn't travelled well. As he stepped into the house, a few heads fell off and landed on the carpet. She led him into the parlour where her father was waiting.

'Bernard Cavalier,' said her father, getting up to greet him. He said cavalier, like the adjective.

'E – A. Caval E – A, like the French knight,' Evie said quickly.

'Mr Burnton,' Bernard smiled, getting his own back. Mr Brunton didn't correct him, which Evie took to be a very bad sign.

Mrs Brunton emerged from the kitchen, flushed from the range. Bernard gave a low bow.

'*Enchanté, Madame!*' he said and, taking her hand, kissed it in a very gallant manner. Mrs Brunton giggled. Then he held out the wilting posy.

'Thank you. Wild flowers are my favourite,' said Mrs Brunton graciously.

Evie quickly took them from her mother. 'They look as though they need a drink,' she said, keen to escape, even for a few moments. She ran into the kitchen, steamy from the vegetables boiling on the stove, opened a window and leaned her forehead against it. This was going to be a nightmare. She cursed her stubbornness. Bernard had offered her a get-out this morning and, out of pride and obstinacy, she had refused it. Now she would have to suffer the consequences.

When she came back through, Bernard was talking loudly, waving a glass of sherry around as he spoke.

'I didn't actually see active service,' he was saying, 'you see, luckily for me war ended while I was still in training.'

'I see,' said Mr Brunton.

'It feels awkward sometimes,' confessed Bernard.

'What, not getting maimed, gassed or killed?' asked Mr Brunton helpfully.

'I suppose I feel as if I didn't really do my bit.'

'Well, I suppose you didn't. Is dinner ready, dear?'

They moved from the parlour into the dining room. As they made the short silent walk from one room to the other, Bernard spied a piano across the hallway.

'Do you play?' he asked Mrs Brunton.

'A little,' said Mrs Brunton and she giggled again.

The table was set with their best china and cutlery. Evie thought it looked very old-fashioned. Bernard sat opposite her and beside Mrs Brunton. As one, the Bruntons released their napkins from their rings, unfolded them and put them on their laps. Bernard ignored his. Between the grapefruit starter and the roast chicken, it rolled sadly onto the floor. The conversation improved over dinner: Mrs Brunton asked about London and Bernard was full of stories about people he knew and she had heard of. Evie picked at her chicken wing.

Despite snubbing his napkin, Bernard had decent table manners. He managed to polish off his chicken, peas and roast potatoes without talking with his mouth full, spitting or elbowing Evie's mother. This was silently noted by all three Bruntons. After the main course, Evie sprang up, cleared the plates and brought in the jam roly-poly.

The pudding was not one of Mrs Brunton's best. The sponge had dried up, taking most of the jam with it, and the whole thing tasted rather rubbery. The covering of custard did little to disguise the disappointment of what lay beneath. Bernard gallantly pushed his helping around the plate and Mrs Brunton noticed.

'I'm sorry about the pudding,' she mumbled.

'*Mais Madame*,' replied Bernard, reverting to the French of earlier, '*Votre cuisine est magnifique*!'

'I beg your pardon, sir?' Mr Brunton spoke fluent French.

'I feel a song coming on!' cried Bernard.

As Evie choked on the last of her roly-poly, he jumped up and nimbly hopped over to the piano room opposite, leaving the door open. He settled himself on the piano stool and started to compose a ballad for his hostess.

The grapefruit was divine,
The chicken was sublime,
So who cares if the dessert
Is just a little tough?
Yes, just a little rough,
At least it's not as dry
As a desert.

The reluctant audience could hear Bernard loud and clear, but they could only catch glimpses of him smiling at them as he swayed backwards and forwards, coming in and out of view from behind the doorframe, singing his heart out. Mrs Brunton looked confused and embarrassed; an expressionless Mr Brunton took the opportunity to stretch his neck, backwards and forwards, this way and that. Evie thought she might die of excruciation, wished she could, but she would first murder Bernard.

When the ditty was over, Bernard bounded back to the dining room to graciously accept applause and was met with icy silence. He glanced at Evie. She looked like an animal caught in a trap, both terrified and wild with rage. He had failed completely: his lateness, his handkerchief, his frivolous anecdotes had all stacked up against him. But the worst fault was his realisation that there was something missing. Just as Evie had sensed a lack of life in his painting, he had detected a lack of animation at the dinner party. He had hoped to resuscitate things with his little ditty. How wrong he had been. What the London set applauded, the Devon set were appalled by. As he took his seat back at the table, he realised that an evening at the undertakers would have been more inviting than sitting back down with these prim parents and their seething daughter.

He smiled at Mr Brunton, 'Where did you find such a fine cook?'

But Mr Brunton had had enough. He pushed back his chair, left the room and marched upstairs. They could hear his feet striding along the landing and the click of the study door.

'Well, I think we're all finished?' Without waiting for an answer, Mrs Brunton got up and started clearing the table, keeping her head down and her eyes on the tablecloth.

'It was lovely,' Bernard said, gesturing with his hands to the empty dishes, trying to catch Mrs Brunton's eye.

'I'll see Bernard out,' said Evie, keeping her voice even but glaring across the table at her guest.

'Would you, dear?' said Mrs Brunton, not looking up, her head bent over the pudding bowls.

Bernard stood up and followed Evie out of the dining room. It reminded him of being put off the train at Crewkerne. He was being ejected again, but this time there was much more at stake. Evie led him out of the back door and down the path to the back gate. She stalked ahead of him and he lumbered uneasily behind her. When they reached the gate, he hesitated before opening it.

'I'm sorry.'

'No you're not.'

'Look Evie, I am sorry. I warned you it was hopeless. I just can't behave at these kinds of things. All those middle-class expectations, they make me nervous and I end up doing something silly, or mischievous.'

'It was just like the train all over again. It was torture for me, watching you insult my mother. How could you do it, Bernard? It was bad enough when it was me—'

'But your mother is a good cook. She needed celebrating.'

Evie wanted to hit him. 'Do they let you out in public in London? Or do you live in a zoo?' she snarled.

'London's different, people are more—' He managed to stop himself.

'More what? More *avant-garde*?' Evie was furious.

'More friendly.'

She knew he was referring to her father.

'It seems to me, Bernard, that we are not suitable friends for each other. We are too different. I was brought up to make people feel good about themselves, you were brought up to humiliate them. I was brought up to placate people, you were brought up to shock them.'

Bernard was silent.

'And as for our deal, well you couldn't manage a decent, civilised meal with my parents and I won't sit for a portrait. You didn't keep your side of the bargain and I won't keep mine.'

'Whatever you say.' He turned, opened the gate and then: 'I just can't help it, Evie. It's like a red rag to a bull, all that—' he paused and, lost for words, gestured in the air, 'all that stuff.'

'You are a bull, Bernard, a bull in a china shop. You have run roughshod over everything I hold dear.'

'Everything you hold dear?' He looked surprised and then sad. He slowly disappeared down the lane.

Evie was still incandescent with rage. She wanted to shout after him: 'I wish I'd left you to die in the shed!' but she was conscious her parents might be listening. She slammed the gate shut, clenched her fists and went inside.

Her mother was washing up at the sink.

'I'm so sorry, Mummy!'

Mrs Brunton sighed stoically and looked out of the window. 'Your father's taken it worse,' she said. She spoke as if there had been a bereavement and, in a way, there had. A dinner party had been ruined. People relied on dinner parties as a means of keeping the wheels of society in motion. One came, one brought a gift, one ate, one paid compliments, one left, one wrote a thank-you note. Bernard had dared to challenge this assumption: he had turned a dinner party on its head by introducing spontaneity and risk taking. He had stuck his neck out and he had made a mistake. It was shocking, unforgivable.

Evie helped her mother to do the dishes. The two ladies worked in silence. What could they say? Then Evie went into the parlour to face her father. Mr Brunton was hidden behind *The Times*.

'Daddy?'

'A most unpromising youth. I hope we shan't see him here again,' said Mr Brunton, without lowering his newspaper.

Evie went upstairs and lay on her bed. Bernard had betrayed her, completely. Now, to all the other Bernards that crowded her mind, she added a new one – Bernard the betrayer. She had trusted him to behave well, just for a couple of hours, just so her parents would approve of him. But he couldn't do it. He didn't respect them enough. He didn't respect her enough. If he couldn't behave at a dinner party, then where could he behave?

Perhaps a friendship with Bernard would only work outside of society, away from everyone else. Perhaps if they had met on a desert island, with no one to witness his eccentric behaviour – his mole touching, his dreadful ditties, perhaps that would have worked. But she herself was a product of the society who condemned his behaviour. She was as horrified as the rest of them. Even on a desert island she would have been cross if he slighted her customs, her standards. No, there was no doubt about it – they were incompatible. She lay awake for hours nursing her anger. Then, just as she fell asleep, she saw his face, the way it had looked at the end of their quarrel – puzzled and sad. It had the same vulnerability as when he emerged from the shed. Yet another Bernard. How many were there?

The Wheatsheaf

After he left Evie's, Bernard felt completely at a loss. He certainly didn't want to go home. An empty house and a stack of blank canvases would demoralise him completely. He had messed up yet again. What was it about these sorts of events that made him behave so badly? He knew what was expected but he couldn't bring himself to perform. He was like a child who knew a second language but refused to speak it.

As soon as he went into the Bruntons' pokey parlour, he had felt like a dog on a lead, and like a dog he had strained and pulled to get off again. During dinner, he had felt the lead tighten till it was like a noose around his neck and he had been compelled to wriggle out of it. Ironically, he had felt exactly the same at Phoebe's. He only visited her once – once was enough. He sat in her stifling parlour with several portraits of vicars staring down from the walls at him. Then her father, the Reverend Carson, came in looking just like one of his ancient ancestors, except older if anything. Whatever Bernard said to him was met with: 'I don't think so,' and a large clock on the mantelpiece ticked: 'Nit-wit! Nit-wit!' at him. Phoebe fussed with the tea tray and smiled nervously, but the two men couldn't find a single subject in common or a single point to agree on. Eventually Bernard made a sweeping gesture with his hands that took in every single vicar and said, with a brilliant beaming smile: 'Sir, with a house full of old men, it must be a relief to have a young lady around.'

The Reverend Carson replied that he didn't think so and the clock repeated its earlier refrain and Bernard knew it was time to go.

Phoebe had been cross with him and the failed tea party had dented their friendship, but only temporarily. After a couple of letters, they were back to the cheerful witticisms of old and they even started to meet again in the town's tea rooms, although the invitation to the vicarage was not repeated. A failed tea party in Saffron Walden, and now a ruined dinner party in Colyton. There were certainly similarities between the two, but there were differences too. Phoebe had worn a dreadful gown – a heavy purple covered with large lilies, whereas Evie had looked as fresh as a daisy in a blue cotton dress. Also Phoebe lived alone with her father whereas Evie had a mother.

Bernard always felt nervous with mothers. They were a strange animal to him and he was never sure what to say or how to act around them. Mothers in London tended to be rather pushy. It was these sorts of mothers that he fobbed off with his witty songs – and usually got away with it. But Evie's mother wasn't like that at all. She was quiet, gentle, unsure of herself in a charming way. She had anxious eyes, but behind them something else was dancing. A sense of mischief – that was it. She had responded to his French with giggles and she had been charmed by his posy of flowers. Why then had he made up such a ridiculous song about her pudding? What had possessed him? She had looked completely crushed afterwards. How dreadful. How callous he had been; no wonder Evie was livid.

Bernard realised his lack of a mother had turned him into a kind of Peter Pan. Benedict's guidance was vague and he often viewed Bernard's waywardness with amusement rather than concern. Like Peter, Bernard was left to his own devices. He was a free spirit and a free-thinker and his art had been enriched by this, but he hadn't learned the boundaries that mothers taught their children.

Bernard chewed all this over in his mind as he slowly walked the mile back to Hollybrook. As he entered the village, he rounded a corner and there in front of him was The Wheatsheaf. It was an old pub, half-covered with an enormous thatch, the rest of its white exterior broken up by crooked windows. It looked friendly and inviting. When had he last had a drink? A proper drink, not the clawing sherry he had been offered in Evie's parlour. A drink would be nice.

He pushed open the heavy wooden door and went into a dark, low-ceilinged bar. Whitewashed walls were broken up by dark wooden beams. The windows, smeared with dust and grime, glowed orange from the last of the sunset. Wooden tables were scattered around a stone floor, all empty except for one by a low window where three lads and an older man sat talking, drinking large mugs of cider. When Bernard came in, they all fell silent and stared at him.

'Good evening,' said Bernard, approaching the table with a smile. The young men looked away but the older man got up and offered his hand in greeting.

'Welcome to Hollybrook,' he said with a smile. 'Join us if you want, but it's your round.'

'But of course.' Bernard bounced over to the bar, feeling in his pockets for some change.

'Five of what they're having,' he asked a toothless man at the counter.

This was easy. These lads weren't stuck up like London types and they weren't stuffy like the Bruntons. He would make friends with them. He tipped his coins onto the counter – there was just enough for the drinks. He handed it over, picked up the mugs, three in one hand, two in the other, sticking his fingers in to carry them, enjoying the feel of the frothy cider, and plonked them down on the men's table.

'May I?' but without waiting for a reply he pulled up a stool and joined them. The older man looked at him.

'So you're staying at High View.'

'How do you know that?'

The others smirked into their drinks.

'Walls talk around here.' A pause. 'Actually I'm Mr Wilson.'

'Oh I see,' Bernard grinned. 'Your wife, sir, makes wonderful soup.'

'And you, sir, make a terrible mess.'

Bernard grinned again, more sheepishly. 'I'm not very good at domestic duties,' he admitted, smiling round at the young men.

Not a flicker.

'I'm all fingers and thumbs in the kitchen.' He grinned at them again. He felt like a fisherman casting a fly over a stream, hoping for a bite.

The men smirked into their drinks again but didn't look at him.

'Well, cheers!' said Bernard, raising his mug of cider.

'Cheers!' replied Mr Wilson. The younger men mumbled but didn't lift their mugs. They hunched together at one end of the table. They looked about his age yet he felt a yawning gap between them and the gap seemed to be widening.

'So what do you lads do for a living?'

'This and that,' said one of them, scowling at Bernard through his eyebrows. 'You?'

'I'm a painter,' said Bernard, realising how pretentious artist would have sounded.

'And in the war?' asked another.

A shadow crossed Bernard's face but he didn't miss a beat. 'I just caught the last of it.' He took a gulp of cider.

'Where?'

Another gulp and then: 'Actually, I was still in training when it ended.'

'How come?' asked the scowling youngster.

'I had an accident,' said Bernard quickly. 'I fell off a roof.'

'Were you thatching?'

'No.' He knew that if he wasn't honest it would lead to more questions. 'I was playing the fool,' he admitted, looking sheepish again.

'To get out of the war?'

'Not at all, it was before war started.'

'Sure it was,' the scowler said, quite sarcastic. 'What were you doing on a roof? Trying to find a white feather?'

Bernard stood up quickly, knocking the table legs. The cider bounced out of the mugs and onto the table top.

'Say that again and I'll punch you!'

'Now, now,' warned the older man.

'White feather,' said the scowler, getting slowly to his feet. 'I know your sort, you're a trench dodger.' He glanced round at the two young men for support and they nodded into their drinks. 'It's no good looking for a fight now the war's over,' he goaded.

Bernard was furious. He clenched his fist, pulled back his arm to throw a punch and then, at the last minute, he realised the scowler's right arm was missing. The sleeve of his cotton shirt hung down limply by his side, like a broken wing. Overcome with confusion, Bernard hesitated then lowered his fist and, as he did so, the scowler suddenly lashed out and hit him with his left hand, punching him hard in the face.

Stunned, Bernard reeled backwards and staggered away from the table. He put his hand up to his nose and felt blood. He quickly wiped it and glanced at his hands, smeared with red. Despite the blood, despite the stinging pain, his anger had completely evaporated. The last thing he wanted to do was fight a one-handed man.

'You win,' he said.

'But we've only just started,' replied the scowler.

'Forget it Sam, sit down son.' The older man tugged on the scowler's good arm till he grunted and sat back down again.

'Trench dodger,' he muttered again into his drink.

Bernard took his chance and made for the door. Once outside he walked quickly up the road, dabbing his face with his sleeve. Yet again he had been brought face to face with the suffering he had somehow managed to avoid. They were right, he was a trench dodger. Why hadn't he fought? The same old question came back again and again to haunt him.

Two Mothers

'You're not a ghost then?'

Mrs Wilson heard the bottom stair creak, but she didn't bother turning round from the sink where she was preparing vegetables. Bernard came meekly into the kitchen, smiling sheepishly at her bent back.

'Mrs Wilson,' he began, 'I'm so sorry about last night.'

'You certainly make the mess of a poltergeist,' she continued, ignoring his apology.

Bernard felt really awkward. He had been here nearly three weeks and it was the first time he was up early enough to meet his housekeeper, but she had her back to him and her voice had an edge to it that was both sarcastic and tetchy, the sort of voice Bernard imagined only a mother could do well.

'I'm sorry,' he said again.

'Sorry you got punched or sorry you bought the drinks?' she retorted, not looking round, peeling the potatoes with great ferocity.

He was surprised at how frank she was with a paying guest, and yet this frankness gave him permission to offload his guilty feelings. He seized the moment. 'Sorry I upset your son.'

Bernard's voice had a tone of real contrition in it and this seemed to incense Mrs Wilson. She threw the potato peeler down and swung round to face him. 'And are you sorry he lost his arm too?' She glared at him, dark brown eyes flashing in her tanned, lined face. She was small in size yet she seemed to tower over him in the tiny kitchen. Bernard was silent, worried she might send the potato peeler flying in his direction.

'I wish I could have done my bit and contributed in some way,' he said eventually.

'Really? And which bit? What would you have given the cause? A leg, an ear, an eye perhaps?'

Bernard tried to change tack. 'I'm a lazy oaf,' he mumbled.

'Yes, and a romantic one,' she replied, steering the conversation back into dangerous territory.

Bernard took in her tired face, her thin dark hair scraped up into a bun, the circles around her eyes. He wondered how many other jobs she did besides this one.

'I wish I could have gone, instead of your son.'

'And how long would that have lasted? Five days, five hours, five minutes?'

Bernard felt the force of her comments in his chest and was winded by the truth of them. He stood miserably in the kitchen, looking down at the floor, unable to meet her eyes.

'To be honest, I wish you had,' she said, half to herself. 'I mean I wish you'd gone instead, any mother would.' A pause. 'But I wouldn't want you to go as well.' She turned away from him, back to the sink and, picking up the potato peeler, gazed out of the window. She was thoughtful for a minute as if reviewing what she had said.

'I'm not needing the work here mind,' she muttered, glancing at his reflection in the window.

Bernard caught her eye in the glass pane. 'Well I need you, Mrs Wilson, I couldn't paint without your help in the house.'

As he said it, he realised how lame it sounded. How many pictures had he actually finished? One? Two at the most?

He gestured to a saucepan simmering on the range. 'The soup smells nice.'

'It's chicken,' she said and a smirk crossed her lips. 'But you're not one, Mr Cavalier.'

She put one hand into the bowl and one hand under it and drained the water out, deftly catching the peel with her fingers; then she added the chopped potatoes to the simmering pan.

'You need to get over your good fortune, stop tripping over your lucky star and get on with your painting.'

With a final glare, she stormed past him and made for the front door. He stood and watched her stomp down the drive towards the gate. Well, at least he had finally met her. He sighed and sat down at the table. The painting he had done the day before was still propped up against the empty jam jar. He picked it up and, with another sigh, took it into his studio.

* * *

The Bruntons' silent wake for a ruined dinner party continued through breakfast. It was Sunday so the door to the piano room was firmly shut. Despite the chilly atmosphere in the dining room, the weather looked promising and the sun was already hot. Mr Brunton got up from the table to water the hanging basket outside the front door and there it was: a brown paper parcel, sitting on the doorstep. A small, flat, oblong package, addressed to Mrs Brunton.

The three Bruntons crowded round the dining table as Mrs Brunton opened it. Evie's heart was in her mouth. She alone recognised the handwriting, but they all surmised it was from Bernard and they all thought the same silent thought: Now what? Mrs Brunton snipped the string with her dressmaking scissors and the brown paper fell away to reveal a small picture, painted on card – a watercolour. Wild flowers sat in a jam jar on a windowsill. An early morning sun slanted in at the window behind them, making multi-coloured patterns both on the windowsill and in the jam jar itself. Some of the flowers fanned out expansively; others bent their small heads with a delicacy that was breathtaking. Mrs Brunton let out a gasp of surprise and delight.

Mr Brunton took control. 'A letter of apology would have been sufficient – and more appropriate.'

But Mrs Brunton looked radiant. She picked up the painting and went upstairs.

Looking for a bit of peace and quiet, Mrs Brunton took her picture into the bathroom. She propped it against the window frame and gazed at it, quite lost in the beauty of the flowers. After a few minutes, the usual doubts began to gather in her mind: Bernard had insulted her, but now he had apologised. And what an apology, what colours. That silly song, but now this touching present. What was she supposed to think?

If Mrs Brunton was rather confused by the picture, her daughter was rather moved by it. Perhaps because it was such a surprise, perhaps because she had slept so badly, something about the delicate flowers made her want to cry. They were exquisite: pale, subtle, soft, gentle. They showed a side of the artist completely at odds with his buffoon-like behaviour of the evening before. The tension this created in Evie made it difficult for her to breathe. Last night, she had condemned him completely and written him off as someone who had offended her mother. This morning he had delighted her. Such a turn-around made Evie feel unsteady on her feet. She had meant him to serve years in purgatory, but his picture had invoked almost immediate forgiveness. With such a beautiful painting Bernard had surely atoned for his brash behaviour. But what about her behaviour? What about the unpleasant things she had said? How could she make up for those?

Mr Brunton looked up from his paper when Evie stuck her head round the study door a couple of hours later.

'I'm going out for a cycle,' she said. 'I'm not sure when I'll be back.'

'Where's your mother?'

'Still at church.'

'What will you do for lunch?'

'I've made a chicken sandwich.'

'I see.'

Of course he did. Evie smiled weakly and closed the door again.

The Raspberry Patch

It was a glorious day and she wasn't in a hurry. Evie meandered down the country lanes, enjoying the freedom of not carrying a postbag. The sun bounced off the road and the hedgerows shimmered in the heat. She was wearing a white lacy summer blouse and cream skirt to keep as cool as possible. She had chosen the blouse because of the weather conditions, not because it had a flattering neckline, not because it complemented her hair. If her mother had known about the trip she would have advised Evie to wear a hat, but Evie didn't like hats; she didn't look good in them. She cycled slowly but purposefully, enjoying the journey, refusing to think about what she would say when she arrived at her destination.

High View seemed unusually quiet. Evie parked her bicycle at the gate and crunched up the gravel to the front door. She took a deep breath and rang the doorbell. No one came. She rang again. Still no one. She hadn't envisaged this scenario. How frustrating; she had cycled a mile for nothing on her day off. She turned and started to walk back down the path again when she heard it – a loud snoring sound in the front garden, just behind the hedge. She crept across the grass and peeped round the privet. There was Bernard, stretched out on a blanket, dead to the world. She stood and looked at him. A round face, reddish from lying in the sun, clashing slightly with his copper coloured hair. And a mark – a bruise on his nose. She hadn't noticed that last night. How had he got that?

Never mind, it was nice to have the chance to just look at him without worrying about what he was going to do or say. If only he could always be this quiet and peaceful; how easy things would be.

As if on cue, Bernard opened an eye, saw her and jumped up.

'Evie!'

'Bernard,' was all she could say. Why hadn't she rehearsed this? Now it would be awkward.

'I came to tell you that my mother appreciated your picture.'

'Good, good.'

Bernard looked at a bit of a loss – bewildered even. He had his vulnerable face on again. Was it because he had just woken up, or was it because he was feeling wounded?

'I spoke a little hastily last night,' she began.

But Bernard had recovered himself. 'You spoke a little hastily and I sang a little hastily,' he laughed. 'Friends again?'

'Friends.' Evie was relieved but also surprised how quickly he could forgive and forget. If he remembered her remarks, he certainly didn't bear a grudge.

'You look hot, Evie. You must come inside out of the heat. I'll make some tea. Have you had lunch?'

He was off, buzzing and bumbling, shepherding her into the cool of the kitchen.

'I have lunch!' laughed Evie, pulling a packet of sandwiches out of the deep pockets of her skirt. But the heat of the day had affected them and they smelled suspicious.

'Mrs Wilson to the rescue!' Bernard took the lid off the saucepan of soup.

'I had a long chat with her this morning,' he smiled. 'I was up early.'

Evie was impressed. So he had painted the picture this morning and then delivered it, on foot presumably, and all before breakfast.

'You worked fast!'

Bernard didn't answer. Instead he put the saucepan on the hotplate, found the bread and butter and put bowls and plates on the table.

'I had to do something,' he said suddenly, breaking the silence. He paused. 'I'm afraid I don't have much idea of etiquette, Evie. The thing is – I didn't have a mother.'

This was new information. Evie looked up, startled.

'My father brought home a succession of 'aunts', all of them very sweet, but none of them permanent.' He started slicing the bread. 'And my father's friends are, well, fairly unusual.'

'I see.' She sounded like her father.

'You could say I had an unconventional upbringing.'

'Yes.' She couldn't think what else to say.

They sat quietly and ate their soup.

He looked at her. 'I'd still like to paint your portrait.'

Evie felt herself blushing. 'Yes, of course.'

'Excellent, excellent,' Bernard smiled, 'but pudding first. Do you like raspberries?'

The raspberry patch was at the back of the house, twenty canes covered in ripe, pink berries. They wandered through them, each carrying a basket, eating more than they picked. The sun was really hot now; Evie could feel her forehead prickle with perspiration. Bernard beamed at her.

'Here!' he exclaimed. 'We'll paint it here! Wait Evie! Stop! Don't move a muscle, I'm coming back!' He ran towards the house, still carrying his basket, scattering raspberries over the lawn.

'What?'

'Your portrait! We'll paint it here! Don't move!'

He returned a few minutes later with a small gardening stool and a sketchbook. He found a spot near her and dug the legs of the stool into the ground till they were level. Then he plonked himself down, pulled a pencil from behind his ear and opened his sketchbook.

'Don't I get to sit down?'

'No Evie, you are the peasant girl, toiling in the heat, bringing in the raspberry harvest.'

She grimaced. She was baking in the sun. How long would this take? She should have brought a hat.

'Could you possibly agree to—' Bernard made awkward movements with his hands, 'wearing your hair down?'

Evie was too hot to care. She shook out her bun and her long blonde hair tumbled round her shoulders.

'Lovely.' He put down his sketchbook and stared at her.

'Aren't you going to get started?'

'Hold on!' Bernard got up and came over to her. He gently placed his hand under her chin and titled her head ever so slightly to the left. 'There.'

He returned to his gardening stool and took up the sketchbook again.

'Hurry up!' laughed Evie, 'I can't hold this for long.'

Bernard set to work, looking at her, measuring the perspective with his thumb and pencil, scribbling in his book, looking again. After a few minutes, he suddenly got up again and came up very close.

'Your hair,' he explained, 'can I just rearrange it a little?'

Without waiting for an answer, he gently picked up a loose strand that was falling over her eyes and lifted it out of the way. He was so close she could feel his breath on her cheek.

'You have such beautiful hair. Don't ever cut it!'

'What? Why would I?'

'So many girls do these days—' He stopped suddenly and gazed at her mouth. 'Keep still.'

Quickly and gently he brushed her top lip with his thumb.

'Just a little fly,' he whispered, 'from the raspberries.'

The soft touch of his thumb made her lips tingle and she started to feel giddy. She had to break the spell.

'You'd better hurry up. I'll be needing tea in a minute.' She was smiling but suddenly businesslike.

Bernard quickly stepped away from her. 'All done.' He

went back to the gardening chair, picked up his sketchbook and snapped it shut.

'What, you've finished?'

'I've everything I need.'

'Oh.' She felt cheated. Was that the extent of her career as an artist's model? Five minutes in a raspberry patch picking fruit? Surely he needed to make a few sketches, otherwise he would never remember what she looked like. Perhaps he had lost interest? She had set aside the afternoon, but the sitting was already over.

'Well, I should be getting home.' She sounded slightly peevish.

'Don't go. I was hoping you'd show me the beach.'

'It's too far to walk.'

'I found a bicycle this morning – in the shed!'

***

The bicycle was much too small for Bernard, more of a child's bicycle, and the only way he could ride it was with his legs almost doubled up. He had to cycle twice as fast as Evie, but it didn't stop him playing the fool on the country lanes, dawdling far behind, then shooting past her and then dawdling again. He wove around her, trying to make her wobble, singing songs from the music halls.

'Evie, Evie, give me your answer do,' he crooned, racing past her, his legs going full pelt, pedals spinning.

When they reached the beach at Seaton, the tide was in. They sat on the shingle and looked out to sea. Bernard recounted stories from some of the crazy beach parties he had been to at Brighton and Eastbourne with the Charleston set. He told her about art school and his fall from the roof. Away from home, Evie could throw her head back and laugh at his exploits, and her hair shook out behind her as she laughed. The sea air invigorated her and loosened the knots of her parents' expectations. She felt rebellious and free – a kite flying in the wind. They didn't need a desert island, just time together outside, far from the stifling air of her parlour.

'Do you have a best friend?' he suddenly asked. Evie was taken aback by the directness of his question.

'I do,' she said eventually. 'Cassie, the girl I was with on the train, we've known each other for ages, but…' her voice trailed off.

'But what?'

'Well, she lives in London, so I don't see her much, but also…' A pause. 'I'm not sure I can always trust her. I mean, I think she sometimes breaks confidences.' Evie winced at the way she was maligning her friend. 'But it's always to protect me,' she added quickly.

'If you're not sure, she can't be a best friend.'

Evie sat and looked out to sea. She had obviously painted Cassie in the wrong light. It was true that Cassie had told her parents about Bernard, but she had also gone to a lot of trouble to find out more about him. Both these actions had been inspired by concern for her and Evie felt guilty and anxious to change the subject.

'And you?'

Bernard looked thoughtful. 'I have a friend – Toby. I mean I have lots of pals in London, but only Toby has bothered to write to me here. Toby cares about me, but he's a terrible talker and I wouldn't tell him my secrets. So maybe he's not a best friend.' Bernard paused and looked at her. 'Maybe I'm still searching.'

Evie looked back at him. His eyes were an unusual colour – a cornflower blue. She hadn't noticed them before.

It's too hot!' he said suddenly. 'Come on! Let's get wet!' He jumped up and, grabbing her arm, started to pull her down to the water.

'No!' Evie laughed. 'Look, Bernard, I'm sorry, I have to get home.'

He released her. 'You go and I'll paddle.' He sat down and started pulling off his boots and socks.

'Goodbye, Bernard.'

'Goodbye!' He started to roll up his trousers.

Evie knew she had to leave before someone spotted him and she was somehow implicated in his mad dash to the water. Perhaps her kite was not as free as she had thought.

Itchy Legs

After Evie left, Bernard messed around in the shallows for ages, but he couldn't seem to cool down. He waded in deeper, letting the sea splash high above his knees, but the water wasn't cold enough. His chest seemed to be burning up, as if his heart was being consumed by a bizarre chemical reaction that was steadily growing in intensity. Something had happened in the raspberry patch, something that had nothing to do with the weather. He gave up and made his way back to the beach. He sat on the stones and unrolled his trousers, soaking after his paddle. As he picked his way back over the shingle, they flapped round his legs like wet wings. He got back on the tiny bicycle and headed for home. Cycling with doubled-up legs uphill was hard work. On the way, he was keen to impress Evie and the route sloped downward towards the sea. Going home, on his own, proved more difficult.

Bernard's trousers were made of canvas. The salt water had stiffened them and, as he pedalled along, the wet material started chaffing the tops of his legs. It was only two miles to the house, but by the time he got home the salty slacks had done quite a lot of damage. He alighted from his bicycle in the manner of a cowboy getting off a horse. Then he walked into the house very carefully – his legs splayed out sideways like Charlie Chaplin. By the evening his thighs were on fire. He couldn't bear to have a sheet touch them and he had to sleep on top of the bed.

The next morning they were no better – worse if anything. Great wheals of red skin covered the insides of his legs. He couldn't bear the thought of getting dressed, but he couldn't risk wandering around the house without trousers on, not when Evie might arrive at any moment. He decided to lie low until she had been with the post. He lay on his bed, trying to decide whether his heart was hotter than his legs or whether his legs were hotter. After what seemed like an age, he heard the swish of wheels on the gravel and the click of the letterbox. He got carefully out of bed and crawled to the window, making sure his naked body was well out of sight. He peeped through the panes. There she was, cycling away, over the brow of the hill. He was safe.

He threw on a shirt and made his way downstairs, one step at a time, reverting to the Chaplin walk of the day before to keep the insides of his thighs away from each other. He picked up the letter on the doormat. It was postmarked London and he recognised Carruthers's slanting handwriting. He knew what it would say: How's it going? Have you finished? His itchy legs would keep him indoors today, so he might as well get on with some painting. He locked the front door from the inside so he couldn't be disturbed, buttered himself a piece of Mrs Wilson's fresh bread and walked gingerly to the drawing room. He could hide himself away and paint uninterrupted all day while he waited for his legs to recover.

Perhaps because he had no other option, perhaps because of the unopened letter from Carruthers, Bernard set about painting with gusto. He found standing much more comfortable than sitting and he could forget the heat in both his heart and his legs while painting. He worked solidly through lunch, too caught up in his art to think about eating. When the sun moved round to the back of the house, he was able to open the French windows on to the garden. A smell of late summer drifted in. Delightful. He started to hum. Wait, he could do better than that. In the corner of the room, by the fireplace, was a gramophone player and a few records. He flicked through them. Mozart's clarinet concerto? Maybe, what else? Ah – Verdi. Perfect. He slid the record out of its sleeve, put it on the gramophone and wound it up. Suddenly the room was full of music. Bernard moved his brush in time to the beat. This was the life; this was artistic endeavour at its finest. He was a Renaissance man – a master of painting and a lover of music.

Evie got back from her round to find the Post Master waiting for her.

'I'm afraid there's a telegram to deliver,' he said. 'Cavalier, High View.'

Her heart sank. She had already been there and had been only too glad just to pop the letter in and slip away. She didn't want to see Bernard every day. It made her feel like a jack-in-the-box, appearing all the time, especially when he wasn't expecting it.

'What about the telegram boy? Can't he take it?'

'He's off sick,' said Mr Thornber. 'You can fit it in with your four o'clock delivery. You'll be going right past the house.'

'I suppose so,' said Evie, doubtfully.

Telegrams reminded her of the war. She had watched the telegram boy deliver hundreds of them in the conflict and she knew that almost all of them brought bad news. The boy told her how he hated having to ring the bell and hand over the small envelopes.

'When people open the door, I never look at them,' he said. 'I don't want to see their faces.'

She had often noticed him in this predicament as she passed with the post. He would hand over the envelope as quickly as possible and take off on his bicycle. Missing. Wounded. Prisoner. Dead. There were really only four possibilities and they were all bad news.

And so Evie always dreaded this particular job. She rarely had to do it – only when the telegram boy was off sick or on holiday, but she hated being the harbinger of doom. Of course telegrams brought good tidings as well – births and marriages as well as deaths. Bernard's telegram was probably innocuous but she still felt trepidation. She sighed, put it in her coat, picked up the mail bag full of the afternoon's mail and cycled back out to Hollybrook. She delivered all the letters first and only when the postbag was empty did she head to High View. This time she left her bicycle by the roadside. She had no intention of staying. She walked up the drive and rang the doorbell. No one. Well, she wasn't going to peer round hedges today. One more try and then she would leave the telegram and come back tomorrow. She rang again and then she heard the sound of singing from the back of the house. Perhaps Bernard was painting and hadn't heard the door.

She walked round to the back garden. The music was getting louder and, on top of the strains of an operatic chorus, she could hear a loud voice warbling. Smiling to herself, she reached the French windows of the drawing room and peered in. An unholy sight met her eyes: Bernard – naked from the waist down. Fortunately he was facing away from her, engrossed in his canvas. His shirttail covered some, but not all, of his ample buttocks and below them his large, hairy legs swayed in time to the aria. This unexpected exposure made Evie start and take a step backwards. As if he sensed an intruder, Bernard glanced in the mirror above the mantelpiece and saw her horrified face. Quick as a flash he grabbed the canvas to cover himself and whisked round to face her, positioning the painting to shield her from another shock.

'Evie! I thought you'd been already?'

She could hardly hear him above the roar of the record. She reached into her pocket, pulled out the telegram and waved it feebly.

'Hold on!' He reversed his large frame towards the gramophone and, still facing her, fumbled with the knobs until he had turned the record off.

'Evie, I'm so sorry. Don't go away, I'll put something on.' He walked awkwardly backwards towards the doorway into the hall.

'Come in, Evie. Sit down – I'll be back in a second.'

Evie stayed standing resolutely in the garden. She would not go inside. Not after a sight like that. She could hardly bear it. Why was nothing simple with this man? Why couldn't he get dressed before he painted? Surely artists tended to work fully-clothed?

Before she had time to consider this further, Bernard was back, this time in trousers. He waddled carefully into the room, like a very slow duck. Safe in the garden, Evie held the telegram out to him but remained firmly outside. Bernard's face twisted painfully every time he took a cautious step towards her.

'My legs had an allergic reaction to swimming. They're agony today. I waited till you'd delivered the post before I got up – I never imagined a telegram.' He took another step towards her and winced.

'I may take a while to reach you,' he smiled through clenched teeth. 'Could you either come inside or just read it out to me?'

'I can leave it for you,' she said, from the garden.

'It may need a reply.'

'But it might be bad news.'

'Just read it.'

Evie opened the envelope, quickly scanned the contents and then read the telegram out loud.

16.8.1920 LONDON

A NOTICE FOR YOUR OPENING APPEARS IN THE TIMES TODAY. ONLY TWO WEEKS TO GO. C

'Carruthers from the gallery. He's trying to put the fear of God into me. I've already had one letter from him today which I haven't opened.'

'You mean you don't read the post I bring?'

'Normally I do,' he said hurriedly. 'But I knew a letter from Carruthers would just be full of questions – How many, how big, how much can I charge for them?'

'But these are questions that need an answer.' She imagined the agent in London, anxiously waiting for news. 'How many paintings have you actually finished? I mean, how many are ready?'

Bernard hesitated. 'A few,' he said, vaguely.

'How many do you need?'

'The thing is, Evie, I've been a bit distracted.' He looked at her strangely. 'I've been distracted ever since I got here,' he said, not taking his eyes off her.

Evie was worried what he might say next. After his indecent exposure, any sort of declaration felt wrong – inappropriate. She imagined her father's face. If Bernard was going to profess his feelings for her, it shouldn't be like this. She needed to escape.

'Well, I won't keep you another moment then. You have lots to do, Mr Cavalier.'

'No, Evie, don't go.' His voice was urgent, desperate almost. He tempered the desperation with an awkward smile.

'I mean, don't go just yet, you've only just arrived. Come in for a moment. Give me the telegram at least.'

He put his hand out as if coaxing a bird in from the garden. She took a few cautious steps towards the French windows and held the telegram out. He waddled towards her, keeping the smile on, although it was lopsided with pain.

'Thank you,' he said gently, as he took the envelope from her, and then she was in the room with him and she could feel a thudding sound starting in her head.

'I love your hair,' he said softly. 'Did I mention that yesterday?'

The thudding in her head grew louder.

'I'd like to touch it.'

'You have a painting to finish.'

'Kiss me, Evie.'

He smelled of oil paint, turps and clean cotton. Close up his skin was pale pink and his lips were dry. The thudding noise was deafening now.

'Just kiss me, Evie.'

She could see his lips moving but she couldn't hear him. He reached out and put a hand round her neck, pulling her closer. She closed her eyes and then, through the thudding, she heard the sharp sound of a bell – a front door bell. Her eyes shot open again and she pulled away from him.

'Someone's here!' She lurched back towards the French window.

He gave a little laugh. 'Can't you get it?' he teased, but he turned away and started walking slowly towards the hall.

'Coming!' he called. 'Just a minute!'

Evie stood rooted to the spot. How had this happened? Her bicycle was at the roadside. Whoever the visitor was, she hoped they hadn't noticed it. What a nightmare. She had to get away.

She slipped back through the French window, crept along the side of the house and peered round the corner. Mr Wilson was standing on the porch, holding out a jug of something.

'My own brew,' he was saying, 'it doesn't taste as good, but it does the job.'

Bernard said something inaudible.

'Her bark's worse than her bite,' came the reply. 'I can see your legs are sore. I'll carry it into the kitchen.'

Mr Wilson disappeared into the house and Evie took her chance. She ran across the front lawn, keeping close to the shrubbery so she wouldn't be seen from the kitchen window. Then she tiptoed down the drive, jumped on her bicycle and shot round the corner.

When Bernard returned to the studio a few minutes later, it was empty. The bird had flown. Had she really gone? He stood and waited. 'Evie!' he called. A blackbird darted past the window, a cacophony of chirping and then silence. He waited a few minutes more. Still no sound. He dropped his trousers, stepped out of them and returned to his painting.

Life presented itself to Bernard as a series of images, some brighter than others – Evie's horrified face, reflected in the mirror. He considered it as he painted. She probably hadn't seen a man's legs before – and certainly not a man's buttocks. Was her look of horror due to surprise, or did his anatomy not meet her expectations? Before he had time to decide, the image changed – there was Evie on the beach, throwing her head back and laughing at one of his jokes, her long hair fluttering in the breeze like a golden flag. And now a different Evie, with a face like thunder, sitting at her parent's dining table. And now her face, up close, eyes closed, eyelids trembling. Bernard's heart began to boil over. He put down his brush and lit his pipe. Yet another painting day truncated by the arrival of his post lady.

A Man of Opposites

Cycling back to Colyton, Evie's head was teeming with thoughts. Safely away from Bernard's legs, she began to see the funny side and wished there was someone she could share the joke with. Certainly not Cassie; she would imagine the worst and there was also the chance she might gossip. Certainly not her mother; she would have a heart attack. But it wasn't just his legs that had unnerved her. His urgent request for a kiss had shocked her in a different way, amplifying the throbbing noise in her head, making her close her eyes. What on earth would have happened if the doorbell hadn't rung? Evie cycled slowly home, both confused and excited. She wished she had a sister she could confide in, but there was no sister back at North Lodge; just her father, sitting in the parlour, reading the newspaper. Evie scanned the advertisements on the front page of *The Times*. There it was, under a notice about a charitable ball, a small box:

THE ECHOED IMAGE
A NEW EXHIBITION OF CAVALIER PAINTINGS
SEPTEMBER – OCTOBER
CARRUTHERS GALLERY
CORK STREET
LONDON

It was obviously a grand affair. What if he wasn't ready? He had said he was too distracted to paint. Was she the distraction? The idea was both disturbing and delightful. She was twenty-two and, up to now, she had never been a distraction. War had started when she was sixteen and, quite suddenly, all the young men in her area had disappeared and Evie had found herself with a responsible job. There had been no time or opportunity for distractions. The very sound of the word was delicious. She had tried not to dwell on it, but for years and years she had secretly longed to be distracted. And now Bernard had arrived in her life, she most certainly was distracted – not always in a good way – sometimes he tormented her with his pranks and scrapes, but he was definitely a distraction. So if they distracted each other, what next? Would he try to kiss her again?

At dinner that evening, she struggled to do justice to her brisket and afterwards she wandered into the garden to think. Bernard was impossible, but he had prospects. Impossible-prospects, the two words melded in her mind till they became a new kind of flower, like holly-hocks. He was a man of opposites: overconfident yet vulnerable, deeply absorbed in his work one minute, flighty and distracted the next. He often acted without thinking but he was never unkind; in fact, he was very sweet and sensitive. And he seemed to like her. He seemed to like everything about her – even her mole. And he seemed to live – really live. While others tiptoed through life, he sang and swam, painted and partied. This bold approach was the bit about him that worried her the most, but it was also the bit of him she felt jealous of. She would love to stop caring so much about everything.

Evie had been brought up to care about all sorts of things, but she suspected that none of these things really mattered. They mattered when she was sat at the dining table with her parents, eating brisket; they didn't seem to matter when she was with Bernard. In his studio, she didn't worry so much about what other people, particularly her parents, thought about 'all that stuff.' Every little thing she did was done for other people, as if other people were watching, checking, nodding their approval. Instead of living her life she was acting it. Her life was a play. She had been given her lines and she had to be sure to remember them and trot them out at the appropriate moment, when it was her turn to speak. If she forgot her lines then there was a prompter, off stage, just out of view, who would hiss them to her until she picked up the thread again. If she changed the lines or missed her cue, there would be a general gasp from the audience, and the other actors in her play would glare at her as if she had betrayed them completely.

How different it was with Bernard. With Bernard she never knew what her lines should be. Anyway, he was always changing the plot – that was part of the excitement of being with him. She couldn't fall back on well-versed patter; she had to think on her feet and she had to think for herself. He spoke to her directly and, when she was brave enough, she spoke directly back. There was muttering from the stalls – the audience never liked surprises; they liked a predictable storyline. But maybe she was learning to ignore the mutterings, or perhaps she didn't notice them as much. Being with Bernard was a bit like being under the sea, the din of the everyday was muffled. She was swimming in inky depths and below her shone treasure. She just had to ignore the noise on the surface, dive down and touch it. She realised that if she had the courage to do this then everything would change for her. Perhaps he would give her the strength she needed?

Evie tried to remember what her life was like before Bernard arrived. She was happy enough before she met him. But now he was here, well everything was different. And he was only staying five weeks. How long had he been here already? She racked her brains. Two weeks? Three? He was almost certainly halfway through his stay. And then he would be gone. What would life be like when High View was empty again?

As Evie strolled thoughtfully through the garden, Mr and Mrs Brunton watched her warily from the kitchen window.

'A most unpromising youth,' Mr Brunton reminded his wife.

'But an accomplished painter,' said Mrs Brunton, remembering her picture.

Mad with Desire

The trouble with Phoebe's letters was that they kept coming, and replying to them was definitely a chore rather than a pleasure. Bernard received them respectfully, but not joyfully, and they weren't always opened the same day. They were put ceremoniously on the dresser where they sat and looked at him with the broodiness of an unpaid bill. As he passed on his way to the studio, he would give them a sideways glance.

'I really must do something about Phoebe,' he would say to himself. Then he would stick a paintbrush behind his ear and forget all about her. A few days later, he would seize the envelope, tear it open, glance through Phoebe's letter, dash off a jovial reply and stuff it in an envelope. As he stuck on the stamp, he would feel a combination of relief at having completed his task and exasperation at having to do it.

One evening, just as he was licking Phoebe's envelope, Bernard caught sight of a *Dear Evie* at the top of the letter. His heart missed a beat. He quickly ripped the whole thing up and threw it in the wastepaper basket. Then he opened the window, loosened his collar and took a few gulps of the cool night air. After that he started addressing Phoebe as *Dearest*, just to be on the safe-side. He chose *Dearest* in the hope she would find the old-fashioned salutation mildly ironic. He thought the term suggested fondness, but not affection, or at least not the sort of affection that would give a young lady any false ideas about her correspondent. And all the while, his feelings for Evie smouldered under the surface until the incident in the raspberry patch ignited the bonfire in his heart. And the bonfire grew quickly in size and intensity until it was a raging bush fire and he began to wonder if his heart would be consumed completely. He had to do something.

The day after the itchy legs, Bernard woke up early with an idea that might resolve his quandary. He would write to Miss Carson and Miss Brunton and be completely straight with both of them. But how to let down Phoebe as gently as possible and declare himself to Evie, whose feelings he couldn't quite read. He began wording the two letters in his mind during breakfast and, impatient to get started, took his bread and butter up to the writing desk in his bedroom. Although he was dying to declare himself to Evie, he knew he should write Phoebe's letter first. It was important not to rush such a delicate task. Phoebe would be very disappointed and his words, rather than wounding more than necessary, should contain the balm that would make a quick healing possible.

He glanced at the clock. He had a good two hours before Evie would arrive with the midday post. He would begin with the envelopes. He addressed Phoebe's more carefully than usual, for it was important that the letter of rejection reached its destination. *Miss Phoebe Carson, 82, Summerhill Road, Saffron Walden, Essex*. He held the envelope at arm's length and blew on it. Then he picked up a stamp, licked it, placed it in the top right-hand corner and thumped it down with gusto. Now for Evie's. This was easy; after all, he would be giving it to her in person. He carefully selected the creamiest envelope in his stack, refilled his pen, shook it to remove the slightest chance of an ink blot and wrote in large curly letters: *Evie*. Carried away by the beauty of her name, he added a little flower, just after the dot. Then he put the two envelopes to one side and started on Phoebe's letter. It was difficult to get it right and the wastepaper basket under his desk was soon filled with discarded drafts. Finally he came up with a version that seemed more or less acceptable. Thank goodness.

He left it to dry and started on his letter to Evie, which flowed much more easily.

High View, Hollybrook, Devon
Tuesday 17th August 1920

My Darling,

I hope you don't mind me addressing you as my darling. I have tried to contain my feelings for you over the past few weeks, but I cannot bear it any longer, I must speak the truth. You have captured my heart, you occupy my every waking moment and I cannot live without you.

I know I am embarrassing, difficult, and I don't know how many other awkward adjectives, not to mention an appalling show-off. I know your parents don't approve of me in the slightest and that the promise of an exhibition in London hardly counts as 'good prospects' for a young man, yet some madness in me makes me dare to ask the impossible: Could you bear to consider me for a husband? I dream of you as a wife, a muse, a companion – besides, I am quite mad with desire for you –

Bernard paused and reread this last phrase. A little bold perhaps, but he liked the way it tripped off the tongue: *mad with desire*, the two ds clinking together so pleasingly, like two wine glasses. He stood up, trotted downstairs to the piano and began to compose a few bars to go with his romantic lyrics. 'I'm quite mad with desire for you,' he crooned. He paused and thought for a moment before continuing: 'And I know that my heart will stay true.'

An over-educated musician might have considered his composition to be just a fistful of notes, but Bernard was not over-educated. He swayed and hummed and added a few twiddles, then he started again from the top, relishing what was fast becoming an achingly good melody. He pictured Evie reading the letter in front of him, reaching that line, rushing at him with outstretched arms, and he managing somehow to hug her and sing to her at the same time. The minutes passed as he perfected his ditty. When he finally paused for breath, he heard the ring of a bicycle bell. Evie! She was early! He pulled out his pocket-watch – no, she was late! He could hear the crunch of gravel on the drive and the tick-tick of a bicycle wheel. He raced out onto the porch.

'Hello!'

'There's just one thing for you, and I can't stop to chat, Mother wants me to run some errands after my round.'

She held out the letter but stayed on her bicycle, wobbling around with one foot on the gravel to steady herself. He knew she would be circumspect after yesterday. How he loved her shyness. He took the letter and smiled at her conspiratorially.

'Evie, could you give me a second, there's a couple of things I need to post.'

'Be quick then.'

Bernard ran up the stairs two at a time. He hadn't finished her letter! He grabbed the pen and quickly scribbled *and I know that my heart will stay true*. Then, with a flourish: *For ever yours, Bernard.*

'Hurry up!'

'Coming!'

Thank goodness he had already addressed the envelopes. He pushed Evie's letter into one and the letter for Phoebe into the other. Then he ran back downstairs and, leaning breathless against the doorframe, held the two letters out to her.

'Sorry,' he gasped, 'but I wanted to get these off.'

'Always in a rush,' she laughed and, without looking at the envelopes, she popped them both into her bag. Then she jumped back on her bicycle and started cycling down the path, towards the gate.

'I say,' called Bernard, 'one of them's for you!'

'Oh, right.' She kept cycling.

'Only, it doesn't have a stamp.'

But she had gone.

As soon as Evie rounded the corner, out of sight of the house, she applied her brakes. The bicycle screeched to a halt. She got off the saddle and stood, with the frame between her legs, fishing in the postbag. There it was, a cream envelope with Evie on the front, and a little flower. For some unaccountable reason the flower made her hands shake as she opened the letter.

High View, Hollybrook, Devon

Tuesday 17th August 1920

Dearest,

We have known each other quite some time now and I have so enjoyed getting better acquainted with you. You really are the sweetest creature and I admire you enormously. However, I have to be totally honest with you, because I really do like and respect you.

The thing is, I have recently met someone else and we have become very friendly and I am beginning to realise I am in love with her. I don't know if she cares for me, but the point is that I can no longer care for you as I ought to. I wanted to let you know as I don't want to stand in your light and spoil your chances. I can only hope that one day you will meet a boy who will make you very happy.

Please forgive me.

Your sincere friend,

Bernard

When she had finished reading, Evie stood and gazed over the hedgerows for several minutes, the letter still in her hand.

Then she folded it carefully and put it in her bicycle basket. She opened the postbag again and looked for the other letter that Bernard had given her. She was almost sure this letter would be addressed to Miss Phoebe Carson, 82, Summerhill Road, Saffron Walden, Essex. She knew the address by heart. She found the letter, leaned the bicycle up against the hedgerow, sat down in the long grass by the roadside and carefully opened it. The envelope had been stuck down hurriedly and it popped open like a ripe pea pod. *My Darling* it began.

Evie read the letter three times. After the third time, she dropped it and lay back in the long grass, eyes wide open, not moving, not even blinking. The clouds raced past, far, far away. She could feel the earth spinning under her; it was turning so fast she had to grab hold of the grass and hang on. There was a strange wheezing sound, like air rushing out of a broken bellows. The noise grew louder and louder. How could she stop it? She sat up, ripped Phoebe's letter up into tiny pieces, threw it in the ditch and lay back down again. What was it he had said? 'I've been a bit distracted.' Distracted certainly, but not by her. The wheezing sound was quieter now and the earth was slowing down again. Evie lay there for ages and then she remembered the post. She would be late today and it might miss the train. She hurriedly got up off the grass and picked up her bicycle. She forgot all about Phoebe's empty envelope, and leaving it where it lay on the verge, got on her bicycle and started for town.

As she pedalled furiously away, a soft summer breeze came from nowhere and whispered in the hedgerow. It picked up Miss Carson's envelope, lifted it slightly and flipped it onto the road. So when Evie glanced back over her shoulder, she saw it lying in full view of any passers-by. She applied her brakes and screeched to a halt. She couldn't leave it there; she would have to take it with her. The envelope twitched. Was it a sign? Perhaps tearing up Phoebe's proposal had not been cruel enough, perhaps there was more she could do to hurt the man she suddenly despised. The breeze got up again and the envelope flipped over once more, creeping nearer. Evie went back and picked it up. It was still quite clean. She blew carefully on it to remove any traces of dust and dirt. Then she opened it, slipped her letter of rejection inside and folded the edges of the flap inwards to close it again. It looked good as new. She put the envelope back in the bag and cycled to town as fast as she could.

The Chop

There were grumbles about her time-keeping at the sorting office. Evie apologised, blaming her delay on a puncture. She was never normally late. Too busy to notice her flushed face, the Post Master accepted her story without question. The bag was emptied and the letters and parcels were stamped and transferred to a sack for the mail van which would meet the mail train at Axminster. Evie watched the van leaving the yard, waiting for guilt to engulf her, but it didn't. Instead she felt a new blast of fury – she had another job to do.

She marched along the street to the barber's shop and pushed the door open. The grey-haired barber was sweeping up when she came in and looked up startled at her red face and blood-shot eyes. Evie plonked herself down in the barber's chair, pulled her hair out of its loose bun and glared at herself in the mirror, trying not to cry.

'Cut it all off!' she ordered. 'As short as you can.'

'Are you sure?' the old man asked gently. 'It's taken years to grow and it will take a long time to grow back again.'

'I've never been so sure of anything.'

The barber glanced at the clock. Ten to four. He wished he had shut early. He decided not to cut her hair as short as she had asked, just high enough above the shoulders so it would swing, like a curtain of gold, around her slender neck. He was a good cutter and he was hopeful that this new style would torture any man it was meant to punish, but not in the way the customer was expecting. His optimism increased when his fast-moving scissors revealed the most delightful mole at the nape of the young lady's neck.

When it was all done, Evie got up slowly and, averting her eyes from the long blonde tresses lying on the floor, paid the barber and left. He watched as she dashed across the road in a very self-conscious manner, head-down. The driver of a passing car hooted his horn eagerly; Evie didn't notice. She rushed back to the sorting office, pausing outside to jam her hat down on her head and put her collar up; then she crept inside to collect her four o'clock postbag. She slung it over her shoulder, picked up her bicycle and headed out of town, back to Hollybrook.

Bernard was waiting anxiously, yet optimistically, for Evie's return. Too excited to paint, he had spent his time deciding where to receive his fiancée. Should he be on the balcony as she cycled up to the house, à la Romeo and Juliet, or should he be playing the piano, leaving her to run into the house and find him? It was a close call and he was still deciding when he heard Evie arrive. But there was something about the sound of her bicycle on the gravel that made him go quickly to the door to meet her.

'Evie!' He peered closer. 'Good God, what happened to your hair?' For it had gone – almost all of it, leaving a sharp line at her chin, making her look so different he could hardly believe it.

Evie threw her bicycle down and marched up to him.

'What happened to my hair?' She flushed with anger. 'What happened to my hair? Your letter is what happened to my hair!' She was shaking with fury and very close to tears.

'But Evie, I had to confess – I couldn't wait any longer.' He was desperate to hold her. Surely this was when the bride-to-be kissed her future groom?

'Oh yes, certainly,' agreed Evie, wincing. 'You had to confess. But why couldn't you have told me earlier, before—' Instead of finishing her sentence, Evie kicked a plant pot with all her might, sending it flying against the porch where it smashed into pieces.

'And as for your so-called maiden aunt and your feelings for her – I find your behaviour unforgivable.'

Bernard blanched. He had been found out. But at least he now knew the reason for her anger. He could iron this out.

'You're right, Evie, she's not my aunt, but you have no right to be jealous when I clearly feel—'

'I know what you feel, Bernard Cavalier, you see, I read both your letters.'

He was stunned. 'You read my letter to Phoebe?'

'You read my letter to Phoebe?' Evie repeated, mocking him, and then: 'You are a cad, a fickle cad, a man of the lowest order.'

Another plant pot flew towards him, hitting the door, leaving a deep dent in the wood.

Bernard could feel his own face flushing. 'I say, steady on, you have no right to read other people's correspondence.'

'And you have no right to play with other people's lives!' She came up very close to him and spat the words out: 'But I've got my own back!' She paused dramatically. 'I swapped the letters round!'

Bernard started as if he had been shot. His body buckled and he grabbed hold of the doorframe.

'Oh my God, then I am undone!' he cried.

His reaction seemed to both thrill and horrify her in equal measure.

'Now she can react the way you wanted me to,' she snarled.

Still clutching the doorframe, Bernard fought for breath.

'That was a cruel trick, Evie,' he gasped. 'I'll need to write and explain to Phoebe. Tell her I didn't mean it.'

'Well, good luck with that!'

She was triumphant, exultant in her fury. Despite her hair, despite her cruelty, she had never looked more beautiful.

'I can't believe your reaction to my letter – it's so unreasonable!' he cried.

'Unreasonable?' Now it was Evie who seemed to be lost for words. She turned away from him and staggered back towards the gate.

'I would rather go to hell than marry you!' she finally shouted over her shoulder, as she got on her bicycle and cycled off, her new hair flying in the breeze.

Her parting shot wounded Bernard to the quick and her speedy departure ignited his anger.

'I could report you!' he shouted, as she sped away from him.

'Go ahead!' she shouted back.

He struggled to think of another riposte, and then it came to him: 'I would never marry a criminal anyway!'

Bed Rest

Once home, Evie quietly let herself in the back door. There was no one in the kitchen. The curtain had been pulled across to keep the afternoon sun off and the room felt cool. A fly buzzed around the shelves, seeking out the light dancing through a gap in the curtains. On the table, another fly buzzed around a vase of roses from the garden. She had picked them yesterday, was it only yesterday? She found an old shopping list and wrote on the clean side of it: *Feeling unwell so gone to bed. See you tomorrow. Evie.* She propped it against the roses and crept silently upstairs.

In the safety of her room, she lay on her bed and reviewed the dreadful events of the afternoon. How could she have done it? She shut her eyes, but words swam before her so she quickly opened them again. What was she thinking of? How could she have been so conniving? She had broken the fundamental rule of her profession. If it were discovered that she had intercepted the mail, she would lose her position, or worse. Bernard was right – she was a criminal. She had acted very rashly, without thinking, without considering anything else but her own pain. He had discarded her, cast her off, thrown her away, and her reaction had been to become as impulsive and volatile as he was. Was she turning into him? Would she start painting next?

She ran her hand over her bob, smiling ruefully as she remembered Bernard's look of dismay. She sat up and peered into the mirror on her chest of drawers. She was surprised by the look, but not shocked; it wasn't that bad. Her parents would hate it, but Cassie would like it. Dear, dear Cassie. Cassie had guessed, right from the start. She had tried to warn her parents about Bernard and she had tried to warn her. Why hadn't she listened? Anyway, if she had hoped to literally cut Bernard out of her life, it hadn't worked. Her neck felt cool and free, but her heart was full of hard, cold, boulders. Of course she would get over him; it was just a matter of time. She just had to remind herself of his letter of rejection, his condescending *Dearest* – and the rest. She lay back in the dark room, turning it all over in her mind until, exhausted from the day's events, she fell asleep.

Evie was almost never ill. Worried by her note, Mrs Brunton decided to put her head around her daughter's door and check everything was all right. She was met by a scene of carnage. Evie's uniform lay on the floor, screwed up handkerchiefs lay all over the eiderdown, and there, in the middle of it all, lay Evie – a shorn sheep. Mrs Brunton stood at the door, immobilised by the horror of it all. Mr Brunton noticed and joined her.

'Bernard,' he said after he had looked in, surveyed the scene and quietly closed the door again. 'I'll go down to the Post Office and say she's ill. She won't be able to work tomorrow.'

Mr Brunton strode quickly down the stairs and out of the house. He walked briskly through town, trying to think things through. As a solicitor he had seen it all: estrangements, divorces, broken-off engagements. This was a break-up, of that there was no doubt. But a break-up of what? If there had been a proposal, even a promise of a proposal, he would surely have been told about it. Something dreadful had happened to Evie; her hair was testimony to that. But what? The only thing he knew for certain was that the cavalier was at the bottom of it.

Shattered

It arrived in the afternoon mail, such a mean little letter. Phoebe was glad she had had lunch because swallowing supper would be impossible after such a dry, dismal note. There was so much wrong with it. Firstly it was too thin: Phoebe could tell right away just by feeling the envelope. It was only half the weight of Bernard's usual letters. As soon as she picked it up, she felt a strange, ominous dismay seeping through her. No was a thin, light little word; yes was more bunched up. This letter was as thin as a wafer. Usually she tore Bernard's missives open, but today Phoebe played for time and hunted for her father's letter opener. It was a wooden one, with the head of a buffalo on the end of it. She kept it in her hand as she opened the envelope, and the buffalo read the letter over her shoulder.

'There,' she said, when she had finished, 'we are better off without him.'

It would need a reply. That was the dreadful thing about letters. With a phone call, the two people could each have their say and then put the phone down. Of course it was annoying if you forgot something you wanted to mention, but once the receiver was replaced that was the end of it. But with a letter like this one – Bernard would be anticipating, if not a reaction, then at least some kind of acknowledgement. Well he couldn't expect any jokes; she was through with those. She would be polite and prim and that was already more than he deserved. Of course she could be very rude to him, but there was no point. Today she felt angry and hurt, tomorrow she would feel sad and hurt; and perhaps, maybe in a few months, just sad.

Phoebe sat for a good hour composing her response. She wanted her letter to be even thinner than his. She wanted it to be so dry that, when he had finished reading it, he would click his tongue in his mouth like a parched man in need of a drink. She was good with words and, after a few wrong turns, she came up with a suitable reply. She waited for the ink to dry and then she folded it very neatly and exactly in half and slotted it into the envelope. What a waste of a stamp, she thought as she licked it and stuck it on.

Then something dreadful happened: a single but rather large teardrop dripped onto the address, smudging *High View*. No doubt it was the waste of the stamp that had made her almost cry. Yes, it was a vexing business wasting money. As she found another envelope, and yet another stamp, the tears started coming in earnest and she had to be careful that she didn't ruin a second attempt. She wrote the address on the envelope while keeping it at arm's length, well away from her face. Then she blew her nose, put on her coat and headed out to the postbox.

The last post left at five o'clock. When Phoebe got to the letterbox, the postman had already emptied it and was locking it up again.

'Would you mind?' Phoebe held out her letter, smiling tentatively.

'I'm afraid you're just too late, Miss.'

How did he know she was a Miss?

'Couldn't you just pop it in the bag?' she smiled again.

'It says on the box, Miss. Five o'clock. It's now five past.'

'But you're still here, so could you take it.'

'I'm only here because you're talking to me. Rules is rules. If we wasted precious minutes like this every time we opened a box, the post would never go anywhere.'

125

Phoebe felt in despair. She was suddenly desperate to be rid of the letter. It felt contaminated and it was contaminating her, the bitter response seeping through the envelope. Acid. She could feel it burning her glove.

'It's from the vicar,' she said quickly.

The postman appeared to swither. 'The vicar?'

'The Reverend Carson. He said it was urgent.'

'Give it here,' said the postman. 'I'll do it once and once only.'

He grumpily untied the postbag and stuffed the letter into it.

'Thank you,' said Phoebe. 'The Reverend will be pleased.'

She gave a little bow and turned away. Then a thought occurred to her.

'It's going to someone in Devon,' she ventured. 'Will they get it tomorrow?'

'Not at this rate,' he retorted. 'Not if it misses the train, but if you stop talking and let me get on, it has a chance.'

'Good, good, I'll let the vicar know.'

There was just one more thing to do and for that Phoebe waited for the Reverend Carson to go out to Evensong. Then, when the house was quiet, she selected a jar of gooseberry jam from the larder and took it upstairs to the bathroom. She climbed onto the bathroom windowsill and forced the top of the sash window open. She stood for a few moments, gazing out over the back garden; then she took hold of the jam, held it high over the rockery and dropped it. The jam jar hit the ground with a terrific smash, but it didn't fly far into the garden. Instead it imploded – collapsing in on itself, as if exhausted from its fall. The shattered glass stuck to blobs of fruit and the jam shone greasily in the sunshine. Phoebe looked down at the greeny-brown mess. She felt quite sorry for the gooseberries. What a waste.

Bad Dreams

Back in Hollybrook, Bernard was feeling extremely sorry for himself. He had every reason to be. He had been rejected out of hand by the woman he cared for more than anything. He had proposed to a beautiful angel, and she had rewarded him by diabolically forwarding his proposal and shearing her hair off. But even more worrying than Evie's unexpected rejection was Phoebe's expected acceptance. Phoebe would jump at the chance to marry him. What was he to do? He paced up and down the balcony, the very balcony he had hoped to use to great effect just a few hours earlier. Dusk came and went and only the midges forced him indoors. He couldn't eat; he couldn't settle.

Up to now, he had tended to shy away from long-term relationships. He always liked a girl, but never quite enough, never enough to really commit to her – until he met Evie. It was extremely cruel that now he finally wanted to marry someone, everything had gone so terribly wrong for him. It was as if the universe was telling him that it was better to stay single. And the cruel twist was that he now wouldn't be able to stay single. Destiny had coached him and moulded him until he was ready to pledge himself to his true love. And then destiny had snatched away the bride he wanted and replaced her – with Phoebe of all people. Bernard had many lady friends and he could think of no one he would least like to marry than his correspondent in Saffron Walden. A friend, yes; a bride, heavens no! How could Evie have been so heartless, so callous in her response to his declaration?

That night he had a dreadful dream. There was a curtain of golden hair which fell in long waves from the ceiling down to the floor. He walked through it and found himself in a church. A wedding was taking place, and as he walked down the aisle, he realised that there was a bride waiting at the altar, but no groom. Then he looked down to see he was wearing morning dress and a buttonhole. The bride turned round to smile at him, and it was Phoebe.

He rose at dawn and continued his pacing. He could hardly bear the wait for the post. He chose a position on the balcony from where he could see anyone coming at a distance. What time was the first post again? Evie had told him way back when he first arrived. Seven o'clock? But seven o'clock came and went and no one appeared with a letter. Mrs Wilson arrived and seemed surprised to see him. Bernard disappeared into his studio but couldn't even contemplate picking up his paintbrush. The morning dragged past.

At midday, he resumed his position on the balcony, scanning the road for a bicycle. Nothing for him again. Then it dawned on him – Phoebe might only just have got the letter, in which case, even if she replied today, he wouldn't receive her answer till tomorrow. He groaned. Another night of torment lay ahead of him; he didn't think he could bear it. He lay on his bed waiting for the sun to set, willing time to accelerate. After staring at the ceiling for hours, he fell asleep and dreamt that Phoebe had given birth to triplets and they all looked exactly like her father.

Exhausted by his nightmare, Bernard slept in and woke mid-morning. He rushed downstairs but there was nothing on the doormat. He went into the kitchen and gloomily ate the breakfast Mrs Wilson had left for him. At noon, he posted himself just inside the front door, so he could peer out at the drive. After a few minutes, he heard the familiar tick-tick and rushed outside. But it wasn't Evie who delivered the mail; an older man opened his bag and handed Bernard a letter from Saffron Walden. He accepted it gingerly, holding it at arm's length as if it were an unexploded grenade.

'Is Evie on holiday?' he asked the man doubtfully.

'Indisposed,' was the reply.

As soon as the postman had gone, and fearing the very worst, Bernard tore the letter open.

82, Summerhill Road, Saffron Walden, Essex

Wednesday 18th August 1920

Dear Bernard,

I have received your letter. Of course I will step aside. I can only hope that the fates will grant you all that you desire, and that time will help me to recover from my disappointment.

Yours sincerely,

Phoebe

What could it mean? He read it again and again. Step aside? So Phoebe didn't want him either. Hold on, she did want him. Oh heavens! What had happened? Slowly the truth began to dawn on him. There had been an appalling mix-up, one which Evie had inadvertently righted. But that meant he had given Phoebe's letter to Evie by mistake.

Bernard rushed upstairs to the bathroom and was violently sick. Then he lay on the floor, clinging to the bath tub, retching and sobbing. But it was for Evie that he wept. Over and over again his mind replayed the moment when she would have opened the letter destined for Phoebe and first read the word *Dearest*. He felt every emotion – her shock, disbelief, disgust, anger, hate. He remembered their row afterwards and his crass comments which must have ripped right through her. With a groan he recalled his final jibe; in fact, he was the criminal. He had behaved thoughtlessly, callously even, and broken two hearts. Phoebe had been dignified in her distress; Evie had been incandescent. He had thought love was a game to be played between paintings. It was unforgivable behaviour – Evie's words. Whatever he said, she would never believe him. After what seemed like hours lying on the cold floor, he got up and went downstairs. He couldn't stay here, not now. It would be impossible, intolerable, especially for Evie. He started packing.

As he wandered around the house gathering his possessions, he began to wish that his nightmares really had come true. If only Evie had rejected him and sent his proposal on to Phoebe, and if only she had accepted. He would rather marry Phoebe than hurt Evie. But he had hurt Evie – and he had to admit that he was well-practised in the art of hurting others. He had been hurting women for years, not badly, not seriously, just little slights, little knocks, here and there. This one huge mistake was the accumulation of thousands of smaller ones. He had been careless for as long as he could remember and up to now he had always got away with it. But every transgression, every missed date, every forgotten birthday had somehow rolled together, like a snowball. Layer upon layer of mistakes and the snowball had silently grown in size and momentum. Finally, the gods had unleashed it on Evie and it had injured her badly. He hadn't aimed the snowball, but he had created it. He had to take the blame.

Perhaps because he knew that Evie had read his letter to Phoebe, Bernard found himself picking it apart. He analysed it with the unflinching precision of an anatomist working on a particularly unpleasant cadaver. Now it was under the spotlight, he realised that his letter of rejection had been unfeeling and inconsiderate. The worst of it was that he wouldn't have given the tone and style a second thought if it had just gone to Phoebe, as intended. It was the fact that Evie had read it first that forced him to judge it so honestly. But how awful for Phoebe to have received such a mealy-mouthed end to their friendship.

He returned to the wastepaper basket and took out the screwed-up drafts. They were all slightly different, but they were all as bad as each other. He thought of Phoebe's reaction to the letter, her courageous, unselfish honesty. How little he deserved such a well-considered reply. He read it again, this time with tears streaming down his face. How could he make it up to her? How could he apologise? But he knew he was only considering her at all because if he was thinking about Phoebe's bruised heart, then he couldn't think so much about Evie and what she might be feeling. The bonfire in his own heart was out. The heat had been replaced by a heavy, constant ache, as if someone wearing large boots had stamped on the bonfire and was still stamping.

He went into the drawing room and gathered up his paints, brushes and one or two watercolours that he could fit into his suitcase. He couldn't face shipping the canvases at the moment; he would figure out what to do with them another day. He glanced at the work he had finished. There wasn't much to show for his time here – most of the canvases were blank. There seemed to be an obstacle between him and his art and one he couldn't be bothered to cross. And Bernard knew it was the same with people. There'd always been a gap between him and everybody else. He had never quite connected with others – never really needed to. And now he had made this terrible mistake he could feel the gap widening, minute by minute. The distance between him and Evie was growing, as if she was on a boat that was leaving the shore and there was already a gulf separating them.

But perhaps it wasn't too late. Perhaps if he wrote to her now and explained everything, there was still a chance she might forgive him. He rushed back upstairs to the writing desk, found a sheet of paper and pulled the lid off his fountain pen. The pen was almost out of ink, so the first few words came out scratchy and faint.

My very dear Evie,

A terrible beginning, but what else could he say? My own dear Evie, was what he longed to write. That was no longer possible. And darling felt like another country. Where the deuce was the ink? He hunted in his half-packed suitcase and found a dried-up bottle. He squeezed the nib into the dregs at the bottom, willing the remains up into the reservoir of the pen. A large, almost solid blob got stuck in the nib and he wiped it hurriedly on the sleeve of his shirt. He would have to be quick, before the ink dried up again.

Evie, I don't know how to begin. I can't think what to do, which way to turn, how to make amends for my dreadful, dreadful letter. You see you weren't meant to get it. It doesn't excuse it – the letter I mean, but it wasn't meant for you, and now I can't see how to undo it – all your hurt, all your anger, all the terrible things I said. I can't imagine how you must be feeling. I would do almost anything just to wind back the clock and start again. The thing is Evie, I love you. I've ruined everything and I'm so, so,

The ink was starting to fade and the *sorry* was almost invisible, but he kept writing anyway, scribbling *sorry* again and again on the paper, harder and harder, until the end of the nib split and the two halves carried on independently, mirroring each other in an invisible scrawl. Then the letter ripped: a large curl of paper got caught in the gap between the two bits of nib. Bernard pulled it out and watched it float to the floor.

Back to London

Bernard was desperate that no one should notice him leaving. He wanted to slink silently away. He would walk into Colyton, buy a ticket and catch the 4.40pm to Seaton Junction to meet the London train. He sidled through the town. He had another burden now, not just the suitcase, but something else, holding onto his legs, making every step a tremendous effort. He kept going, one foot in front of the other, looking down at the pavement, trying not to think about the pain in his chest. He had one final street to negotiate before the station and there was Mrs Brunton coming out of the butchers.

'Bernard.'

'Mrs Brunton.' He stopped dead in his tracks. He didn't know what to do. He wanted to fall on his knees in front of her. Instead he raised his hat.

'Could you tell Evie,' he hesitated, 'could you tell Evie that I made a terrible mistake.'

'A terrible mistake,' she repeated.

'And that I'm leaving,' he continued miserably, wanting to confess everything to this gentle lady and her packet of sausages.

'I'll tell her, Bernard.' A pause. 'Thank you for the picture.'

He raised his hat again, but surprisingly Mrs Brunton was the first to move off.

She nodded her head at Bernard and crossed the street with quick, decisive movements. Here was a change indeed, she thought, as he disappeared slowly round the corner. It was an awkward situation, but she had felt in control. She had been polite, but not friendly. She knew he had done something horrible to her daughter, yet she had maintained her dignity. However, after this small triumph, indecision and anxiety began to creep in again. Should she actually impart this message to Evie? All of it? None of it? Some of it? Evie was in terrible distress, but which bit of his message would make her feel better? After dithering across several roads, she decided to just tell her the first bit – that he had made a mistake. Mistakes could surely be put right. They offered the chance of patch ups and reconciliations. Whereas leaving – well, she wasn't sure Evie would want to know that.

Mrs Brunton waited until dinner was over and her husband was in the garden, watering his vegetables. She and Evie were clearing the table.

She took a deep breath: 'Bernard said to tell you that he made a terrible mistake.'

The plate Evie was carrying wobbled and two green beans fell onto the carpet. She glared at her mother. 'Never mention that man's name again,' she said and stalked out to the kitchen.

This was not the reaction her mother had been hoping for. 'I bumped into him outside the butchers,' she explained, following her out with the gravy boat. 'He's leaving,' she added. There – it was out.

'Good,' said Evie. She banged the plate down on the kitchen table and ran upstairs.

Mrs Brunton didn't follow her. She stayed in the kitchen, staring into the garden, letting her fingers play scales around the sink. It had been hard to say but it would no doubt help. Now Evie could eventually go back to work. Mrs Brunton had not shirked her task. The guy ropes that held up her sagging courage tightened. She felt tauter, taller.

Evie slammed her bedroom door shut and then stood leaning against it. So he had gone. He had ripped up her hopes, her dreams, and then he had taken off, back to London.

He had destroyed her and then he had disappeared – he was a hideous locust, consuming everything in his path, laying waste to her life. At least she wouldn't have to see him again. She could go back to work now; except that he had wrecked her job for her too. Every day she would have to pass High View and remember him. And worse than that – she would also remember her crime. Because of him she had lost all pride in her position. In fact, the post lady role that might have helped her was yet another obstacle to recovery. Before Bernard she had been honest, now she was a criminal. For the rest of her life she would divide everything into Before and After Bernard. Before he came she was happy; after he left she was miserable. Before – self-contained; after – vulnerable. She wandered over to the mirror. Her eyes looked sunken and her cheeks were pale and pinched. Before Bernard she was young; after old. Before – lively; after – lifeless.

And what was it he had said to her mother? Tell Evie I made a terrible mistake! He made a mistake? What about her? She was the one who had made a mistake – the worst mistake of her life, getting involved with such a cruel, uncaring monster. But as Evie looked into the mirror, she knew she had made two mistakes. The first mistake was getting to know Bernard. The second was dabbling with fortune, intercepting the mail and interfering with destiny. She had thought herself a god who could meddle with the lives of others. This was not a small mistake; it was a big one. She would pay for it. And so the two mistakes wound themselves around each other, weaving together into a rough rope which knotted up and became a horrible tangle in her gut.

Bernard's Bill

'Well, you'll have to get on with it.' Mr Carruthers dipped a wafer in his lemon mousse and considered the miserable man opposite. Then he leant in closer and, in a voice he usually saved for the dim, or the hard-of-hearing: 'Bernard, you have a show. In twelve days.'

Bernard was staring into space.

'It's all very well coming back from Devon early, when did you get back by the way?'

'Yesterday,' mumbled Bernard, as if in a dream.

'Well it's all very well coming back early, but where is the work?'

'I left it in Devon.'

'You left it in Devon?'

'There wasn't much and what there was wasn't any good.'

Carruthers tried not to choke on his wafer. 'Then you'd better get painting now. You've wasted more than three weeks, so you're well behind.'

'I'll never paint again,' Bernard muttered.

Carruthers realised that although Bernard sounded dramatic, he meant to be sincere. This worried him greatly. He tried a new tack.

'Well in that case I'm afraid you have a few bills to settle.'

Bernard looked out of the window.

Carruthers took a pen out of his pocket and started scribbling on the back of the menu.

'Now let's see – five weeks' rent on a house in Devon, plus housekeeping, plus,' (he eyed Bernard suspiciously) 'unexplained but not insignificant damage to the front door, reported to me this morning. Then there's the cost of a month's gallery space, the framing to be completed, the invitations, oh and the money I lent you in the spring…' Carruthers made calculating noises, glancing at Bernard out of the corner of his eye. 'I make that £157 pounds, not including the train fares.'

As Carruthers suspected, the figure startled Bernard out of his reverie.

'I don't have any money.'

'Then paint.'

'I can't paint. Not anymore. I'll have to find another job.'

'Another job?' Carruthers sneered. 'What, down a coal mine? Bernard, you're not qualified for anything else.'

'I can't,' said Bernard simply, looking away again.

Carruthers had another idea. 'What about we come to an arrangement – we could put your new work in the exhibition and then fill in the gaps with your old work. No one will remember.'

'But it didn't mean anything.'

'I'm sorry?'

'The old work – it didn't have any point to it.'

Carruthers stood up, yanked off his napkin and threw it on the table.

'Listen to me, Bernard. You have three options. Either you work like billy-oh to fill my gallery with new work, or you include your old "pointless" work, or you owe me £157, plus interest.' He glanced round at the hovering waiter. 'And two lunches at Claridges, starting with this one.'

***

After his meeting with Carruthers, Bernard went straight to his studio. He had spent his first night back in London at Toby's, unable to face his bachelor pad; now he was forced to. Carruthers would have put his change of heart down to his threat of a large bill and congratulated himself on his ruse. But it was something else. One word: Pointless. Bernard had finally articulated Evie's devastating observation of his work. And Carruthers hadn't contradicted him. So it was clear: his work, up to now, had no real point to it. It was meaningless, a waste of time and a waste of space. Well – he would show them. He had messed up his life, but he could still save his art.

The first time he tried to open the wooden door to his studio, the key stuck in the lock and he had to yank it out and have another go. He fiddled with the lock, pushed against the doorframe and finally forced the door open. The studio was in darkness and there was a horrible smell of mould. He groped his way to the window and opened a shutter. A shaft of light shone in through the mottled Georgian windows. He looked around. He must have left for Devon in a hurry all those weeks ago because the place was in chaos. A pile of clothes lay on the floor and round it unwashed plates orbited like satellites. One plate had a piece of green cheese – presumably where the smell was coming from. He would deal with it later; right now he had to start work.

Bernard put down his suitcase and immediately began looking for a blank canvas. There were rows of half-finished pictures stacked against the walls, but nothing actually finished – nothing worth finishing. He couldn't find a clean canvas and he thought wistfully of the pile still in Devon, leaning against the wall by the fireplace. Too bad, he would paint over what he had here.

He picked up a canvas with a profile sketched on it and positioned it on his easel. It was easy enough to paint over the half-hearted portrait, but then what? He stared at the canvas and waited for his daemons. They didn't appear. Perhaps he had left them in Devon? He pursed his lips together and tried to summon them with his distinctive hum. Nothing. He waited. Still nothing. Where were they? On their way up?

He wandered over to the window and peered through the half-open shutters. In the late afternoon light everything looked dull and grey. Cars and carriages rushed past on the road, making the windows rattle. No inspiration there. He returned to the canvas and started humming again, keeping the tune light, not wanting his daemons to think he was impatient, worried, desperate even. If this was a game of hide and seek, then he just had to keep calm and unperturbed; they would get bored and emerge from their hiding places.

Bernard left the canvas but didn't quite turn his back on it. He started tidying the studio, picking objects up off the floor, returning books to his make-shift bookshelf on the windowsill, all the while peeping at the easel out of the corner of his eye, keeping his mind blank to welcome any image that might suddenly manifest. Any moment now he would hear the rasping sound of an idea in his ear; a picture would appear in his inner eye and he would rush to the canvas and start painting.

Hours passed and the studio was clean and tidy, but Bernard's mind remained dull and blank. The daemons were playing truant, ignoring him, passing him over. But why? He walked down to a public house on the corner where no one knew him, ordered a glass of beer and a steak pie and sat in a corner, gloomily consuming them. A terrible realisation was dawning: his daemons were offended. They felt affronted by his condemnation of the work they had inspired. *Pointless.* This was the word that had done the damage. Evie had questioned his work but she had left the word unsaid. Today he had voiced her doubts and Carruthers had agreed with him and the daemons had felt rejected. They had flown. They were gone and they probably wouldn't be back. So now what?

Bernard paid for his supper, left the pub and returned to his studio where he lit a couple of oil lamps. He would work through the night tonight. His daemons had deserted him, but he would press on regardless. He had less than two weeks to prove himself, relying only on himself. The days of copying were over; he would have to start painting what he felt. He stood in front of the canvas and slowly tried to prise open the door to his heart. The door to his studio had been stiff and hard to open; the door to his heart was jammed solidly shut. He felt like Blue Beard's wife in front of her husband's closet – terrified, yet driven on by a need to know what lay behind it.

Bernard found a space on the cluttered floor of his studio, sat down with his back against the wall and made himself think of Evie. Immediately, the pain that had followed him back from Devon intensified and became a harsh grating ache, like a muscle tearing. He sat through the pain, determined to endure it, waiting to see what lay beyond it. After a few moments, a picture flashed into his mind – a young woman standing in a raspberry patch, pushing long strands of blonde hair out of her eyes. In the old days he would have jumped straight up and started to copy it, but he knew from experience that images of Evie could quickly fade. Instead he stayed where he was, shut his eyes and held on tight to the vision of her.

Then he began to feel her with his whole being, slowly and painfully opening himself up to her, allowing her into his chest, letting her beat inside him like a second heart, letting her fill his lungs with her own air, in and out, rising and falling. He sat quietly, eyes closed, watching Evie grow in size and strength and take on an energy of her own. And as her presence solidified, he gained strength from it. Now he knew what to do, without looking, without copying. He stood up very slowly and returned to the canvas.

An Exchange of Letters

The day after Bernard left for London, Evie woke with a strong feeling that she should write to Cassie. She hadn't written for ages, not since she discovered that Cassie had spilled the beans. Evie had been annoyed with her then and decided, in a fit of pique, not to write for a bit. How silly all that seemed now. Compared to Bernard's deceitful behaviour, Cassie's slip seemed inconsequential. Evie also felt a bit guilty. On the beach, she had told Bernard that Cassie wasn't always loyal. In fact, Cassie had shown great loyalty when she had written to warn her about him. And she, Evie, had ignored the advice of a loving friend.

She sighed and got out of bed, avoiding her reflection in the mirror opposite – she knew her short hair would be sticking out all over the place. Yes, she would write to Cassie, but she wouldn't mention why she had taken so long to reply to her last letter, it would seem churlish. Nor would she mention her hair. She couldn't tell Cassie that she had cut her hair to punish Bernard; Cassie would be offended. She loved her own short style and wouldn't understand why Evie had used the same look to shock. But she would tell Cassie that her prediction about Bernard had unfortunately come true, and she would ask her for forgiveness and help. Cassie would feel her distress and would come and see her. When Cassie arrived, she could pretend her new hairstyle was weeks' old and nothing to do with Bernard at all.

Evie's letter arrived in Kensington the next morning and it was propped up against the toast-rack when Cassie came down to breakfast. She was in no hurry to read it. There was always the chance that Evie's relationship with Bernard had blossomed. Cassie didn't want to read about romantic strolls or furtive hand-holding before breakfast. So she ignored the letter and poured herself an orange juice. Her mother came in, sat down beside her and rang a little bell.

'Aren't you going to open it?' she asked, nodding at the envelope.

'I'll read it later. I've a headache this morning.'

A maid appeared.

'I'd like some coffee,' said Cassie's mother, 'and some fresh toast.'

'Certainly, Ma'am.'

The maid picked up the toast-rack and the letter flopped onto the tablecloth face down. Cassie's mother picked it up and leaned it against the marmalade pot. Then she unfolded *The Times* and started reading the 'Births, Marriages and Deaths' column.

Cassie lifted the woollen cosy off a boiled egg. She gazed with pleasure at its brown, freckled top. Then she picked up a small silver spoon and gave the egg a sharp tap. The eggshell cracked. She smiled at the crumpled dome, then she took a silver knife and skilfully cut the top right off. She made a clean job of it and there was no sign of even a dent in the remaining egg. She liked things to be neat. The maid returned with toast and coffee; Cassie's mother looked up from the paper.

'I see Lavinia's cousin is to be wed. Do you know her, Cassandra?'

It was a double-edged sword – both a reminder that another girl was going to be married and a hope that Cassie might at least be invited to the wedding.

'Really? No, I don't,' Cassie answered as vaguely as possible, waving the knife around so it caught the light, keen to get back to her egg. She smiled at her mother but she had returned to the paper. Cassie put the knife down, picked up the spoon and tucked into the egg with gusto. It was cooked to perfection, the white firm to the touch, the yellow yolk runny, warm and smooth. She scraped the last of the egg from the shell, popped it into her mouth and stood up. Then, picking up the letter, she left the table and glided upstairs.

North Lodge, Key Lane, Colyton, Devon

Friday 20th August 1920

My dear Cassie,

I'm sorry to have taken so long to reply to your letter. Things have been very difficult here, as I'll explain shortly. But first let me thank you for your thoughtful advice. How right you were my wise friend and how foolish I was to ignore your warning. You told me that Bernard was unfaithful and inconstant and, when I read your letter, I was sure you were right. Yet, like many girls before me, I was reeled in by his charm and then left high and dry.

And so my news is short and sad – Bernard flirted with me, wooed me, all but declared himself to me and then proposed to someone else. He enchanted me and then he deceived me. I hate him and I hate saying that I hate him. I would rather have no feelings for him at all, for being hated is still more than he deserves.

Dear friend, please help me. Forgive my idiotic behaviour and come and see me. I need your help and encouragement if I'm ever to get over this disaster. One mistake leads to another and I am in a dark place. I'm having some time off work to try and recover – it would be wonderful if you could keep me company.

Your desperately sad but still loving friend,

Evie

Cassie finished the letter and gazed out of the window. The news was good and bad. She was relieved that Evie's friendship with Bernard was over, but the break-up had obviously left Evie feeling needy, and she didn't want to go back to Devon for a while. The last visit had been tiresome enough but it would be worse if Evie was low. She couldn't face nursing Evie back to health. And if she went down to Colyton, it would be all about Evie: Evie's adventure, Evie's romance, Evie's broken heart. No, she couldn't stomach that. She needed to concentrate on her own future, not waste time comforting her friend. It wasn't fair – Evie just had to catch a train and she had an escapade. Other people had to make much more effort to attract attention. She would have to delicately decline Evie's desperate request. She sat down at her writing desk, found an attractive notelet, filled her fountain pen and wrote a few comforting lines to her friend.

72, Fairholme Road, Kensington, London, SW.

Saturday 21st August 1920

My dearest Evie,

I was devastated to hear your news. I can't believe Bernard could have behaved in such a fickle and caddish manner. I only wish that my suspicions hadn't come true. Evie, don't be hard on yourself; this could have happened to anyone – and no doubt, in the case of Bernard, it has happened many times before.

I wish I could come down and see you. Unfortunately, I'm completely tied up for the next couple of weeks – a flurry of engagements and a succession of visiting relatives have all conspired to keep me trapped here in the capital. All I can do is send you my sympathy and love.

What you must do, Evie, is recover as quickly as you can and then come up and see me, and I will spoil you.

I'll distract you with lots of fun activities that will take your mind off that despicable man. We can shop and go out for tea and to the theatre.

In the meantime, I promise I won't mention this to anyone I know. Evie, I wish you a very speedy recovery and I hope to see you up here as soon as possible.

All my love and thoughts,

Cassie

She blotted the handwriting, folded the notelet, slid it inside a stamped envelope and scrawled the address on the front. Then she rang for the maid.

'Could you?' Cassie smiled, handing her the envelope. She stayed at her desk and watched the maid pop across the narrow street to the postbox opposite. As she watched, she thought about Evie's intriguing line: *One mistake leads to another*. It was a curious thing to have written, but it certainly wasn't worth the trip down to Devon to investigate.

Cassie's letter was posted on a Saturday, so it didn't arrive until the seven o'clock post on Monday morning. Evie, who was already awake, heard the swish of the letterbox. She dashed downstairs, snatched up the letter and ran upstairs again. She was pleased that Cassie had replied promptly, it was a good sign – perhaps she could come and see her this week. She threw herself on the bed and tore the letter open. She read it quickly through and then again, more slowly. It wasn't what she was expecting, and certainly not what she was hoping for. As she read it through a third time, Evie began to detect other messages couched behind the words. *Fickle and caddish* – Cassie had repeated the words she had used in her letter of warning, as if to underline that she had been proved right. Then there was the condescending *don't be so hard on yourself* and the phrase *it has happened many times before*, suggesting Evie was just another gullible idiot. Of course she was a gullible idiot – she didn't need Cassie to remind her; she needed Cassie to comfort her and cheer her up.

But there was something else in the letter too: another timbre hidden between the lines. *I only wish that my suspicions hadn't come true.* This was the bit that really grated. It hinted at victory, rather than sympathy. And then the final *I wish you a speedy recovery*, as if Evie was suffering from a bad dose of the flu, rather than a broken heart. Evie tried to stay level-headed. Cassie had never been in love, so perhaps it was hard for her to understand just how she was feeling. But despite her attempts to rationalise Cassie's response, Evie felt wounded. It was another blow to add to the pain inflicted by Bernard. First Bernard had disappeared; now Cassie's support had evaporated. Evie shoved the letter back in the envelope. She had never felt more alone. She couldn't face another week off work, kicking around the house. She would just have to put a brave face on things and return to the sorting office.

Toby's Treat

'So glad you're painting again!' Toby beamed. 'And from what I can see, it's marvellous.'

'It's a bit early to judge,' mumbled Bernard, 'I've only been at it a couple of days.' He eyed his dinner partner gloomily. The infuriating Toby: tousled hair, dandy clothes, a charming smile and a bulging wallet. The annoying thing about Toby was that he had absolutely no concept of deadlines or having to earn a living. Thanks to a family investment in the chocolate industry at the turn of the century, Toby didn't have to work at all. And so he floated through life, bobbing along like a helium balloon, splashing his money around, full of advice and encouragement. And tonight was no exception; tonight Toby was treating Bernard to steak tartare at the RAC club. Bernard thought he might choke on it.

'Here's to your triumphant entry into the world of serious art!' Toby cried, raising his glass.

Bernard took another gulp of his red wine. He hadn't drunk that much, but after his frugal lifestyle in Devon he wasn't used to alcohol, and already it was going to his head. He had forgotten to eat lunch and the Bordeaux hit him on an empty stomach. He could feel his tongue slowing and his hands and feet felt heavy.

'And how is your father's ex – the lovely Molly?' Toby asked.

'She's too old for you, Toby! Anyway, I have no idea how Benedict's cast-off is doing.'

'It's so strange,' Toby mused, 'how you call your father Benedict. I call my father father, pater – daddy, even.'

'Well I call mine Benedict.'

'But why?'

'Because I'm a foundling, remember. Benedict is my adopted father and as soon as he could he dropped the father bit.'

'I don't know how you put up with it,' said Toby. 'That baby in a basket story sticks in my throat.'

Bernard drained his glass before answering, 'If it sticks in your throat, how do you think I feel?' He reached for the bottle and gave himself a little top-up, swilling the red liquid round the glass so it caught the light from the candles. 'I've always hated not knowing how I started – where I came from.' He tipped the glass back and gulped the wine down. 'I know it sounds like a poor excuse, but I think it's really held me back – not knowing anything about my origins. Having such a blank past makes it hard to envisage any sort of future.'

Toby wasn't sure he agreed. He knew exactly where he came from, but his future was possibly blanker than Bernard's. He had no need to blaze a trail; he could just fritter away his time and money. Whilst less fortunate friends carefully charted their career paths, he could safely take his hands off the tiller and gaze at the view. Toby was undismayed by the empty skies ahead, but he knew this wasn't the night to argue with his friend. He could see the red wine was making Bernard morose.

'Perhaps you should confront him,' he suggested. 'Have it out with Benedict once and for all.'

'Why?' Bernard looked gloomily at his plate. 'I've tried to broach it so many times. He always dismisses my questions and changes the subject.'

Toby suddenly thought of something. 'Did it affect your proposal? I mean I know you said it went a bit—' Bernard looked up quickly as Toby reached for the right word, 'haywire.'

'No,' said Bernard. 'I can't really blame him for my disastrous proposal.' He picked up the wine bottle, studying the label. He seemed to be fighting back tears. Then he sighed and emptied the dregs into his glass.

'Perhaps if you told me about it,' Toby said, 'perhaps if you explained what went wrong, we could work out how to put it right?'

'No!' cried Bernard. He made a sweeping gesture with his arm and knocked his wine glass over. Red wine dribbled onto the tablecloth. 'Sorry.' He looked at Toby apologetically. 'Look, I'd rather talk about my father.'

'Rather than talk about your father, why not talk to him!' Toby exclaimed. 'Because you need to do something! You're as miserable as sin – you need to cheer up, get a grip on yourself.' He put out a hand and touched Bernard's arm. 'You're no fun anymore.'

Bernard looked at his friend. In the candlelight of the dining room, he seemed to be revolving slowly round the table. He also had two of everything: two sets of cufflinks from Gerrard's, two red bow ties from Harrods, two lots of pearly white teeth. Bernard suddenly felt sick and tired of him – tired of life in London, tired of life full stop. His head hurt from the Bordeaux, his mind felt sluggish from too much painting, his heart – well, never mind his heart. He stood up.

'You're right, Toby, I'm going to confront him – right now.'

'Hold on. We haven't finished supper. Don't you want a dessert?'

'No,' said Bernard. He smiled ironically. 'No, I'd rather find out where I came from.' And with that he left the dining room, swayed his way through the RAC club, hailed a taxi and made his way to Chelsea.

Benedict Cavalier

Benedict Cavalier lived above his King's Road studio, or rather his studio lived below him; for he was first and foremost a successful wine importer, and was thus able to furnish his apartment in a way that many sculptors would struggle to do. Sculpting was his second love, or perhaps his third, as a love of women came immediately after his love of the grape. As Bernard's taxi trundled towards Chelsea, Benedict was uncorking a bottle of rare champagne to impress Penelope Armstrong. In the tastefully decorated drawing room, a fire was blazing, underlining an understated opulence. On the gramophone, the *Moonlight Sonata* was tinkling, indicating an interest in classical music. And now Benedict was adding the magic ingredient – romance. He took Penelope's hand in his and looked into her eyes.

'Of course a clothed statuette would be charming but I would love to sculpt you nude,' he whispered. 'I dream of that.'

'Really Benedict!' Penelope laughed and looked suitably shocked. She knew her lines just as he knew his. Act One of this particular drama was playing out as expected. There would be an interval in which he would open more champagne; then at the end of Act Two, he would declare his undying love and she would fall into his arms.

There was an unexpected knock on the drawing room door. Jones entered from stage left, disrupting proceedings.

'Excuse me, sir,' he began, 'but Mr Bernard is here to see you, sir. He's in the study.'

Benedict did his best to hide his annoyance. He had heard Bernard was back from Devon. What a pain the boy could be.

'We're rather busy, Jones. Could you ask Mr Bernard to come back tomorrow.'

'He seems keen to talk to you,' said Jones. The butler's voice was level, but there was an urgency in his eyes. With his fingers, he made a delicate gesture down his nose which he then tweaked in a clockwise direction.

'I see,' said Benedict. He smiled at Penelope, 'If you could just excuse me for one moment, my dear.'

'But of course.'

Benedict stood up, bowed slightly to the young lady and swiftly followed Jones out of the drawing room. He crossed the corridor and barged into his study. Bernard was standing with his back to the room, looking out at the dark street through the wide Georgian window. Benedict bristled. Bernard had interrupted his evening, so why couldn't he at least look round and acknowledge him.

'If you've come for money, I'm afraid—'

At the sound of his father's voice, Bernard swung round. 'Money? No. Well, at least not this time.' He gave a lopsided smile.

'So to what do I owe the privilege of a visit?' Benedict's voice was full of irony. 'It's rather late Bernard, so I presume this is urgent. Are you ill?'

Bernard shook his head. 'I'm not ill, but I do feel low,' he admitted. 'But not because of the show. I feel down because I've never taken anything seriously.'

Bother, thought Benedict. This was not the night for Bernard to get philosophical; not with Penelope in the drawing room.

'Look Bernard, I have a guest. Couldn't we discuss this another time?'

'And I've never taken anything seriously,' continued Bernard, undeterred, 'because I've never considered my future.'

Benedict caught a whiff of something in the air – something dangerous.

'And I've never considered my future, because I've never understood my past.' Bernard swayed forwards into the room and grabbed the curtain to steady himself. 'Because I don't know what it is. I mean, I don't know where I came from.'

'But I've told you a thousand times—' began Benedict.

Bernard took a step towards his father and pointed menacingly with a finger. 'Don't fob me off with more of that baby in the basket stuff. I need facts, not a fairy-tale.'

'Well I'm afraid it wasn't a fairy-tale. I can still remember finding you on my doorstep—'

'But why *your* doorstep?' said Bernard, raising his voice, taking another step forwards, drunkenly poking Benedict in the chest. 'And why did you pick up the baby and take it inside?' A pause. 'If it wasn't yours.'

Bernard had never talked to him like this before and Benedict felt winded, both by his direct questioning and the accusation that lay beneath it. He took a step backwards and put a hand up to his chest.

'So this is the thanks I get,' was all he could manage. He knew it was a pathetic reaction and a sort of admission, but he couldn't bring himself to say more. He thought of Penelope, waiting for him in the drawing room, like a hot drink going cold. It was ironic that Bernard had interrupted the delicate start of his latest liaison. Perhaps it was a punishment from the heavens. The gods had sent him a baby to interfere with his amorous dalliances and, although the baby had grown into a man, they were still using him to disrupt his love life. Benedict felt a wave of fury sweep over him, turning his thin lips white.

'I think you should leave now,' he said, with a quietness that cut through the air like a knife, 'before one of us says something they regret.'

Bernard's eyes clouded over. He shrugged and took a step past Benedict, aiming uncertainly for the door, then he stopped.

'I won't be back,' he said, 'until you've told me.' He pulled open the study door and staggered into the hall.

Benedict stood with his head down, gripping the back of a chair. He heard the front door open, the momentary swish of a passing car, then the sound of the front door being banged shut again. Silence, then a gentle knock on the study door and Jones put his head in.

'Miss Armstrong has had to leave, sir. She said she would call you tomorrow.'

Benedict gave an imperceptible nod and Jones quietly closed the door again.

Benedict wandered over to the window and looked out onto the street. Nearly twenty-five years of pretending. Why? What was he so ashamed of? And if he kept up this pretence he would alienate Bernard for good. Is that what he wanted? As he turned away from the window, he noticed something silver lying on the carpet. He bent down and picked it up. A key. Blast. It was the key to Bernard's studio. Now he would have to go and find him. Or would he? Bernard would almost certainly go home on foot. If he sent Jones in a cab he could easily overtake him. And perhaps this would give him an opportunity. Benedict hurried over to his writing desk, found a sheet of writing paper and filled his fountain pen. He paused and thought for a moment. Then he put pen to paper, scribbled a short note and rang the bell to summon his butler.

* * *

Bernard decided to walk home. He needed the air. And now he couldn't seem to handle his drink, taking a cab was a bit risky. It took a while to walk from Chelsea to Pimlico. He got lost twice and then he tripped over a particularly high kerbstone and lay for a few minutes, gazing at the stars, before getting up again. When he finally made it back to his studio, he spent ages searching for his key. It wasn't in the inside pocket of his jacket where he usually kept it. Where the deuce was it, then? It was very dark outside the studio so he returned to the nearest gaslight to have a proper look. He checked every pocket of his coat and emptied out every pocket of his jacket. Nothing. Oh no. He couldn't go back to Benedict's tonight. He returned to his door and then he saw it, the key – in the lock. Good grief, he was an idiot. Hopefully no one else had spotted it. He opened the door and went inside.

As he walked over the threshold he felt something underneath his shoe, some kind of paper. He bent down and picked it up, took it inside and lit an oil lamp. Closer inspection revealed a folded up note with Bernard on the front in Benedict's handwriting. He must have set off soon after he left – or perhaps he had sent Jones to deliver it? Whoever it was, they had beaten him home. But what did it say? Bernard's heart raced as he unfolded the paper and read the contents.

Her name was Sophia. She was from Dublin. She modelled for me. I never saw her again. I'm sorry but it was so long ago and I can't remember her surname. She was very beautiful and very kind. I trust you will keep this to yourself.

Benedict

Bernard finished reading, folded up the note again and pushed it into a drawer in his bureau. Sophia. The name filled him up completely, whizzing through his body, coursing through his bloodstream, thumping loudly in his head. Sophia.

'Her name is Sophia,' Bernard addressed the empty room. 'I'll never know her but now at least I know her name.' He paused. 'And I have a father,' he added, 'a real one.'

His drunken stupor was gone, giving way to a bracing certainty. So he had a past after all, not exactly respectable, but certainly artistic. Now he had a past he could finally plan his future – not in a slapdash way like before, without really caring, but with real intent. And he had two women to paint for.

The New Boy

When Evie returned to work, there was a general gasp at her new look. She ignored it, behaving with calm dignity, as if her strange haircut had been planned for months. It would grow, eventually. Despite the unfavourable reaction to her hair, she was glad to be back. The smell of leather and varnished wood, the squeak of boots on the floor, the rows of pigeonholes that letters flew in and out of, they all gave her a sense of belonging. She found her postbag and had a quick peep inside. There on the top of the pile was a letter for Bernard Cavalier, postmarked London. It was inevitable. She sighed and started to pick up the bag. Mr Thornber, the Post Master, emerged from his office.

'So glad you're back, Evie. Are you quite better?'

'Yes, thank you.' She turned to go.

'It must have been a particularly bad flu.' He said it simply, matter-of-factly, as if making an observation, but Evie blushed.

'It was,' she said, 'but I've completely recovered.' Again she turned to go.

'Evie, before you get started, if I could just have a word?' Mr Thornber indicated his door. 'In my office.'

Evie's heart stopped. She had been found out. Someone had discovered the letter in the ditch, or worse, someone had reported her. Bernard.

Inwardly shaking like a leaf, she followed the Post Master into his office. A young man was standing before the fire, nervously warming his hands even though it was August.

'Miss Brunton, I would like you to meet Mr Dixon; Mr Dixon, Miss Brunton.'

The young man turned, smiled and came forward to greet her.

'Please call me David,' he said.

'Please call me Evie.' She smiled back at him.

'David has just returned to the area. I have agreed to let him come in and help out a bit to gain some experience. Would you mind if he accompanies you on your midday round, just for a few days?'

'Delighted!' Evie beamed.

What a relief if this was all Mr Thornber wanted to see her about. And how nice she would have some company for a change; how fortunate she wouldn't have to face High View alone.

'Well then, I will let the two of you get started.' Mr Thornber opened the door of his office and, smiling, saw them both out.

'Do you have a bicycle?' Evie asked.

'Round the back.' And so he did. A shiny Post Office bicycle.

'Where did you get that?'

'I worked for the Post Office in Seaton for a few weeks in 1916, then I got conscripted.'

'You were in the war?' Evie was astonished. 'You look too young!' she laughed.

But it wasn't his youthfulness that surprised her. It was the fact he looked so good – perfect physically: no limp, no scars, no outward sign of having fought. There were so many men, even just in Colyton, who bore the signs. Yet David was strong, upright and good-looking. He was a little awkward, with a slightly gauche way of moving, but that was his age; he would mature in time and then he would look marvellous. Evie was thrilled: he felt like a good omen, sent by the universe just for her. David was a symbol of survival – so, it *was* possible. They cycled companionably along the road, chatting away. He told her he was married with a four-year-old daughter, born while he was at the front. Good Lord, so he was married too! A married soldier and so young – what an extraordinary chap!

'That must have been difficult for you, being away from your family, not seeing your baby.'

'It was.'

'And now you're back, safe and sound!'

'It's a great relief to be home.' He smiled weakly.

Evie was enchanted by his story. She had never needed a happy ending so badly, and here it was, delivered to her by the heavens like a longed-for letter. She wanted to celebrate it, sing out loud, ring her bicycle bell. Here was a tale of love fulfilled, the happy ever after that had eluded her. David was a gallant knight, a real-life chevalier who had survived the battle and returned to his family. How she admired his courage and determination to see the war through. As they cycled along, she mentally compared him to Bernard. Bernard hadn't seen any suffering; he hadn't fought for his country. Bernard was a worthless loser, a no hoper; David was strong, valiant and worthwhile.

It was strange but pleasant to have a companion and the round seemed to go quicker than usual. She made him laugh with an anecdote about each household they stopped at with post. And all the while they were getting closer to Bernard's and Evie was starting to get a strange feeling in the pit of her stomach. She slowed down considerably; David kept getting ahead and having to stop and wait.

'I feel quite tired,' she said, as way of explanation. 'Would you mind taking the next letter in?'

'Of course.' David leaned his bicycle up against the hedge and walked up the drive to High View.

Evie stood and listened, leaning breathlessly against a tree. She heard the crunch of the gravel under his feet, the flip of the letterbox and the crunch of gravel again.

'What a lovely house, but it looks empty.'

So he really had gone.

***

When they got back to the sorting office, David went straight home while Evie went in with the mail. Mr Thornber appeared at her side as she sorted out her bag.

'How did that go?'

'David was first rate – very helpful.'

'Do you think he would make a good postman?'

'Definitely. But he's already been one. He told me he worked in Seaton, just before conscription started.'

The Post Master didn't reply. Evie looked at him. He had turned his back to her and seemed busy sorting a pile of papers.

'Did you know he had worked in Seaton?'

'Yes, yes,' he said vaguely.

'Perhaps when he's trained up, he can apply for a local position,' she suggested.

'Perhaps.'

'I'll do a good job showing him the ropes, Mr Thornber.'

'I'm sure you will, Miss Brunton.'

'I'm just nipping home before the next post, is that all right?'

'Of course. See you later, Miss Brunton.'

Back at his desk, Mr Thornber watched Evie open the back door, pick up her bicycle and wheel it across the courtyard to the back gate. She obviously had no idea; she wouldn't have been so cheerful otherwise. Well then, it had gone as well as could be expected – the first stage of a delicate manoeuvre that had to be undertaken. It was out of his hands. A new Substitution Policy had winged its way from the Postmaster General's office and landed on his desk. London had come up with a plan, one that would mop up the remaining ex-servicemen. They had issued an edict: take the jobs from the women and give them back to the men.

It was a simple but devastating solution. The Postmaster General would no doubt be congratulating himself on such a logical, quick fix. But for Post Masters all over the country, substitution was very difficult to carry out. Still, they would have to.

Mr Thornber stood up too abruptly and his chair fell backwards onto the floor. He sighed and stooped to pick it up. It was so difficult to handle the frustration of it all and keep the lid on things. At work he had to keep quiet; there was no one to confide in. At home he couldn't risk telling his wife about his predicament. Mrs Thornber was a talker and she had too many friends, friends that knew Mrs Brunton. The news might slip out and that would never do. Mr Thornber sighed again. Evie had been an excellent post lady, but David had a family and Evie lived at home. He needed the position more than she did. What a dreadful war. The young men had suffered so much and now it was the turn of the ladies. All those jobs, handed out so liberally, snatched back again.

To make it worse, he was sure that Evie was the better worker. She was probably more capable and certainly more confident than her apprentice. The new boy would improve with time, but would he ever be as good as Evie? Mr Thornber doubted it somehow. There was something holding the young man back and, whatever that something was, it was the real reason why Seaton sorting office hadn't wanted to re-engage David Dixon. They were keeping something from him. He had asked questions but he hadn't got clear answers. And when he had tried to argue the case for keeping Evie, citing her hard work, her level-headedness, her professional manner, he had been made to feel it was wrong to keep a woman when so many men needed a livelihood.

He wandered over to his filing cabinet and opened and shut the drawers in an absent-minded fashion. He felt it too, just as much as the rest of them: an obligation to all the soldiers returning home. But Evie had done the job for four years. It would take more than patriotism to persuade him that this Dixon fellow could match her. So why bother? Why substitute something that worked with something that might be broken? Yes, that was it; he had finally put his finger on it. There was something broken about Mr Dixon, something broken on the inside. You couldn't tell on the outside, not by looking at him, or talking to him, but there was something missing, a spring, a cog – the thing that made the insides of people work smoothly. With Dixon it was missing. There was a jerkiness under the surface; he didn't have the fluidity one would expect in a young man. When he moved, it was as if his muscles were rubbing against each other, as if the war had strained and chaffed the ropes that held him together. Nervy, that was it. Dixon was nervy. Well, he couldn't employ a nervy postman and he wouldn't. He would keep a close eye on him. If he spotted any trouble, he would hold back from hiring him. After all, he didn't really want to lose his post lady.

***

At dinner that evening Evie was much cheerier. Her parents sensed the change in her.

'You look better dear,' said her mother, patting her arm. 'Daddy and I are planning to go and see Aunt Maud on Saturday, in Torquay. I don't suppose you'd like to come with us? We might stay overnight.'

Aunt Maud was very old and very miserable. And she would no doubt have an opinion on Evie's new hair. Then she would ask her when she was planning to marry.

'I think I'll stay here.' She glanced at her father. 'I can water the geraniums.'

Mr Brunton nodded his approval and Evie stood up, smiled at her parents and went upstairs. She would write to Cassie while she was in a good mood.

North Lodge, Key Lane, Colyton, Devon
Tuesday 24th August 1920

Dear Cassie,

*Thank you for your letter. What a pity you're too busy
to come down to cheer me up. Anyway, I'm finally back
at work which helps take my mind off things. I have an
assistant now, a young man called David. He served in
the war, but you'd never know it – he's so tall and
handsome. It feels like a good omen for me, seeing
someone who has suffered so much and come through
without any scars. He's a really nice chap and I'm
looking forward to getting to know him. He's serving
some sort of apprenticeship so I don't think he'll be
here long. By the way, he's married – fortunately! I
really don't want anything to do with men at the
moment. In fact, if I never meet another man it would
be fine by me – I have my job, my parents and you my
dear!*

Do write me news of London.

Your friend,

Evie

When Cassie got the letter she tried to feel pleased. As a
friend she was, of course, glad for Evie. She could sense that
Evie was still very upset, but at least she now had something
else to think about. She was back at work and coping with
life. It was all good news, as good as could be expected given
the circumstances. But as a young woman, and a young single
woman at that, Cassie felt dismayed by Evie's letter. No sooner
had Bernard disappeared than another young man had
appeared to take his place. And not just any young man: a
tall and handsome one; a brave soldier and a nice chap to
boot. It was sickening. So what if David was married, he

162

would still be giving Evie plenty of attention. Why was Evie always surrounded by men? What was so special about her? Cassie suddenly had a terrible vision of Evie squeezing through a kissing gate and the new boy watching her, leaning on his bicycle. News of London? Well, Cassie would wait until she had something really exciting to tell her friend. She would hold off from replying until she could impart something that would really make Evie sit up and take notice.

Two Shocks

The next day, Evie and David got on better and better and Evie was beginning to find delivering the midday post really enjoyable. Everything went smoother and quicker with two people. Opening and closing farmyard gates, carrying bicycles over styles, it was all simpler and easier as a pair. Having a companion also gave her more time to look around and enjoy the countryside. The heat of summer was dying down and everything was turning a golden colour: the corn, the leaves, the apples. David insisted on carrying the postbag and Evie enjoyed cycling behind him, looking up into the treetops, stretching her neck right back so she could gaze straight up at them.

Halfway through the circuit, while cycling up a long hill on a deserted track, they passed a farm cottage. There was no one at home except the dog who, unused to seeing a man with the postbag, rushed to an open window, barking madly. At the sudden explosion of sound David gave a start and his body jerked oddly to the left. He lost control of the bicycle and it swerved wildly off course. There was a squeal of brakes and a crash of metal as bicycle and rider collapsed onto the road. Evie rushed to catch up. The postbag had fallen off and letters were flying everywhere. She jumped off her bicycle and ran over. David was lying in a crumpled heap, shaking uncontrollably.

'David, what happened? Are you hurt? Let's get you up.'

She got him into a sitting position but she couldn't pull him up; he was heavy and his legs kept giving way. Heavens, what had happened?

'David, are you all right?'

He looked at her, grimacing horribly, still shaking, unable to move. Evie knew she had to retrieve the post. Leaving him where he was, she ran around, chasing the envelopes that were being blown back down the hill. Eventually she caught them all and returned. David was sitting on the track with his head in his hands. He hadn't stopped shaking.

'Are you any better? What happened?'

He opened his mouth and uttered a series of low guttural sounds, but no words came out.

'David, please tell me what happened? Are you ill?'

He tried again. 'D-d-d-d,' was all he could manage.

'The dog gave you a fright?'

He nodded. He was sweating profusely.

'Was it the sudden noise?'

David's face crumpled and he started to cry, swallowing down sobs in great gulps.

'Don't worry. If you're not hurt then we can just stay here till you feel better.'

Shell shock, Evie just knew it.

She sat down on the track beside him. 'That was unlucky,' she began quietly, 'because on this particular round there are only two dogs who bark and this dog is one of them.'

He was still shaking like a leaf but the sobbing had stopped.

'It's my fault really for not warning you.' She sat silently for a few minutes and then: 'A dog unseated me once. I flew into the ditch. Luckily no one saw me.' She paused. 'And luckily no one saw you either.'

The shaking was decreasing in intensity.

'Now there are just too many blackberries in these verges and I'm too tempted. So I'm going to eat my fill and when I'm finished, and if you're feeling better, we'll carry on.'

Evie got up and started ferreting in the hedgerow, humming to herself, and all the while wondering about the mail train and if they would make it back in time. She picked a handful of squishy blackberries, sat down on the grass verge and ate them. They left tiny purple bruises all over her palms. She stood up, wiped her hands on the pockets of her jacket and returned to David. He looked much better. He had stopped shaking but he had a woeful expression on his face.

'Ready for the off, Mr Dixon?'

He nodded.

They set off again, riding two abreast to finish the round. Evie carried the postbag and chatted amiably about nothing in particular. David was quiet but she could tell he was listening. When they got back to the sorting office the van for the mail train had already left. Mr Thornber looked at Evie quizzically.

'It's all my fault, I fell off my bicycle and felt dizzy. David was a gentleman and stayed with me.'

David gave her a grateful glance.

'Well, thank you, David,' said the Post Master doubtfully. 'It was fortunate you were there. See you tomorrow.'

David left the office but Mr Thornber hung around Evie's desk.

'Do you find Mr Dixon to be nervous at all?'

'Nervous? No. What do you mean?'

'Oh, nothing, I was just wondering – the war, you know. Anyway, I'm glad he's doing well. By the way, there's a letter for you.' Mr Thornber gestured to the office notice board. An envelope was pinned to it, an envelope with a London postmark. And the address: Miss Evie, Post Lady, Colyton Sorting Office, Devon. Evie unpinned it with her heart in her mouth. Who was writing to her? Someone who knew Bernard? She put the letter in her pocket. She would open this at home, in the privacy of her bedroom.

***

The mailbag for the four o'clock post was full to bursting and it took Evie ages to deliver it all. She cycled up hill and down dale and all the while she could feel the letter in her pocket getting heavier and heavier. Miss Evie, Post Lady. Who on earth was it from? When she finally got home, dinner was on the table. Mrs Brunton was serving up ox-tail casserole and mashed potatoes. It was Evie's least favourite meal. She tackled it as bravely as she could but the potato kept getting stuck to the roof of her mouth. She pushed the meat around her plate for a while and then asked to be excused.

'A headache,' she said, before her mother could question her further, then she stood up and left the room, avoiding her mother's searching eyes. She went slowly upstairs, leaning on the banister like an old lady, and flopped exhausted on her bed.

19, The Mansions, Berkeley Square, Mayfair, London, SW.
Tuesday 24th August 1920

Dear Miss Evie,

Please forgive my presumption for writing to you in this way. But first of all, allow me to introduce myself. My name is Toby Whittington-Smyth and I am a friend of the artist Bernard Cavalier. As you know, Bernard was recently living in Hollybrook and has now returned to London.

I have known Bernard for a number of years. He has always been a fun-loving character, brimming over with confidence and enthusiasm. Imagine then my astonishment when I met him off the train at Waterloo last Thursday and discovered he had turned into a quite different man. He was hunched, sad, quiet and anxious. The strange thing is that he refuses to tell me what has happened to him. From the odd slip he has made, under the influence of alcohol, I have been given to understand that he wanted to propose to a young lady of whom he had grown very fond. I am not sure who this person is, but, as far as I can work out, she never received his offer of marriage.

The thing is, Bernard has returned home really out of sorts. He doesn't go out, he doesn't socialise and he barely eats. Just yesterday he walked out of dinner at the RAC club when we were only halfway through. As far as I can tell he is at least working – fortunate as he has a show in the near future. I spent the weekend with him and it wasn't much fun. When he wasn't painting he just gazed out of the window. During the night he kept shouting in his sleep: 'Evie! No! Don't open it. It's not for you.' When I asked him who Evie was, he refused to answer. When I pressed him repeatedly he finally muttered – 'my post lady'.

So you see, you are the only clue I have, but I do mean to solve the puzzle. Can you help in any way by shedding some light on what this terrible mix-up might be? Why did his proposal go awry? Do you know? I mean to find the young lady that Bernard is so keen on and try and reunite the two of them. Perhaps you have some idea to whom Bernard was writing or who was writing to him? I know it might be difficult for you to remember an exact address, but even the name of the town or village would assist me in my search. I realise these things are confidential but I do think that, given Bernard's situation, desperate measures are called for. Only love, and thwarted love at that, could wreak such havoc in a man.

Please let me know if you can help in any way.

Yours sincerely,

Toby Whittington–Smyth

As soon as she had finished reading, Evie tore the letter up into tiny pieces, determined that not a speck of evidence would remain. But the irony of this action was not lost on her. The last letter she had ripped to shreds had been the one addressed to Phoebe. As she stuffed the little bits of paper into her wastepaper basket, hiding them under some orange peel, she wondered if she was going to be doomed to carry out this action in perpetuity. Perhaps she would be forced to destroy a letter every few weeks for the rest of her life. Perhaps, even after her death, her ghost would return to rip things up.

She retreated into bed and pulled the covers over her head. 'No, Evie, don't open it! It's not for you!' Was this Toby chap recounting the words in all innocence, or had he guessed that she had played a sinister role in Bernard's disappointment? What a dreadful man, no wonder he was a friend of Bernard's. But what was she to do? She had torn up Phoebe's letter in a moment of madness, now this moment of madness was threatening to overwhelm her whole life. It would always follow her around, like a shadow creeping behind her. On cloudy days she wouldn't notice it, but in the glare of the sun it would appear, scratching at her back with its long dark nails.

Evie was beginning to feel more and more like Lady Macbeth. She had led an exemplary life up to now, but this one 'damn spot' wouldn't leave her in peace. It was sticking to her and, no matter how often she scrubbed her hands, it wouldn't disappear. She could blame Bernard for hurting her, but not for causing this terrible muddle, that was her own doing. If she carried on trying to cover it up, she would have to cover it up her whole life. Lie would be added to lie and the coverings would get bigger and more brittle. One day they would crack and her evil deed, for that was what it was, would be exposed for all to see. By then she would be a bitter old maid, sitting all alone in a parlour putrid with the smell of guilt.

No, she would have to do something. But what? She wouldn't admit her crime to Toby, but she could let Phoebe know that there had been a mix-up with the post. She could go and see Phoebe and let her know that the cold, callous letter of rejection was not meant for her at all. She could still remember Phoebe's address. Saffron Walden was a fair way, but she could do it in a day. On Saturday her parents would be safely in Torquay with Aunt Maud and she didn't have to work. It would be an opportunity to put things right. It would be very hard, but it would mean she would be released from her guilt. Once she had made amends she might be able to forgive herself. Then, maybe, she could begin to forget.

Scavenger

'Are you still employing that scavenger?'

'I beg your pardon?' As he locked up the sorting office that evening, Mr Thornber had suddenly had an urge for some raspberries and had stopped at the greengrocer's on the way home to buy some. His own crop had been very poor that year because of the blackbirds that kept squeezing under the netting, so when Mr Franklin said scavenger he had immediately thought of them.

'That scavenger,' repeated the greengrocer, moving closer to him, 'the one taking an honest man's wages.'

'If you are implying that I have a dishonest post worker then you are very much mistaken,' said Mr Thornber stiffly. This was a very unpleasant accusation and not one he wanted to hear right now. Right now, all he wanted to do was to go home and sit in the garden.

'I don't mean they're dishonest, but it's dishonest to keep them.'

Oh dear. The greengrocer was referring to Evie. Mr Thornber didn't know what to say, so he said nothing, he just handed over the punnet of raspberries.

'There are men in Colyton in need of a position. Decent men, hardworking men.' Mr Franklin paused dramatically while he slipped the punnet into a brown paper bag. 'Heroes.'

Mr Thornber knew the greengrocer was right. It added weight to the belief already growing in his own mind. It was true: the few servicemen that had survived the war were all heroes.

'And now,' said the greengrocer, taking the ends of the brown paper bag and flipping them over to seal it, 'and now there's nothing for them, because of the bread snatchers.'

Mr Thornber gave an uneasy cough. 'I think you have a girl working for you as well, Mr Franklin?'

'Had, Mr Thornber, I had a girl working for me,' he flipped the bag over again, 'but I let her go. Now I have a soldier in her place.' Another flip of the bag. 'And you should too.'

'How much do I owe you?' said Mr Thornber, weakly.

'A penny.'

The Post Master fumbled in his pocket for some change. Mr Franklin moved closer.

'They say young Evie always stops for a while at High View.' There was a smell of mothballs coming from his green overalls.

'I beg your pardon?'

'Every day, they say.'

Mr Thornber felt a rush of anger and his face flushed the colour of the raspberries.

'Mr Franklin, if you are insinuating—'

'Oh not me, Mr Thornber, I'm not insinuating anything. I'm just passing on what other folk are saying.'

'Well I won't have it. Evie has worked for me for four years now and she's as honest as the day's long and very professional.'

'Whatever you say, Mr Thornber. But remember the war's been over nearly two years now.'

Mr Thornber found a penny and slapped it down on the counter. Mr Franklin handed over the raspberries.

'Goodbye Mr Franklin.'

'Goodbye Mr Thornber.'

***

The Post Master was really rattled by the conversation; he couldn't get it out of his head. He was sure that Mr Franklin had been very unfair to Evie, yet it was a worrying rumour. What if it were true? Much later that evening, when his wife popped out to see her sister, he decided to take a look at High View and see who was living there. He found his bicycle in the shed. It had got tangled up with the rake but he managed to detach it. He jumped on and set off down the road towards Hollybrook. Before he had even got to the house, he saw a big TO LET sign in the trees. He got off his bicycle and peered up the drive. The house was all shut up. So it was balderdash. Thank God. It was terrible what people would say.

He turned round and headed home, his mind free at last from the worries of the evening. Then, as he reached his driveway, he remembered that a couple of weeks ago there had been a telegram. So someone was living there until recently. His mind clouded over again. Oh well, whoever it was, they'd gone.

He parked the bicycle in the shed. On his way round to the back door he passed his raspberries and heard a rustling under the netting. How frustrating, those pesky birds just couldn't leave his fruit alone. He rushed over the lawn, stamping the ground with his feet. There was a frantic chirping and then silence. He looked in through the netting. A blackbird looked back at him, head cocked to one side, beady eye shining, beak bright yellow – such a pretty little thing.

'Scavenger,' he said, quietly.

He walked slowly over the grass to the house, weighing everything up in his mind. It was hard to believe the rumour. Evie had only missed the mail train twice in four years – once the day of the rain storm and then today. What was the reason she had given for being late? 'I fell off my bicycle and felt dizzy.' It was so unlike her. And then there was the letter that arrived earlier: Miss Evie, Post Lady. Could Evie be in love? He hoped so. He hoped to goodness that she had something else in her life, because sooner or later he would have to let her go.

Saffron Walden

On Saturday, and after several complicated changes, Evie finally boarded the train to Saffron Walden. She sat nervously, watching the fields of sheep rush by. She felt like a lamb going to slaughter. This meeting could go so wrong, but it had to be done. She couldn't live her whole life knowing that two people were suffering because of her. If she looked at it selfishly, she knew that making amends would help her own recovery. If she looked at it unselfishly – but she couldn't bring herself to do that. It was too awful to consider what she had done; all she could do was try to put it right. But would Phoebe believe her? As the miles sped by, she tried to recall what the proposal letter had actually said. Perhaps if she could remember a line or two, she could quote them to Phoebe and give her hope. She racked her brains, but only one phrase emerged: 'mad with desire for you'. No, she couldn't quote that.

Summerhill Road was only ten minutes from the Railway Station, but it took Evie ages to find it. She kept losing her bearings and had to ask several passers-by. Finally she found herself outside number 82. It was a large, rambling house, set back from the road behind a red brick wall and hooded with mature trees. She lifted the latch of the gate and walked slowly up to the front door. The garden path seemed to be sticky with glue and she had to make a huge effort just to get one foot to move in front of the other. There was an old-fashioned bell. Evie rang and waited, her heart in her mouth.

After a couple of minutes, the door opened. A tall, bespectacled woman in her mid-twenties peered out, squinting at Evie.

'I'm afraid the vicar is out,' she began.

'Miss Phoebe Carson?'

'Yes?'

'My name is Miss Brunton. I actually came to see you.'

'Oh,' Phoebe took off her spectacles. 'I'm sorry, these are reading glasses. I can't see a thing with them on. Do come in.'

She led the way through a hallway that reminded Evie of her own, then into a small parlour where a fire was burning.

'Quite an unnecessary luxury at this time of year,' Phoebe nodded at the fire, 'but I love a luxury!' She gave a little laugh, revealing rather rabbity teeth. She seemed charming and Evie was horrified to realise she already liked her.

'A fire and a book,' she grinned. 'There's nothing like it! Do you read?'

'A little,' said Evie, nervous about letting her guard down with this disarming lady.

'I'm afraid I read a lot,' laughed Phoebe. 'I devour books. So, what can I do for you, Miss Brunton? Let me warn you now that I am a no-hoper. If you have come to invite me to join any sort of group, society, guild or indeed any kind of charitable institution, you are wasting your time.'

'I haven't.'

'Excellent!' beamed Phoebe. 'Then I shall make you tea and crumpets.' She jumped up and started towards the door.

Evie was horrified – afternoon tea was the wrong ambience for a business-like chat.

'I must hasten to the point of why I am here.'

'Only once you have a cup and saucer in your hand,' smiled Phoebe. 'I wasn't born in a vicarage for nothing! Do sit down.' She waved hospitably at an armchair and disappeared.

This was bad, very bad. Phoebe was delightful. If only she had been astonishingly attractive and rather dull, or, even better, superior and unpleasant. Then Evie could have hated her as she imparted her 'good news'. Instead Miss Carson was quite plain but really charming – the sort of girl one could get very fond of. No wonder Bernard was so keen on her. Evie sat down gingerly on an armchair and waited. She could hear Phoebe crashing about in another room. A clock on the mantelpiece ticked loudly. 'Trai-tor, trai-tor!' it ticked. She looked around. The walls, heavy with dark flock wallpaper, were covered with portraits of old men in dog collars. On the floor was an Indian rug; on the mantelpiece, beside the clock, a porcelain shepherdess. Evie wondered whether Bernard had ever been a visitor here. She glanced again at the rows of vicars in their ornate frames. The ticking grew louder. 'Trai-tor.'

The door opened again and Phoebe came in wheeling a wooden trolley stacked with tea cups, buttered crumpets and, oh no, a jar of gooseberry jam.

'Allow me,' she said, busying herself with plates, knives, and the sugar bowl.

Evie felt desperate. 'It's extremely kind of you, Miss Carson, to be so friendly and hospitable, but—'

'I'm not kind,' interrupted Phoebe, 'I'm a show-off. I made some gooseberry conserve and I want you to try it.' She twisted the lid off the jar and it opened with a pop. 'Father can't stand the stuff!' she laughed.

Powerless, Evie sat and allowed Phoebe to butter her a crumpet and lavishly cover it with jam.

'It's so kind of you, Miss Carson,' Evie struggled to pick up her thread, 'especially as I have come on business.'

'Business?'

'Yes.' Evie started gabbling, trying to get it all out as fast as possible, 'You see, I work for the Post Office. I'm here to represent the Colyton sorting office. I understand that you have recently had a correspondent in our part of the world?' And before Phoebe could answer, 'We have unfortunately had a problem with a member of staff who works in our branch.

It appears that this member of staff has tampered with some letters. The other day, for example, a letter was found torn up in a ditch.'

'Dear, dear, but what has that got to do with me?'

'It was discovered outside a house rented by a Mr Cavalier.'

Phoebe, who was pouring the tea, gave a start. A spurt of brown liquid gushed out onto the lace cloth which decorated the tea trolley.

'How do you know I know him?'

'We are contacting all the people he corresponded with,' Evie lied.

'Does Mr Cavalier know then?'

'Mr Cavalier is very upset that there may have been a problem with his mail and is co-operating with us. He gave us your address.' She was pirouetting on the rim of a volcano. One false move and she would tumble in.

'And this letter – was it possible to read it or repair it?'

'No, it was completely ruined by the water in the ditch. But we at the Post Office are worried. Someone who has sufficient gall to destroy a letter might also,' Evie paused to swallow, 'mix a letter up.'

'Mix a letter up!' Phoebe looked horrified. 'But why?'

'There are a lot of disappointed people around at the moment, Miss Carson. Bitter people. People who, having had their own happiness ruined, want to spoil things for others.'

This flood of honesty bolstered Evie. She took a sip of tea and a bite of crumpet.

'That's shocking!' Phoebe exclaimed. 'I guess the war—'

Evie didn't contradict her. 'Anyway, I – I mean we at the sorting office wanted to warn you. Miss Carson, if you have received a letter from Mr Cavalier recently, it is possible that – it's just possible that it's the wrong one.'

'The wrong one?'

'The wrong one, Miss Carson.' It was like lancing a boil – excruciating, but now Evie had started she just wanted to get it over with. 'If you received a letter from Mr Cavalier recently, it is just possible that it wasn't meant for you.'

'Good heavens.' Phoebe sat back in her armchair and gazed at the young girl before her. She was a pretty thing, despite a rather severe haircut. There was something about her – her directness, her smile that Phoebe really liked. She wished she lived in Saffron Walden. She suddenly found herself wanting to confide in her.

'I did get a letter from Mr Cavalier recently,' she began, 'of a very serious nature.' She paused and looked wistfully out of the window. 'I only wish it hadn't been for me.'

Evie blanched. The ordeal was certainly proving as painful as she had expected. She took a deep breath. 'Perhaps it wasn't,' she suggested, gently.

'Oh, I'm afraid it was,' said Phoebe. 'Mr Cavalier came to see me a couple of days ago to apologise.'

'Apologise?' Evie's heart began to beat loudly in her chest. The sound was deafening. Could Phoebe hear it?

'He said he had made a mess of it – the letter I mean. He felt it was too brusque, too insensitive. He wanted to make sure I was all right about everything, which of course I am.' Phoebe smiled weakly, out of the window. 'Our friendship obviously wasn't meant to be.' A shadow crossed her face. 'Funny, he never mentioned anything about a mix-up with the post.'

'We've only just discovered it,' said Evie quickly.

'I see,' said Phoebe, relieved. 'He's lost a lot of weight,' she said, half to herself. And then to Evie: 'We're having a clean break.' A pause. 'It's better like that.' She smiled, 'More tea?'

'No thank you. I should get going.'

The patterns in the Indian rug were starting to spin, whirling up towards her. Evie looked away before they could swallow her up.

'I have a train soon,' she managed, staggering to her feet.

'What a shame.'

Evie knew she meant it and her heart went out to this sweet woman. If she could have, she would have stopped time, spun the earth backwards, reached into the ditch, found the letter, stitched it together and presented it to Phoebe.

'Take it!' she would have said. 'Take this chance of happiness. You alone deserve it.'

'Did you know Bernard?' Phoebe asked.

'Bernard?'

'Mr Cavalier.'

The patterned rug leapt up at Evie again.

'No, he wasn't on my round.' And that, she promised herself, was the last lie she would ever tell in her whole life.

'Thank you so much for the tea, I've really enjoyed meeting you, Miss Carson.'

'Please call me Phoebe.'

'Thank you, Phoebe.'

Phoebe showed her out. They smiled at each other again and then Evie turned and followed the path back down to the gate.

'I say,' called Phoebe, from the door. 'What happened to the postman who tampered with the letters?'

Evie pretended not to hear and walked briskly away.

* * *

Safely back on the train, Evie stared out at the darkening landscape. She could do no more. The boil was lanced. She was too numb from the ordeal to feel anything, but she knew the pain would begin again tomorrow. So Bernard had gone to see Phoebe. He had had a chance to put everything right and he had decided it would be better to leave things as they stood. He must have thought that keeping quiet about the mix-up would be simpler, kinder to Phoebe, less unsettling. She realised it would have been very difficult for him to make amends. It would have been almost impossible for him to kneel on the Indian rug and propose to Phoebe after a letter like that, especially with all those clergymen watching. Evie could still hardly believe she had ruined three people's lives. She had spoilt Bernard's and Phoebe's chance of happiness and she had wrecked her own career. She was a sham, a post lady who interfered with the mail. She had single-handedly undermined her profession.

If only she had gone to see Phoebe earlier, before Bernard's visit; she could have changed everything with her story. She could have sowed the seed of doubt in Phoebe's mind and given her the impression that there might have been a mix-up. Then, when Bernard came to see her, Phoebe could have quizzed him, found out the truth and flown into his arms. The timing was wrong; she had tried to put things right but she was too late. Funny how Phoebe had assumed the dishonest post worker was a man. If only she knew that the dishonest post worker was in front of her, drinking her tea, eating her crumpets. Evie had hoped that going to see Phoebe would assuage the guilt she was carrying around with her everywhere, like a postbag. But she felt worse than before. She hadn't managed to untangle the terrible mess. It rolled like a ball of barbed wire alongside the train, knocking against the window.

* * *

Back at the vicarage, Phoebe was washing up and thinking about the extraordinary visit. She slowly scraped the remains of Miss Brunton's crumpet into the dustbin. Miss Brunton hadn't eaten much. No wonder she was so slim; slim and attractive. She was just the sort of girl that would have turned Bernard's head, had he known her. But Miss Brunton had been quite clear about that. She had been adamant that Bernard was not on her round – fortunately for her. Phoebe smiled ruefully as she washed the dishes. She was almost sure that 'love' was the reason someone had tampered with the post. Perhaps someone was trying to get their own back on Bernard; perhaps hers wasn't the only broken heart. It helped somehow to imagine that she wasn't alone in her grief and it also made her feel less foolish. Well, whoever it was, they would recover together.

Phoebe gave a little smile. She was feeling stronger. Bernard's visit had been painful, but it had helped. She felt more peaceful now and her resentment towards him was slowly fading. Poor chap, he had looked so miserable. What was it about him that led to so much disorder and chaos? Like an enormous whale he thrashed around, leaving disarray and confusion in his wake. She smiled at the idea of Bernard as a whale; it was a funny but apt metaphor – even he would have liked it.

The Echoed Image

YOU ARE INVITED TO A PRIVATE VIEW
THE ECHOED IMAGE
A NEW EXHIBITION OF PAINTINGS BY CAVALIER
ON WEDNESDAY SEPTEMBER 1ST AT 5 PM.
CARRUTHERS GALLERY
CORK STREET, LONDON

Cassie stared gloomily out of the window of a hansom cab, an invitation to Bernard's upcoming show lying stiffly in her lap. She had noticed it propped up on the mantelpiece as she drank tea in Daisy's drawing room and Daisy had noticed her looking at it.

'Oh, you must come with me!' Daisy had leapt up, grabbed the invitation and pressed it into Cassie's hands. 'I have no real interest in art and it would be much more fun if you came too. Anyway, I remember you asking what Bernard's work was like.'

'I'm not sure,' Cassie had begun.

'Oh do come, an opening is always fun. Take the card, I can use mother's invite.'

Not knowing how to refuse it, Cassie had accepted the printed invitation. As she gazed out at the darkening sky, she realised she would have to attend. Daisy would be expecting her to go. It would seem churlish to miss the opening, especially as she had quizzed Daisy and Lavinia about Bernard; especially as she had told them she had once met him on a train. Well, if she had to go she would at least try and look the part. A trip to Harrods was called for.

Cassie visited the boutique on Harrods' fashionable third floor and chose a black bolero outfit, comprising a black velvet skirt and a pretty black bolero jacket over a gold bodice, with a matching gold hat and shoes. She resolved to save it for the day and put it to the back of her wardrobe. Bitter experience had taught her that even the prettiest dress could lose its gloss after the first wearing. The magic of a new frock was definitely ephemeral and she wanted to sparkle at the opening.

Unfortunately, the day of the exhibition was rainy and Cassie was faced with a difficult dilemma. If she risked wearing the dress without a coat she might ruin it, but a coat would quite spoil the look of the outfit. In the end, she decided to take a cab and an umbrella. She rooted around in the umbrella stand by the front door and discovered a large black umbrella with a gold handle. She was pleased with her find; it looked rather like a long sword and added to the matador look that the jacket suggested. Thus armed, she arrived at Carruthers's gallery in Cork Street as the doors were opening.

There was a queue of people waiting to get in. Cassie quickly put up her umbrella and held it high above her head, so it would protect her dress and hat without hiding it from any potential admirers. She was amazed to see so many people, everyone talking loudly and laughing. She looked for Daisy but there was no sign of her. How annoying that her friend was late. She didn't know anyone else here and now she would feel like a fool on her own. Stifling her annoyance and trying to look nonchalant and confident, Cassie gazed around. At the door stood a stocky man in a dogstooth suit and a spotted bow tie. Only a gallery owner would dare to wear such an audacious mix; this man had to be Carruthers. He beamed at everyone in greeting, occasionally touching someone's arm with a 'Hello, so glad you could come,' like a holy man offering benediction to pilgrims.

Beyond Carruthers the gallery was filling up. People were milling around the pictures and there was a murmur of voices that was slowly gaining momentum. Folk were looking at the paintings and slyly looking at each other sideways, trying to gauge the general mood. There was a feeling of anticipation in the air with everyone waiting for something. Then Cassie noticed a smart lady with a large hat go back to the door and whisper something in Carruthers's ear.

'It's yours, Madame!' he bellowed, whipping a red dot out of his pocket and sticking it to one of the paintings.

The first bet had been placed. Someone had taken a punt on Bernard Cavalier, someone of significance, judging by the size of the hat. There was a split second of silence during which it felt as if time had slowed to a stop. Then, like greyhounds released from their traps, people rushed to Carruthers, clamouring to buy a painting. Carruthers looked beside himself with joy as he dashed about, sticking red dots here, there and everywhere. Cassie felt irritated, though she didn't really know why. It was like a rash of measles. Did the mole toucher really deserve this sort of fuss? She looked more closely at the picture behind her. *A View of Seaton*. She knew the beach well, but in the picture the pebbles were a bluey purple and the sea was ever so slightly orange.

'A little like Dufy perhaps, but bolder I think, more visionary,' said a loud voice behind her.

Cassie turned round. A short man with dark hair and a velvet jacket was holding forth to a group of people, an elegant lady dangling on his arm.

'Anyway, I'm very proud of him, he's a real chip off the old block.'

Chip off the old block? Could this be Bernard's father? He looked very different: small instead of large, dark instead of carroty, but the same booming voice, the same overconfidence. And where was Bernard? Cassie scanned the gallery and spotted him standing in a corner, clutching a glass of wine and holding a cigar which had gone out. He was brightly dressed in a coloured waistcoat and bow tie, but he looked rather out of sorts, almost despondent. People were coming up to talk to him, but he was clearly struggling to engage. What on earth was wrong with him? How spoilt to look so downcast at his own show.

She searched for Daisy but she still hadn't appeared. Cassie decided to whizz round as quickly as possible and then leave before her friend arrived and detained her any longer. She had done the first room already, so there was just the back of the gallery to glance at and then she could slip away. She turned the corner and there it was – a large picture entitled *Picking Raspberries*: an enormous portrait of her friend, Evie Brunton.

Cassie gasped. The frame was a rather heavy gold-leafed affair, but the canvas within it was lovely. It was an oil painting and it danced with light. Evie was standing amongst some raspberry canes, dishevelled and sweaty. She looked slightly grumpy and completely beautiful. Her long blonde hair shone in the sunlight and there were dapples of sun on her face and neck. She was wearing a lovely white blouse and her eyes were a searing blue. Cassie glanced at the price. £75 and there was already a red dot on it.

Cassie felt quite sick. How had he made Evie look so lovely? It must be an artist's trick. How could someone so hot and bothered look so attractive otherwise? She knew what artists were like, always happy to paint over any defect and cover any blemish – all in the name of art. Bernard Cavalier had turned her friend into a fake beauty, a sort of cheap Aphrodite. It was dishonest. It was disgusting. Cassie turned her back on the picture and walked quickly away from it and there, facing her on the opposite wall, was a much smaller painting. A girl with a short bob was sitting on a sofa with her head bent over, reading what looked like a letter. The girl had her back to the viewer but Cassie knew immediately who it was, for at the nape of her neck a mole was peeping over her collar. Evie again. So, she had cut her hair – about time too. But at what cost if it meant the mole was showing? She knew Evie hated her mole, so what had possessed her to reveal it?

She glanced down at the title – *The Wrong Envelope*. What on earth did that mean? And where the price should have been displayed there were three letters – NFS. Cassie had no idea what they stood for. She examined the picture again, looking for clues. There seemed to be a story, a tension lying just below the surface. She would work it out. She would stand there until she had solved the riddle.

'Cassie?'

She looked round and saw Bernard approaching. Goodness, he had remembered her.

'Actually, it's Cassandra.'

'You're Evie's friend. Is that right? I think I met you on a train.'

'That's correct.'

'How is she?'

'I'm sorry?'

'Evie. Have you seen her? Has she written? Is she well?' He looked at her intensely, as if everything depended on her answer.

Cassie hesitated. 'Fine, Evie's fine,' she said vaguely.

'Good. That's good.' Bernard looked pleased and relieved. 'So you think she's fine?'

Heavens, why did he keep asking? After all, he was the one who had cast Evie aside. Perhaps he felt guilty.

'Why is it called *The Wrong Envelope*?' she asked, keen to change the subject.

'It's a long story. And it doesn't matter, because it's NFS.'

'NFS?'

'Not For Sale.'

Of course, she should have known. Now he would think she was an idiot.

'Carruthers insisted I put it in,' Bernard continued, 'and I agreed on condition it was NFS.'

'Oh, I see,' said Cassie, not really seeing at all but anxious to appear knowledgeable about such things.

'So how is Evie?' he asked again.

The man was demented. Cassie felt overcome by irritation. It was always about Evie; she was sick of it.

'Evie's on good form,' she said. 'She's working with a charming new colleague now, a young man who was in the war.'

Bernard looked desperate, but also resigned to this piece of news, like someone receiving the death sentence they were expecting.

'Of course, of course,' he said.

There was an uneasy silence during which Carruthers came along with another man. He nodded to Cassie and then turned to Bernard.

'This is Mr Taylor, Bernard. He's very interested in your painting.'

'It's not for sale.'

'Yes I know.' Mr Carruthers smiled uneasily at Bernard, like an elderly relative dealing with an unpredictable child. 'The thing is, Bernard, Mr Taylor is from The Tate.' He was still smiling but he spoke through slightly gritted teeth.

Cassie could sense the tension in the air and knew she should move away, but there was something compelling about the situation and she stayed rooted to the spot. Mr Taylor had taken off his glasses and was examining the painting close up, peering at the paintwork.

'It's exquisitely executed,' he murmured.

'But it's not for sale,' repeated Bernard and he stood in front of the painting, blocking Mr Taylor's view.

'I'm sorry, but that's how it is.' He motioned with a hand around the rest of the gallery, as if pointing out there were plenty of other paintings and then he glowered at Carruthers. 'I thought we had a deal?'

Ignoring Bernard, Carruthers gently moved Mr Taylor on to the next painting, talking quietly and seriously, gesturing with his hands. Cassie saw him glance back and give Bernard a look full of reproach. Bernard shrugged and started to walk away. Cassie realised he had forgotten all about her.

She picked her way back through the gallery, which was now even more crowded, and made for the door. Still no sign of Daisy. Good. She didn't want to stay a minute longer. On her way out, she passed the man who didn't look like Bernard's father. He had collared Mr Taylor.

'Yes, that's what I say, like father – like son,' he was saying and laughing heartily.

Outside, she breathed in the cool evening air. The rain had stopped and she decided to walk to Oxford Street and take the Underground. The heels of her new shoes clicked on the pavements. She felt utterly empty. How did Evie manage it? There were only two portraits in the whole exhibition and they were both of her. Evie lived in Devon and yet she had appeared, as if by magic, in a London gallery. Not only that, but in one portrait she looked rather ravishing and in another brooding and dramatic, like a fledging film star. It wasn't fair. Bernard had idolised her. It was infuriating. She was infuriated, not jealous. Why, when he had proposed to someone else, was Bernard still soft on Evie? Why, when he had broken her heart, was he still painting her portrait? Why? Why? Why? And why had she allowed herself to be coerced into going to the exhibition by a friend who hadn't even bothered to show up?

It was a cruel twist of fate. And now she would have to write and tell Evie all about it. If Evie found out she was hanging in a London gallery and thought that Cassie was keeping it from her, she would never forgive her. But she would wait a few days, until she felt calmer. She would collect her thoughts and then she would edit the events of the evening.

Which One?

The gallery was quieter now. Most people had wandered off home, but a few stragglers still mingled by the door, catching up with the gossip, draining their glasses. In the second room, Toby sat on the floor with his back against the wall and his legs stretched out in front of him. He wasn't drunk; he could hold his drink. He was tired – it had been a very tiring night.

Bernard, of course, had already left – taken off, probably back to his studio, without saying goodbye. What on earth was wrong with him? He had spent the whole evening struggling to talk to anyone, looking over people's heads when they were talking to him, nodding imperceptibly when they told him they'd bought a painting, or shrugging and turning away. It was his show dammit and yet he didn't seem to care. Was Bernard really depressed or was this some sort of silly persona he had adopted? Was he trying to become the moody artist *par excellence*? He hoped not because there was only so much moodiness a man could take. Toby had spent the evening feeling very frustrated by his friend's attitude. And all he could do was stand and watch, because every time he had tried to get near Bernard he had walked off. Well, he had got away with it – this time. People loved the work and forgave him his offhandedness, but would they be so gracious next time?

Toby suddenly hiccupped and felt very sick. Perhaps he had eaten something dodgy? An oyster? A prawn? What had he had for dinner? Wait a minute, perhaps he hadn't eaten

– in which case he would go in search of some supper.

He lurched to his feet and stood for a few seconds getting his bearings. The sudden change of altitude from the floor to standing made him feel dizzy. Heavens, he must be getting old. And his eyes were going too, the paintings seemed blurry all of a sudden. He staggered over to the nearest one – *Picking Raspberries*. A lovely girl. Toby leaned towards her. She had a beautiful mouth. He put out a finger, suddenly wanting to touch it. Hold on. He mustn't touch. One didn't touch paintings. He stood and gazed at her.

'Was it you? Are you the culprit?'

She didn't reply.

He turned round and looked at the other girl, the one in *The Wrong Envelope*.

'Or was it you?' he asked, more urgently.

The girl ignored him and carried on reading her letter. The sofa she was sitting on was rather shabby and the standard lamp beside her was very old-fashioned. The young lady in the raspberry patch looked aristocratic, but this one was from a different class. Which one? Middle? Lower? She wasn't giving anything away.

'Look at me when I'm talking to you!'

'I beg your pardon?'

Toby jumped. Just for a second, but only a second, he thought the girl in *The Wrong Envelope* had spoken; then he realised there was someone else in the gallery. He swung round to find Daisy standing beside him.

'Oh, it's you, Daisy,' he said, half relieved, half embarrassed.

'Who did you think it was?'

'You're fashionably late,' said Toby, avoiding the question. 'It's all over. I hope you didn't want to buy a painting?'

'I didn't,' said Daisy, a trifle too quickly. 'Actually I'm looking for Cassie.'

'Cassie?' Toby had never heard of her.

'Cassandra Richardson? Oh, never mind, she's obviously gone.'

Daisy turned to go but not before Toby had admired her dress. It was a lovely blue and had a long straight transparent skirt and underneath another skirt, shorter in length. It was worn to tease; he was sure of it.

'Daisy, I need your help.'

'I'm sorry, Toby, I have to find Cassie.' She seemed keen to get away. 'Anyway, you're squiffy.'

Toby lurched towards her. 'You see one of them is guilty – but I don't know which one.'

If Daisy had seemed anxious to escape before, she now seemed desperate. She glanced back round the corner as if she was looking to be rescued.

'Guilty of what, Toby?'

'Guilty of breaking Bernard Cavalier's heart.'

A sudden spark of interest flashed across Daisy's face. 'Bernard's in love? You mean the cavalier has finally been smitten? How did that happen? A love potion? An arrow fired by Cupid himself?'

'Devon,' said Toby gloomily.

'Heavens!' Daisy looked highly amused. 'And it's one of these two?'

'I think so. Can you help?' Toby came up close to Daisy. She had pretty eyes, very pretty eyes; they peeped out at him from under her thick dark fringe, bright green, like a cat's. Why hadn't he noticed them before?

'Well I can try – I love to solve a mystery.'

Daisy walked purposefully backwards and forwards between the two paintings and then she hovered in front of *Picking Raspberries*.

'I think she looks rather posh,' said Toby.

'I'm not sure,' said Daisy. 'She's attractive, but it's difficult to gauge whether—'

'She's one of us?'

'No, whether she's Bernard's type.'

'Oh she is,' said Toby with feeling.

'Is she? She looks rather vulnerable, rather malleable,

whereas this lady,' she hurried over to *The Wrong Envelope*, 'looks more determined, more feisty, more the sort of girl that would capture his heart.'

'Really?' Toby was amazed. 'How interesting you are, Daisy.' So she was clever as well as pretty. How come he hadn't realised before?

'You must think me an oaf for not being more perceptive.'

'Actually, I think you're rather sweet for being so concerned about Bernard.'

'We're very close, like brothers.'

'Really? I had no idea.' Daisy looked at Toby as if she was reassessing him in some way. She definitely had very nice eyes, he decided. He lurched towards her again and she sidestepped him, but she kept smiling.

'So you think it's the one with the mole?'

'I do.'

'Thank you very much.' Toby felt so grateful he wanted to hug her. 'And now, can I take you for supper?'

Daisy hesitated. 'Not tonight, Toby, but another night would be lovely – when you're not so squiffy.' She smiled again and disappeared round the corner just as Carruthers appeared.

'Hop it, Toby,' he said.

'A good night hey, Carruthers?'

'Yes, yes,' Carruthers agreed. 'Now, hop it.'

Just Not That Interesting

72, Fairholme Road, Kensington, London, SW.
Thursday 9th September 1920

My dearest Evie,

I'm so sorry to be so tardy in replying to your last letter. Things have been a bit of a social whirl here in London. I have so much to tell you, but firstly let me congratulate you on finally taking the plunge and cutting your hair! But how do I know? How is your friend aware that you've lopped it all off? Have I suddenly developed the gift of second sight? No, I simply attended the opening night of a new exhibition by a certain Bernard Cavalier.

The exhibition took place in a very fashionable London gallery last Wednesday. My dear, they were queuing at the door to get in. I had no idea the 'mole toucher' had such a following. He must know the right types because the London set were all in attendance and quaffing great quantities of wine. The artist was there, of course, his Liberty bow tie clashing artistically with the colour of his waistcoat. He stood in a corner, with a little cigar in one hand and a glass of wine in the other, and people crowded round him, vying for his attention. He listened, nodded and smiled, but he seemed rather distracted to me, or perhaps he felt embarrassed. The thing is, his work just wasn't that interesting, well not to me anyway. The word 'obscure' comes to mind. I'm sorry to say that, but it's true.

Well Evie, did you know you were the muse for a modern artist? Two of the pictures in the gallery are of you! There is one called 'Picking Raspberries'. You are standing in some sort of a vegetable patch, with beads of moisture on your forehead and above your lip. The colours are pale, almost bleached, as if the sun is beating down. It made me hot just looking at you, especially with the obvious perspiration on your face. The theme was very impressionistic, you know – peasant girl picking fruit, but the result was a bit sketchy, I'm afraid.

The second picture is tiny and very enigmatic. Your hair has by now been cropped (who cut it – a friend?) You are sitting on your old sofa, facing away from the painter. I only knew it was you because you are leaning forward reading what looks like a letter and there, at the nape of your neck, is your mole. Imagine, it has been immortalised! And the title – 'The Wrong Envelope'. Whatever does this mean? Do you know? What a puzzle. My dear, I hope you haven't been tampering with the post! To add to the sense of mystery there was a little sign on it, where the price should have been: NFS. In case you don't know, it means 'Not For Sale.' Perhaps the gallery owner thought no one would buy it.

You must write and tell me all, Evie – you have much to explain! In fact, no – you must come up to London and see your pictures for yourself. And I could take you to my barber, just to tidy your new hair up a bit. It may be modern darling, but it's not the latest style.

Yours in anticipation,

Cassie

Evie got the letter on a Friday when she came home from work and it completely ruined her weekend. It was a double blow, the news itself and the way Cassie imparted it. Cassie's jibes about her hair, the dismissive way she wrote about the portraits and then the thinly veiled accusation. Cassie was clearly not a real friend, not any more. A real friend would have been gentler, kinder. A real friend would have come down and broken the news to her in person. Instead, Cassie had written it in black and white and in a teasing way. She had shown no mercy.

But if Cassie had taken a pot shot at her, it was Bernard who had given her the ammunition. *The Wrong Envelope.* He might as well have called it *The Dishonest Post Lady.* And then he had painted her mole, identifying her to the whole world. It was only a matter of time before someone from her area noticed the picture. Then they would tell everyone and the sorting office would find out and they would question her. She would have to resign. She couldn't go on now, not with her secret hanging in a London gallery for the whole world to see and comment on. She would resign before she was found out. Perhaps they would give her job to David. At least then some good would come of the terrible mess.

The Larger Than Life Portrait

As Evie was deciding how she would hand in her resignation, Toby was waiting for Bernard again. Where the dickens had he got to? From his armchair in the RAC club's smoking lounge, Toby watched taxi cabs coming and going. Rain streaked across the windows of the club, turning headlamps into stars. Still no sign. He sighed, stubbed the end of his cigar into the ashtray, downed his whisky and got to his feet. He would have to go and find him. Again.

Toby walked briskly through St James's Park towards Pimlico. He felt really irritated. He was hungry and cross that supper had been postponed, if not cancelled, by the no-show from his friend. Another Friday night ruined. What on earth had got into Bernard? Why couldn't he just get back to normal? His show was a sell-out and he was now one of the most popular artists in London. There were queues of girls desperate to be seen with him or painted by him, or both. Yet he had disappeared, literally. He hardly ventured out of his studio and he shunned invitations to the theatre and the opera. Bernard was the talk of London, and yet Toby wondered if he was even remembering to wash.

Having reached the mews that housed Bernard's studio, Toby lifted his cane and hammered on the door. No one came.

He banged again, harder this time. 'For pity's sake, Bernard, open the door!'

He heard a shuffle of footsteps on the inside and then the bolt was drawn back. The door opened a crack and Bernard's unshaven face peered out at him. He looked eerie, lit by just one light from the other side which made his stubble shiny. Quick as a flash, Toby stuck his foot out and jammed the door open. 'Let me in Bernard old chap. We had a dinner date, you know.'

'Did we? I'm so sorry.' Bernard opened the door and went back inside; Toby followed.

The studio didn't look as messy as usual. There were no dirty plates or cups littering the floor.

'What have you eaten today?'

'I'll eat later. I'm working on something.'

Leaning against the back wall was an enormous canvas, covered by a sheet.

'Something new?'

'It's something for me. I'm not showing it to anyone.'

'You'll have a job to keep it quiet, it's so big.'

'The thing is, Toby, *Picking Raspberries* has gone. And Carruthers will give *The Wrong Envelope* to the Tate. I don't want him to, but he'll find a way of wheedling it out of me. He'll fabricate some story about another debt or the fact I owe my career to him. So, while I can still remember, I've painted another one.'

'Let's have a look, old boy.'

'As long as you keep quiet about it.'

Bernard flicked the edge of the sheet. It fell away and there, as large as life, gleaming in the oil lamps that lit the studio, was a post lady standing on a porch. She was soaking wet from the rain and water was dripping off her hat and coat. Light danced in the drips and the whole painting throbbed with life. Toby gave a start.

'But this is your post lady!'

'Yes, this is Evie.'

'But she has the same face as the girl in the raspberry patch.'

'Yes.'

'So it was Evie in the gallery?'

'Always Evie,' sighed Bernard.

Toby gulped, 'And in the other picture too?'

'I'm afraid so.'

'So it was Evie you wanted to propose to, but didn't?'

'I messed everything up. I didn't deserve her.'

Toby's mind started working ten to the dozen. So it was the post lady that Bernard loved – the woman who he had unwittingly written to, asking for clues, looking for answers. And he had almost insinuated that she had interfered with the post. Oh Lord, what must she have thought? And all along it was Evie that should have got the proposal. What was it he had written on her envelope – *Miss Evie, Post Lady*. No wonder she hadn't replied. Dear God, what could he do to put this right? Toby felt sick with anxiety. All thoughts of dinner evaporated; he just wanted to get home.

Bernard smiled ruefully. 'I need to do something, Toby, but I don't know what. I keep trying to write and I keep giving up.'

He put his hand in his pocket and pulled out an envelope. It was addressed and stamped, but torn in two. Toby's eyes desperately scanned the ripped envelope. What was her surname? Burnton? Binton? Barnton – that was it, Barnton, New Lodge, King's Lane, Colyton. Bernard sighed and tossed the letter on the ground. It landed face down. Toby started silently repeating the address to himself, like a mantra – Miss E. Barnton, New Lodge, King's Lane, Colyton, Devon.

'Well Bernard, it's too late for dinner tonight, so I suggest we reconvene tomorrow.' Toby waved his arms vaguely in the air as he walked backwards towards the door.

'But you've only just arrived. The pub's open and they serve pies.'

'You know I'm not a pub man. Let's meet tomorrow, at my club.'

'Don't be a snob, Toby. Come and have a beer.'

'Sorry, but I'm not an ale drinker. Good night Bernard.' And with that Toby slipped out of the studio and closed the door. Once on the street he quickly hailed a cab.

'Berkeley Square, as swiftly as possible.'

Miss Barnton, he said to himself, as the driver turned the cab and headed for Mayfair. New Lodge, King's Lane, Colyton, Devon. Dear, dear God.

The Resignation

When Evie went to see Mr Thornber on Monday morning to hand in her resignation, he could hardly believe his ears. He had been worrying all weekend about how to tell his most efficient post worker that her services were no longer needed. How was he to explain that he was taking away the job she had done for four years and giving it to someone with almost no experience? He had lain awake most of Sunday night preparing a speech on the necessity of supporting ex-soldiers. He had rehearsed phrases like 'family responsibilities', 'mouths to feed' and 'War Office priorities'. But there had been no need for this careful preparation. Evie was leaving anyway. The job was being handed back without any need to persuade or coerce.

'I need a change,' was all she said by way of explanation. And then she added: 'I hope you will give my position to David.'

'He is certainly at the forefront of my mind,' Mr Thornber replied, amazed at how well the conversation was going.

'Good,' Evie said, standing up. 'Because I think he possesses both honesty and integrity.'

'Like you, Evie.'

The Post Master smiled at her but she didn't smile back. Instead she bowed slightly and then turned and left. A strange end to a long period of exemplary service. He wondered what she would do now.

As she returned her Post Office bicycle to the shed behind the sorting office, Evie was wondering exactly the same thing. What on earth would she do now she had no position and no bicycle? One thing was certain: she would take her time going home. Her mother would be confused to see her back so early and she would almost certainly have some questions. If she could wait until as near to lunchtime as possible she could break the news to her parents together, kill two birds with one stone. And then? Now there was a question, and one without any answers.

Evie turned left into Market Street. The octagonal tower of St Andrew's beckoned. She walked through the churchyard, opened the heavy wooden door and went into the cool semi-darkness of the ancient building. There were lots of reasons why she liked this church, but the main one was that it was such a mishmash of different styles and ages, all built on top of each other. The Saxons, the Normans, the Elizabethans, they had all had a bash at making the church their own but somehow the church had not only survived their attacks, it had grown stronger because of them. Evie had always taken great satisfaction from this fact; she thought it proved that anything could be integrated into the whole, given time. Today she took particular delight in tracing the Saxon remains and then finding where the Normans had joined in and left off again. Life was a muddle and history reflected this, only on a much grander scale.

She mooched down the aisle to the Pole monument, dated 1587 and the tomb of Sir John and Lady Pole, together in death, but lying back to back. Why, she always wondered, were they not facing each other, or at least lying side by side? Why were they both looking the other way? Was it a row, a family split, a terrible secret? She drifted on to the Courtenay Monument. Legend claimed this was the tomb of Margaret Courtenay, granddaughter of Edward IV, who choked to death on a fish bone. It was a story that had both fascinated and terrified Evie as a child. During the Sunday service, she would sit and look at the tomb and imagine Margaret gasping for breath. Today, it made her feel very uneasy. Life is uncertain, it seemed to say; your fate is unpredictable, you live on a knife edge. She walked hurriedly away. She didn't need any more twists of fortune; things were bad enough already. She left the church and went back out into the sunshine.

She opened the churchyard gate and carried on down the road towards North Lodge. The vicarage lay on her left, one of the oldest buildings in Colyton with a Tudor front. As she peered in through the tiny medieval windows, she suddenly thought about Phoebe. Would Phoebe become a ghost one day, haunting the vicarage on Summerhill Road for centuries to come? Heavens, what a dreadful thought; she couldn't bear to even consider it. She suddenly imagined Phoebe sitting in her parlour, a Miss Havisham figure waiting hopefully in a wedding dress. Oh goodness, what had she done? She took off, running down Vicarage Street, into Key Lane and home. Once through the back gate she stood for a few moments in the garden, trying to get her breath back. Then, bracing herself, she went inside the house.

'Oh!' Mrs Brunton started when Evie came into the kitchen. 'You're back for lunch. Did you finish work early?'

'Something like that.' She would wait for her father before she broke the news.

Mrs Brunton eyed the chops she was frying dubiously. Would they do three people?

'There's a letter for you on the dresser. The address is quite mangled. I'm surprised it got here.'

Evie glanced over, spotted a London postmark, snatched it up and disappeared upstairs.

19, The Mansions, Berkeley Square, Mayfair, London, SW.

Telephone – Mayfair 2484

Friday 10th September 1920

Dear Miss Barnton,

Please forgive me for writing to you at home but I'm anxious to clear up any misconceptions my last letter may have created. The fact is I owe you an enormous apology. But let me cut to the chase as I have already wasted much too much of your time. In my last letter I asked you if you knew the young lady who should have received Bernard's proposal. I now know for certain that the young lady was you.

I hope this news doesn't come as a shock or a disappointment, the point being that Bernard is very much in love with you. He has painted two beautiful pictures of you for his recent exhibition and he has just finished a life-size portrait of you in your post-lady uniform. I don't know how he managed to mess up his proposal. I do know that he has been writing you letters which he doesn't have the courage to post. After my last appallingly inappropriate and inelegant letter, I barely have the courage to write myself. I am doing it only to help my dear friend. He is miserable as sin and only you can save him.

Miss Barnton, I implore you to come to London. Come and see Bernard's exhibition –it's a sell-out show. If you do come, then I would be most indebted if you could let me know you're in town. It would be a privilege to meet you and perhaps I could find a way of showing you the latest life-sized portrait of you that Bernard has just painted. I have included my address and telephone number in the hope I can be of service.

I trust you will forgive my previous impudence and consider me to be your humble servant,

Toby Whittington-Smyth

Evie put the letter down. She had finished reading but the words still rang in her head. Everything in her mind was being reshuffled like a pack of cards. *The Wrong Envelope*. So the picture was a message, not an accusation. The proposal letter was meant for her. And Phoebe would have got it if she hadn't—

'Lunch!' Mrs Brunton called up the stairs.

The Waiting Room

'And what, may I ask, are you going to do now?' Evie had just told her father about her resignation and Mr Brunton had put his knife and fork down a little too quickly, scattering the peas.

'I'm going to London – to see Cassie.'

Evie tried not to blush. She had no intention of letting Cassie know she was going up to town. There were plenty of hotels she could stay in for a couple of days, just while she saw the exhibition. She fingered Toby's letter in her pocket. She wouldn't let herself even imagine any other eventualities. One step at a time.

'I see,' said Mr Brunton. 'And after that? I mean what will you do when you get back from London?'

Evie silently chased her chop around her plate. 'I'm not sure,' she said eventually.

'Well, I'm very surprised,' said her father, in a tone that meant he was very disappointed. 'I thought you were an independent lady, with an independent mind.'

Evie caught her chop, stabbed it with a fork and started sawing at it.

'It seems to me,' he said in a tone used by judges when pronouncing a verdict, 'it seems to me that over the last couple of weeks you have gone out of your way to ruin your life.'

The sawing stopped. The chop slipped away and lay recovering in a pool of gravy.

'You have given up your job and you have,' a pause, 'rather spoilt your looks.' It was the first time her father had made reference to her hair and Evie flinched.

Mrs Brunton, who had been fidgeting with her napkin, suddenly interjected: 'Actually I rather like it.'

A challenge from Mrs Brunton was most unusual and they both swung round to stare at her.

She smiled hesitantly. 'I mean, I wasn't sure at first, but now it's starting to grow on me.'

'That's all very well,' said Mr Brunton, 'but when will it actually grow?'

Evie found strength in her mother's comment. 'Some girls choose this style because they like it, because they think it looks nice!'

Her father looked at her. 'I never liked Bernard,' he said. 'I'm not sorry he's gone. But if you're not going to work, you will have to find someone to marry. And now – well, that might be difficult.'

Evie stood up, faced her father and delivered the short speech which had been forming in her mind during lunch.

'I'm sorry you can't see past a hairstyle. Whatever you think, most modern women now look like this and they will doubtless find husbands, eventually. And whatever you think of Bernard, I have grown very fond of him. He isn't clever or sensible, but he makes me laugh and he makes me feel special. I used to find living in Colyton dull, then Bernard arrived and suddenly there was light and colour. Now he's gone it seems, well it seems much duller than before—' Evie could feel her voice breaking. She grabbed hold of the chair to steady herself. 'Which is why, were he ever to ask me, I would say yes.'

She couldn't possibly sit down again. She left the room, closing the door behind her, leaving her parents to finish their chops in an uneasy silence. She would go to the beach, let it all blow through her, all the anger at her father, all the thoughts Toby's letter had stirred up. She put on her coat and went out.

***

That afternoon, Mr Brunton had a routine appointment with his dentist. It was a relief to get out of the house and he left a little earlier than was absolutely necessary. He felt rather out of sorts – he hadn't meant to be so rude about Evie's hair. Why was it that when he felt worried about her, the words came out all wrong? When he arrived at the dentist, he was the only patient in the waiting room. He sat relishing the quiet and browsing through the magazines left out on the table. As he flicked through the latest edition of *Country Lives*, his eyes were suddenly arrested by an extraordinary colour plate. It was an oil painting of a girl, a girl sitting reading, a girl with a golden bob and a recognisable mole. The caption on the picture said *The Wrong Envelope*. On the opposite page was a review.

What has happened to Bernard Cavalier? When I received the invitation to his latest show I was not overly excited and attended merely to do my duty as an art critic; but I was more than pleasantly surprised. Cavalier used to think it enough to entertain with a clear line and carefully chosen colour; now he is starting to convey emotion. Take his most recent picture – 'The Wrong Envelope'. It has a menacing quality to it. The girl's face is hidden from us, yet we feel there is something important going on. Is she annoyed? Angry even? We are not sure and yet we are drawn into her drama.

'Picking Raspberries' has a similarly mysterious tone. A girl is absorbed in the task of gathering fruit, long blonde hair falling over a face of fragile beauty. It reminds one of Millet and his delightful depictions of rural labour. Cavalier's use of whites and creams, contrasting with the intense vermillion of the

*raspberries, has created a picture flooded with light, yet
it has an unfinished quality suggesting potential loss.
Something has happened to Cavalier, something good. I
predict an upwards trajectory for this once overlooked
artist, in fact...*

'The dentist will see you now.'

Mr Brunton dropped the magazine back onto the table as
if it was hot. He got up and walked towards the door, then
turned back and surreptitiously picked up the magazine again.
He gave a loud cough and, as he did so, ripped the article
out and slipped it into his breast pocket.

Mr Brunton liked a routine, particularly where meals were
concerned. So as soon as she had washed up the dirty dishes
from lunch, his wife always started on the scones for tea. But
not today. Today, when Mr Brunton left for the dentist, Mrs
Brunton repaired to the piano room. Two words swam in her
head: light and colour, two dolphins, diving in the depths of
her mind, turning over and over. Light and colour. She opened
the piano stool and looked for the jazziest tune she could
find.

As he walked down the front drive on his return from the
dentist, Mr Brunton was greeted by the frightful sound of
Alexander's Ragtime Band wafting through the open window
of the piano room. He stiffened, he bristled, but Mr Brunton
was a pragmatist. He approached the window and looked in,
smiling.

'Hello my dear, any chance of a scone?'

Mrs Brunton appeared not to hear him.

'I say—'

The music stopped.

'No chance, I'm afraid,' she said, without looking round.

'How so?' His voice was pleasant, inquiring.

'I burnt them,' she said, still not looking round at him.

'What, all of them?'

'Every single one.' And she took up the tune where she

had left off, hammering out the notes, blasting him with the brash American melody.

The potting shed was too close to the piano room for comfort and his upstairs study was situated directly over it. Mr Brunton retreated back down the drive. There was a lot to mull over. Even during the first weeks of their marriage, when Mrs Brunton's cooking was still quite erratic, he couldn't recall her ever burning the scones. This was a new departure and a very worrying one. But of greater concern was this strange new decisiveness. *Every single one*. So completely and utterly unambiguous. Mr Brunton felt assailed on all sides – his daughter, his wife, the art critic from *Country Lives*, they all saw something in Bernard that he didn't. Three against one; the law of averages told him he must be missing something. He had made a mistake, he realised that now. But how to correct his error without drawing attention to it? How to make up for his put-downs without humiliating himself? He walked purposefully to the railway station.

* * *

Mr Brunton found it very difficult to apologise for anything. He didn't like being in the wrong and he didn't like any sort of fuss. If he committed a faux pas, he liked to make up for it in a subtle, understated way. These compensatory actions were so discreet they were often hard to spot. When Evie, back from her long walk, came into the kitchen, she didn't notice the peace offering he had left out for her.

'Did you see the ticket?' Mr Brunton popped his head out of his study.

She looked at him blankly.

'On the kitchen table.' He disappeared back inside. Intrigued, Evie returned to the kitchen. In the middle of the table lay a return ticket to London, First Class, and a sweet little vase of flowers. Evie flushed with emotion. She picked up the ticket, went back upstairs and knocked on the study door.

'Come in.' Her father was seated at his desk, looking out of the window.

'Thank you for the ticket, Daddy.'

'You must go to London.'

'And thank you for the flowers—'

'That was your mother.'

So no apology then. She would have liked an apology. Still, he had bought her a ticket which must be an admission of something – or perhaps an acceptance, a grudging acceptance of her feelings for Bernard. She laid her hand lightly on his left shoulder. He carried on looking out of the window but his right hand came up to meet hers and gave it a little pat.

'Sorry, old thing,' he said quietly. A pause. 'No one would ever be good enough for you.'

Evie kissed the top of his head and left.

As soon as he heard the study door click shut again, Mr Brunton fished in his breast pocket for the stolen magazine article and quickly and carefully slid it into the bottom drawer of his desk. He smiled ruefully to himself. He had never, in his whole life, pinched anything before. What was it about this Bernard that caused people to behave so irrationally? Evie had cut her hair, his wife had burnt the scones and now he, an upstanding lawyer for thirty-five years, had pilfered a page from a magazine. He wished they could all shake Bernard off, like a cold, but he feared that wouldn't be possible. Anyway, he certainly wouldn't be telling anyone else about his petty crime. His wife didn't need any encouragement, she clearly approved of Bernard already. And Evie would see the pictures for herself soon enough. No, he would keep this review to himself.

The New Curate

'I thought you were doing tea?'

Phoebe's eyes shot open. The Reverend Carson was bending over her, his eyes squinting at her angrily behind thick spectacles. He smelled strongly of haddock. Behind him, tree branches swirled against the sky, knocking against each other in the autumn breeze.

'I said three o'clock and it's now half past.' He knelt down on the blanket beside her. 'It makes a very bad impression,' he hissed, 'on a new arrival.'

'New arrival?' Phoebe's mind was still thick from sleep.

'My new curate is here and waiting in the kitchen.'

Phoebe glanced across the lawn towards the house. Sure enough there was a face at the kitchen window peering out at them, but it quickly withdrew when it saw her looking.

'Heavens, Daddy, I'm so sorry, I was reading and I must have dropped off.' Phoebe jumped up, grabbed the blanket and her book and hurried inside. Of course she knew he was coming, she had spent most of the morning preparing the downstairs bedroom. She had cleaned and dusted and made up the bed and had even placed a small vase of flowers on the dresser. Then she had remembered the previous curate and his irritating hay fever and had taken the vase away again.

'Phoebe, this is Mr Hazlitt.'

'How do you do?' said Phoebe, shaking the new curate's hand. 'I'm afraid I've been shirking my duties.'

'Not at all,' he smiled.

He was a slight man, in his late twenties or early thirties, it was hard to tell. His hair was thinning but he had a round, pleasant face.

'I have a phone call to make,' said the Reverend Carson. 'If I could leave you, Phoebe, to make some tea?' He looked pointedly at his daughter.

'Of course,' said Phoebe.

'Allow me to help,' said the young man.

'Thank you, that's very kind, but there's really no need. Take a seat in the parlour, Mr Hazlitt. I'll be in shortly.'

'Well thank you. It would be nice to rest my weary legs. By the way,' Mr Hazlitt indicated the book Phoebe had brought in from the garden, 'it's my favourite.'

'Sorry?'

'*Pride and Prejudice.*' And with that the curate ambled off towards the parlour.

What a funny chap, she thought, as she set a tray and found the crumpets, having weary legs and liking a woman's book. Her father only ever read the Old Testament or Walter Scott. There was something cosy about Mr Hazlitt. She nipped into the downstairs bathroom and peered in the small mirror above the sink. Her hair was fine, but there were crease marks across her face, from the blanket presumably. How nice that Mr Hazlitt hadn't stared at them. A good egg. Just as well, he would be staying with them until he could find digs in town. Anyway, she had to get on – there was a lot to do: crumpets to toast, a kettle to boil and a fire to lay.

When she went into the parlour Mr Hazlitt was sitting reading the paper, but as soon as he heard her he put it down.

'One never tires of her. I think she's wonderful – Austen, I mean.'

Phoebe liked the way he had carried on the conversation where they'd left off, so easily and comfortably. Was this a new species of clergyman – the kind that didn't stand on ceremony? She thought of her father's stiffness and his dreadfully stilted conversations. Perhaps vicars were trained differently nowadays. She smiled and slipped past him to light the fire.

'I mean the Brontës are marvellous,' he continued, as she fiddled with the kindling, 'but to be honest, they're a bit scary – too scary to read at bedtime!'

He gave a funny snorty laugh, a half bray followed by a sort of sniffing. Phoebe was amazed at the sound and wanted to laugh herself. She looked up grinning and caught his eye in the mirror above the mantelpiece. He grinned back at her and she felt courageous.

'Mr Hazlitt, I'm surprised by your confession. It's unusual for a man to admit to being so sensitive.'

'I know,' he grimaced. 'Oh and please call me Robert.'

'And please call me Phoebe.'

'Thank you, I will!' He grinned again.

Phoebe felt suddenly very comfortable with him, as if she had known him for ages. It was ridiculously early to ask such an impertinent question, but she couldn't help herself.

'Were you in the war?'

'Of course, wasn't everyone?' He paused and looked thoughtfully into the fire as the kindling caught light.

'I was in the Ambulance service.' Another pause. 'Forster is good too, but you can't read him over and over again, like you can Austen.'

How true, thought Phoebe, adding a log to the blaze. She had never thought of that before, but he was right.

'How many times?' asked the curate.

'I beg your pardon?'

'How many times have you read it? – P and P, I mean.'

Phoebe flushed.

'Confess!'

She laughed. 'Twenty-three. Twenty-four if you count this one.'

'Is that all?' he gave another snorty laugh and Phoebe waited for the sniffs that followed it. Extraordinary – the snort shot out like a wave crashing onto a beach and then the sniffing sounded like the sea sucking it back in again. She wondered what her father would think of it. Fortunately, the vicar didn't crack many jokes so his exposure to Robert Hazlitt's laugh would be minimal.

'And you?' she asked.

'I lost count, but at least ten before the war and then, well I took it with me to the Front. It was a marvellous escape. I used to read it at night. It was so wonderfully unlike what was happening around me. I think I probably know some passages by heart.'

'And did it help?'

'As much as anything could.'

It was put so simply and honestly that Phoebe warmed to his frankness. Instead of rushing back to the kitchen, she sat down on one of the armchairs.

'They say the book changes as you get older,' she ventured.

'Changes?'

'Yes, you see new things and also a cynicism in the author.'

'Let's not get old then,' said Robert. 'There's too much cynicism already,' and he laughed again.

This time the laugh drew the Reverend from his study. He came into the room and looked curiously around as if he was trying to ascertain where the noise was coming from. Then he addressed Phoebe.

'Tea?'

'On its way!'

She hastened back to the kitchen. The kettle was boiling; she took it off the heat then popped three crumpets into a griddle and put them on the hob. She fetched down their biggest teapot, opened the tea caddy, spooned in some tea and added water from the kettle. Her head was buzzing. Robert had been so perceptive about Forster. Why had she never thought of that – it was such a good way to judge a book. And what, she wondered, did he think of Hardy? Was he a Hardy man? Had he read *Tess* and, if he had, did he feel even remotely sorry for Angel Clare? She would ask him later. What fun to have a bookworm staying, even for a little while. She buttered the hot crumpets and arranged them on a plate. Now where was the jam? She opened the pantry and routed around for the last pot of gooseberry conserve. There it was, shoved right to the back, behind the mustard. Her hand hovered over it. She dithered, she hesitated, then she closed the pantry again and popped her head round the door of the parlour.

'I'm sorry,' she said, 'but I seem to have run out of jam.'

'That doesn't bother me,' said the vicar, 'as you know,' he added, in case Phoebe had forgotten.

'Nor me,' said the curate. 'I'm not a jam man!' and the laugh erupted again.

The Reverend Carson stared at him in amazement. Phoebe rushed back to the kitchen. She quickly stuffed a tea towel in her mouth, struggling not to roar with laughter. How entertaining he was. She hadn't giggled like this since – well, for a while now. It felt like being on holiday, having someone around who was such fun and so well read. What a blessed relief to have him in the house. She hoped it would take him ages to find somewhere to live. Leaving the tea tray on the kitchen table, she crept back to the parlour and stood outside the door for a moment listening. The two men seemed to be deep in conversation about the size of the parish. Phoebe took her chance. She quickly found the vase of flowers she had prepared earlier, stole into the new curate's bedroom and placed it carefully on the chest of drawers again.

The Bicycle

Bernard tossed and turned on his lumpy bed. He had woken up much too early, again. Every morning he woke at dawn and every dawn he opened his eyes with the same terrible realisation – he was in London, not Devon. Instead of tree shadows dancing on his ceiling, there was a crumbling cornice. Instead of bird song outside the window, there was rumbling traffic. What an extraordinary retreat Hollybrook had been; he had totally squandered his time there. It was easy to look back and miss Devon now, but at the time he had taken it all for granted. He had been handed a trip to heaven and he hadn't appreciated it. Only now, back in the grey reality of London, did he realise the enormity of the gift that had been given him.

At least his show had gone down well. He had sold all his pictures and he was solvent for the first time in ages. More than solvent, for now the critics liked him, he had commissions stretching away as far as the eye could see. It would mean he could start to think about getting out of his pokey studio and renting a proper house. It would be great to escape from his work at night instead of having it leering at him as he got ready for bed. He could even keep his studio and find somewhere else to rent, close by, so he could shut the door at the end of the day, stroll home and forget all about it. The problem being that there was no one to stroll home to. Bernard plumped his pillow in an attempt to make it more comfortable, then he shifted his weight in the sagging bed, trying to find a comfy spot, twisting round like a dog in a basket. He would get a small place, a cosy house where one person could move around without rattling. And once he had found a suitable 'residence', as Toby liked to call it, he might attract someone to share it with. But who? Who could replace Evie?

Bernard sighed and got out of bed. There was no point lying moping; it was high time he tidied his studio. During the big push before the opening, he had an excuse to let things slide; now he would have to address the dreadful state of his living quarters. He wasn't even sure he had unpacked properly since he came back from Devon. He found his suitcase at the back of the studio, shoved behind a curtain. The clasps opened with a snap and there was a sudden smell of summer. He peered inside. There wasn't much left in the case, he must have taken the dirty laundry out on his return. A few bits and bobs, a map of East Devon and a used train ticket. But what was that – a piece of paper at the bottom, a sheet of watercolour paper folded in two. He pulled it out and opened it up.

Dark clouds covered the paper, swathing the hills of Hollybrook in a blur of rain. Scratched onto the blur was a small bicycle and rider fighting along the road, braving the onslaught of the weather. Bernard knelt down and stared at it. As he stared, the rider seemed to move imperceptibly up the hill towards the top of the picture. Perhaps it was a sign. Perhaps he should go back to Devon. He had left in a real rush and he still had things to collect. Yes, it would be useful to get the last of his possessions. And perhaps – but no, Cassie had already told him – Evie had met someone else. Good. He was glad. No he wasn't: he was devastated. Glad and devastated. Glad for her, devastated for himself. He folded the picture up and put it on top of a pile of papers lying on the floor by the window.

Anyway, he would go to Devon as soon as possible. Get it all over with, collect his stuff and draw a veil over the whole sorry episode. But should he try to see Evie? Was there any point? He didn't know how to begin to apologise for his behaviour; and she had a new beau now. On the other hand, if he didn't try to talk to her soon, it might be too late and he would never have another opportunity. Opportunity! Why was he even using that word? He had had his chance and squandered it. Bernard wandered around his studio, picking things up and putting them down again, talking to himself.

As he passed the pile of papers, he absent-mindedly knocked the watercolour and it fell open. The cyclist had moved again: she had gone over the brow of the hill and was now making her way down the other side, the storm clouds chasing her through the valley. Bernard blinked. This was definitely a sign. There was still a chance. He would go down to Devon tomorrow and he would find her. He would explain everything, his mix-up with the letters and his inability to realise what had happened until it was too late. He would tell her exactly how he felt about her. He would declare himself and, whatever the outcome, whatever her reaction, at least he would have tried.

A Fine

Sometimes, when he undertook a journey of great significance, by the time he reached his destination Bernard felt so exhausted he could hardly remember the reason for it. His goal somehow slipped sideways with the passing miles. It was as if he had been holding a ball of wool only to discover he had dropped the end of it near the start and it had slowly unwound until there was nothing left. This is certainly how he felt the next day when he alighted from the train at Seaton Junction to find Evie on the platform. Evie was the only reason for his journey down to Devon, yet all the things he had wanted to say to her disappeared, quite suddenly, as if they had slipped into someone else's luggage.

'Evie, what are you doing here?' was all he could manage.

'I'm going to London,' she said brightly. If she was surprised to see him, she didn't show it.

'Well I'm going down to Colyton to—' Bernard checked himself; it was ridiculous to say he was going to see her when she was going to London. 'I'm going to collect the last of my things.'

There was an awkward silence.

'If you're going to London, I've got—' again he stopped short. Why would she want to see any of his work? Who did he think he was?

'You've got?' repeated Evie.

'I've got a few friends who could show you round.'

'I'm staying with Cassie.'

Of course she was, he was the most pathetic man alive. He tried again. 'You look very well, Evie.'

The tannoy crackled. 'Platform Two for the train to Colyton.' He couldn't believe his bad luck. He had come all the way to see her and now they would have less than a minute together. He couldn't bear to leave her so soon and searched for a way to prolong their chat.

'How are your parents?'

She hesitated before replying. She looked away down the track and her mouth worked furiously but silently, as if she was weighing something up in her mind.

'My father's getting used to the idea,' she said finally. She stood clutching her small suitcase and looked at him. She seemed to be half-waiting, half-hoping for something.

What was he supposed to say? What was the idea her father was getting used to? He racked his brains hopelessly, like a child who hasn't understood a clue in a parlour game. Then it came to him. Of course, she meant her hair.

'And I've got used to it too,' he said. 'I think it looks lovely,' he added, hoping to please her.

Evie put her hand up and touched her bob.

'Thank you,' she said. She looked disappointed and sad.

He had said the wrong thing as usual. Bernard could feel his mind fogging over.

'Platform Two for the train to Colyton.'

'Well, I must be getting going.'

'Quite.'

'So nice to see you again.'

'So nice.' She looked desperate to turn away.

Bernard raised his cap, picked up his suitcase and turned for the stairs. He jogged over the bridge and down to Platform Two. The train was full of holiday-makers and he had to squeeze into a compartment already occupied by a family of four. Two young lads were waving shrimping nets while their father heaved cases into the luggage rack and their mother fussed over sandwiches. Bernard sat by the window, his suitcase on the seat beside him. He was still breathless, both from jogging over the bridge and seeing her again. As the guard came along the platform, slamming the doors, Bernard turned the conversation over and over in his mind. Something didn't make sense. He stared out of the window. He could just see her, over on Platform One. She stood with her back to him, head on one side, golden hair shining under a cloche hat. She put a hand in her pocket, then brought it up to her face. Her back shook slightly, as if she was blowing her nose.

Bernard felt a rising tide of emotion in his chest, a mixture of hope and fear – fear that he had hurt her yet again and hope that she might still care for him. 'My father's getting used to the idea.' He had thought Evie meant her hair. But as the guard blew his whistle and the train jolted into life, Bernard realised that Evie's father would never get used to her hair. It was something else. He jumped up and made for the door of the compartment. It was stiff and it took him a few seconds to prise it open. He pushed through with his suitcase and rushed to the door of the carriage. Too late, the train was moving. Cursing, he slid down the window of the door and started fumbling with the handle on the outside.

'Oi! What do you think you're doing?' A porter had spotted him.

Bernard fought with the door handle and got it open. The train was picking up speed and the end of the platform was fast approaching. He couldn't risk jumping. There was no time to think. He reached up, grabbed hold of the emergency chain and pulled hard. The train shrieked to a halt with a tremendous jolt, throwing him onto the floor. His case flew open and shirts, socks and papers flew everywhere. No time. He jumped up, grabbed the empty case, opened the door, leapt onto the platform and started to run back towards Evie. The porter tried to stop him.

'What do you think you're doing – stopping the train like that, you'll pay for this!'

Bernard dodged past him and back up the stairs towards Platform One. He could see her train coming in.

'Evie!' he bellowed, thumping over the bridge and flying down the stairs towards her. Evie, just about to board her train, looked round startled as Bernard almost fell down the last few steps and into the Station Master's arms.

'I must ask you to come with me, sir. Stopping a train is no laughing matter, in fact it's a serious offence.' He grabbed one of Bernard's arms and the porter, red-faced and out-of-breath, arrived to take the other one. Ignoring his captors, Bernard sought out Evie in the crowd of people staring.

'Evie, please just tell me, what is the idea that your father's getting used to?'

A squall of emotions passed over her face and then she smiled. She turned to step onto the train and then glanced back.

'You, Bernard,' she said, and disappeared inside.

As the guard blew his whistle, she stood by the door, looking out at him.

Bernard started to cry and his nose started running. Pinned between the guard and the Station Master, he couldn't wipe his face and his image of her blurred as the train moved slowly away.

Much later that evening, when he had finally extricated himself from the trouble he had caused at Seaton Junction, Bernard arrived at High View to find a telegram waiting.

15.9.1920 WATERLOO

HOPE YOU PAID THE FINE. I WOULD NEVER MARRY A CRIMINAL. YOURS. EVIE.

A Blessing

The day after Evie left for London and straight after lunch, Mrs Brunton started on the scones. Her mini rebellion was all but forgotten. It had been a short mutiny but it had produced positive results. Mr Brunton had bought Evie a train ticket and Evie had taken her chance and gone to Bernard's exhibition. Mrs Brunton measured out eight ounces of self-raising flour and sifted it into her largest mixing bowl. Then she cut a knob of butter up into little pieces and rubbed it into the flour, humming quietly to herself. It was up to Evie now; she could do no more. Evie was in London and perhaps, right at this minute, she was at the show. Perhaps she was even talking to – Mrs Brunton checked herself. It was no use dreaming. She sprinkled two ounces of sugar into the mixture, then she started to slowly add the milk, bit by bit, stirring it in with a knife, till it formed a gooey dough, not too wet, not too dry. A First Class ticket was generous. She would get the scones just right, just the way Mr Brunton liked them.

Mrs Brunton scattered a handful of flour over the kitchen table, then she picked up the dough and began kneading it into a malleable piece, ready for shaping. As her hands worked to and fro, she realised she had left her rings on. The wedding ring and engagement ring were now stuck together, encased in a thick layer of mixture. She peeled it away, but the gold setting for the three small diamonds of her engagement ring was still full of dough. She prised it off and ran it under the hot tap.

She returned to the mixture, sprinkled on more flour and started cutting out scone shapes. This was the bit she loved – hearing the air puff its way through the scones as she cut them with the metal pastry cutter and shook them out onto a greased baking tray. Once she had filled the tray, she picked it up with one hand and, with the other, she opened the top door of her range. And that was when she saw him out of the kitchen window – walking along the banks of the Coly, swinging his suitcase, his rust coloured hair catching the afternoon sunlight – Bernard. What on earth was he doing here? He was supposed to be in London. Mrs Brunton's baking tray wobbled precariously but she regained her balance and quickly slotted the scones into the oven. Then she shot out of the kitchen into the hall.

'I think Mr Cavalier is here,' she called in the general direction of the parlour.

There was a knock at the front door. Mrs Brunton wiped her doughy hands on her apron and started to walk towards it, but Mr Brunton emerged from the parlour in front of her. She could see his stooping back in the open doorway and, beyond him, Bernard, raising his hat.

'Good afternoon, Mr Cavalier, I'm afraid Evie's away.' He said cavalier, like the adjective.

'Yes I know, Mr Brunton. Actually, it's you I've come to see.' Bernard smiled sheepishly.

'Oh.' There was a pause. 'You'd better come in then.' Mr Brunton opened the door wider and Bernard stepped inside, filling the small hallway with his bulky frame. Mrs Brunton retreated to the kitchen. Mr Brunton went back into the parlour followed by Bernard. The door shut.

Mr Brunton sat back down in his chair and Bernard perched on the edge of the sofa. There was an uneasy silence.

'So then, to what do we owe the privilege of a visit?' asked Mr Brunton eventually.

'Well, Mr Brunton,' Bernard smiled nervously. 'The thing is, the thing is – I want to marry your daughter.'

'My daughter? You mean Evie, the girl you left broken-hearted just a few weeks ago?'

'We had a misunderstanding,' said Bernard quickly. 'We were both broken-hearted,' he added.

'I see.' Mr Brunton looked dubious. There was another silence.

'Well,' he said finally, 'in these modern times it is customary to actually ask the young lady in question.'

'Oh, Evie's accepted,' said Bernard cheerfully.

Mr Brunton gave a start. 'I believe Evie's in London.'

'Yes, but she sent a telegram,' Bernard beamed. 'I came to ask your permission.'

'My permission?' Mr Brunton appeared to be weighing this up. 'If I am to give my permission I need to know what exactly you are planning to offer my daughter. I mean, what are your prospects?'

'I have very little in the way of capital,' Bernard admitted. 'But my prospects are quite good I think. I've got an exhibition on just now and the reviews are—'

'Reviews are not equity. Do you have any assets?'

Bernard blanched. 'Assets?'

'I don't want my daughter living in a garret. Will you be able to keep her in the manner to which she is accustomed?'

'Well I certainly hope to—'

'A hope is not a guarantee. She can't plan her future on a wing and a prayer.' Mr Brunton was warming to his theme. 'Do you have proof of earnings?'

Bernard looked dismayed. 'No,' he said quietly.

'Then I'm afraid—'

Just then the parlour door swung open and Mrs Brunton appeared carrying a tea tray. She was flushed and smiling.

'Then I'm afraid we'll have to rely on the reviews!' She plonked the tray down on the coffee table. 'Bernard, I read in *The Times* that your show is a sell-out. How marvellous!'

She offered him an outstretched hand, still with a bit of scone mixture on it.

Bernard took it in his and bowed gratefully.

'I'm so happy for Evie,' she said.

Mr Brunton spluttered, 'But my dear, I don't think we can—'

'Stand in their way? No, I don't think we can, dear.' Mrs Brunton smiled at her husband but didn't hold his flashing eyes for more than a second. Instead she sat down regally on the sofa, beside Bernard.

'And where will you get married?' she asked.

'I don't think their marriage is definitely settled,' interrupted Mr Brunton.

'It's hard isn't it, when you live in different places,' said Mrs Brunton, smiling at Bernard, ignoring her husband.

'I rather hoped London,' said Bernard quickly. 'I have a friend with a beautiful apartment in Berkeley Square.'

'It's customary for the wedding to take place in the bride's home town,' interrupted Mr Brunton.

'Mayfair – How lovely!' exclaimed the bride's mother. She gave a little giggle, then recomposed herself and smiled at her husband. 'The scones are still in the oven, my dear, but we can start with a cup of tea.'

Bernard jumped up. 'Actually, I must get going, if I'm to catch the train.'

'But of course.' Mrs Brunton graciously held out her hand again and Bernard held it for the second time.

'I'll see you out,' said Mr Brunton gruffly.

They all went out into the hall. Mr Brunton and Bernard turned right towards the front door and Mrs Brunton turned left and sped back to the kitchen. She rushed to the range and pulled the scones out. Dash it. They were burnt – every single one of them. How ironic, she never normally burned the scones, but this week there had been two cremations – one real, one fictional. She wondered if she should leave the tray out on the table as proof that lightning really did strike twice, but there was no need. As he shut the front door, Mr Brunton caught a whiff of burning in his nostrils. He sighed, opened the door again, slipped out into the garden and made for his potting shed.

A Large Cigar

The door to the gallery opened with a 'ding'. Mr Carruthers sighed and uncrossed his legs stretched out on the desk in front of him. Situated at the back of the gallery, the desk's position gave him a double advantage: it allowed him to relax unseen from the street and afforded him a good view of the door and anyone coming in to browse. In case he should happen to nod off after lunch, he had installed a subtle but efficient bell in the doorframe. Subtle, because it didn't frighten away the customer; efficient, because the tone always roused him. Like Pavlov's dog, Carruthers always responded to the bell. With a slight grunt, he heaved himself off his chair and wandered round to the front of the gallery with a ready smile, all in the twinkling of an eye.

Today, Mr Carruthers hadn't quite managed to drop off, the bell to announce his first afternoon visitor being premature, and he felt just a little bit grumpy as he put his smile on to greet the customer. It was a girl, a girl in old-fashioned clothes, goodness – he hadn't seen such a long skirt on someone so young for ages. Her hair was modern though and her face, well her face was familiar. Where had he seen it before?

'Good afternoon,' he smiled. 'Do come in and have a browse.'

'Thank you,' said the girl. She came into the gallery rather gingerly, giving little sideways glances all around her in a furtive manner. Then, once she had made an initial assessment of the layout, she went to the nearest picture and examined it with her head on one side, studying it intently. Mr Carruthers stood watching her in profile. The flash of recognition had gone; if he knew this lady it was only from the front. Perhaps he had seen her before in a painting? She was certainly very interested in art: she hadn't taken her eyes off the first picture she had come to. If she was an art critic he didn't know her, and it was obvious from her age and attire that she wasn't a buyer. So who was she? Not one of the London set, that was for sure. The brown skirt was dated, although the matching jacket had a jaunty cut, showing off a cream camisole and a double string of pearls. The velvet hat was quite wrong, so last season, and Carruthers wasn't sure she should be wearing one anyway. Hats didn't suit her, not from the side at any rate.

After a few minutes in front of the first painting, the girl turned and crossed the gallery to the picture opposite. As soon as she turned away from him, he saw it – a large, but rather attractive mole, at the nape of her neck. Carruthers gave a start. So this was – he hurried to the picture to check, yes, this was the lady from *The Wrong Envelope*. She was either a life model or a friend of Bernard's. But he couldn't remember seeing her at the opening. So why was her face familiar? Mr Carruthers stole a glance at *Picking Raspberries*. There, looking out from behind the canes, was the girl who was now wandering round his gallery. His feeling of grumpiness immediately evaporated to be replaced by a keen curiosity. How intriguing. So, it was the same girl in both pictures, a girl who hadn't come to the opening and who had only visited the exhibition in its third week, and then quietly, unobtrusively, on her own. In one picture she had long hair, in the other short; in one she looked tranquil and languid, in the other she was coiled tight with emotion, like a spring. In both pictures there was something hiding beneath the surface. This was a mystery and he was the man to get to the bottom of it.

He pieced together the clues. Bernard had been reluctant to go to Devon but Carruthers had a feeling that he had met the girl there. She had definitely posed for him, and there was no doubt that the two pictures he had painted of her were the best in the exhibition. But he had come back to London in a depressed state and had condemned his work as pointless. What was it he had said at Claridges? 'I will never paint again.' And when he had said it, Carruthers was sure that he had meant it. Something had happened in Devon, something involving the girl. Carruthers was enjoying himself. He loved a mystery.

'Do you like them?' he approached her with the confident friendliness he used with all his visitors, the aim being to connect and converse without appearing too pushy. Startled, the girl swung round to look at him. There it was again, the raspberry patch face. What was it a critic had said: a face of fragile beauty?

'The recent work is better,' she replied.

Carruthers was astonished by her answer. She was right of course, but how did she know? He suddenly wondered if there was work done in Devon that had stayed in Devon, work which had been rejected, dismissed even. But by whom? This girl, whoever she was, seemed to be growing in power.

'An interesting comment, Miss—?'

'Brunton.'

'Miss Brunton, and a very pertinent one. Do you happen to know the artist?'

'Yes.'

'So, you're a friend from London?'

'No.'

Her answers were disarmingly straight-forward and infuriatingly elusive. Mr Carruthers liked a challenge.

'Well, you obviously know something about art, Miss Brunton, because you are right, Mr Cavalier has indeed progressed to a new level in recent weeks and has become something of a success story.'

Miss Brunton said nothing; she just carried on looking at the pictures. Carruthers would have to try harder if he was to get anywhere.

'Come and see my favourite,' he said, speaking like an old friend and confidant. He led her gently round the corner to where *Picking Raspberries* was hanging. It was a mean trick, but it would unearth more clues and help him solve the puzzle.

Miss Brunton gave a tiny start but quickly regained her composure. The only sign she recognised the woman in the painting was the fact that she put her hand up to her upper lip and wiped away some imaginary beads of sweat with her glove. It was an unconscious act, but one that Carruthers found very exciting.

'It was one of the first to sell,' he said in a quiet voice, just by her ear. 'Why do you think that was?' he whispered.

She blushed slightly, but then she turned to him and smiled, 'The light is well executed,' she replied.

What an answer! Carruthers wanted to clap his hands. Here was a lady whose wit fitted right in to the sophistication of the London art scene. He suddenly didn't care how she knew Bernard; he just wanted to be sure that she still knew him, that she wasn't going anywhere, certainly not back to Devon anyway.

'Does Bernard know you're in town?' Whoops, he had used his first name – that was a giveaway.

'Bernard's in Devon.'

In Devon! Carruthers could hardly believe it. When and why had he gone back there? Really, the man was impossible – so unpredictable and impulsive. He was an artist who could bring him so much, and yet Carruthers felt so unsure of him. This last exhibition had been a punt, a risky punt at that, but it had more than paid off. But what about the next exhibition? Would it be a success, or a failure? Would it even happen? Bernard was a goose that had laid a golden egg, but would he ever lay another one? Carruthers sighed impatiently.

'He's down collecting some things.'

It was as if she had read his mind and wanted to reassure him.

'I see, well thank you for telling me.' He smiled ruefully. 'At least someone knows where he is.'

As soon as he had said it, he realised he had taken the conversation to a new level. His last comment had been a sort of admission and also a confession. Carruthers felt suddenly emboldened by this new departure.

'I find he's quite flighty,' he explained.

'*Was* quite flighty,' she corrected.

Carruthers stared at her. She was holding out an olive branch and a golden olive branch at that, one that a goose would surely land on. He felt a wave of relief washing over him. They had reached *The Wrong Envelope*. He knew he had no business hanging around in front of this particular picture.

'Anyway, I'm getting in your way. I'll be at my desk should you need me, Miss Brunton.'

Carruthers walked away quietly, reverently, as if he was in church. He sat staring into space. How wonderful. He could dare to plan the next one; not right away of course, they must keep people waiting a bit and build up some anticipation. The Echoed Image had been a great title and one that would be hard to beat; but, if he started thinking about it straight away, he might come up with something just as good. Carruthers sat lost in thought. A few minutes later the doorbell dinged. He shot round to the front of the gallery. She was gone. How charmingly mysterious she was. How delightful. He walked back to his desk, swung his feet up onto it and stretched back in his chair. Was flighty. The two words fluttered in his mind like enormous butterflies. Was flighty. The emphasis had been on the *was*. This was a cause of great celebration. Carruthers reached into the drawer of his desk and pulled out a large cigar.

Champagne at Brown's

After the quiet of the gallery, the bustle of Cork Street was alarming. Evie stood for a few moments in the archway of the door, taking it in. Her face in the raspberry patch bounced around on the back of her retina, as if she had been looking into the sun too long. She shut her eyes for a split second and it loomed in front of her, the whites and creams bleeding into each other until they were shimmering. She opened her eyes again and looked at the traffic zooming past. So many cars and cabs. Well, she couldn't stand in the same spot all day; Carruthers might come out any minute. She had managed an air of sophistication in the gallery, but that would quickly evaporate if he found her dithering on the pavement.

Evie surreptitiously consulted the guidebook she had purchased at Waterloo. Where was she now? The thin leaves of the book fluttered in the breeze and she struggled to find the page. There it was – Cork Street. But where was her hotel – that was on another page, what number? 36 or 37? She peered at the index but it was hard to read in the shade of the doorway. Perhaps she would walk back to Piccadilly and ask someone. But which way was Piccadilly – right or left? Evie plumped for left. Then, like a diver standing on a ledge above the sea, she left the safety of the doorway and plunged into the London melee.

She had only gone a few paces when she heard a shout. 'Miss Barnton!'

A young man was running towards her, dressed in a loud, striped green and white blazer and baggy, white trousers. He had a fine crop of dark hair and a long floppy fringe which wafted either side of him as he ran.

'Miss Barnton!' He stopped breathlessly in front of her and gave a triumphant smile, showing pearly white teeth. 'Toby Whittington-Smyth.' He stuck a hand out and grabbed Evie's. 'A friend of Bernard's. I wrote to you.'

He smiled again and pumped her hand up and down.

'Just think, I might have missed you! I got held up. Mother.' He rolled his eyes. 'You see I'd worked it all out. I knew the morning train from Seaton Junction arrived in Waterloo at three, and so I figured you would be at the gallery by four, but of course it shuts at five. It was a small window but a window nevertheless.' He paused for breath and smiled at her again. 'I came yesterday as well and the day before that – how awful it would have been if I'd missed you today.' He shuddered to himself.

'Why?'

'Why?' Toby looked incredulous but then quickly changed the subject.

'So you arrived today? Where are you staying, Miss Barnton?'

'In a hotel. Yesterday. It's Brunton.' Evie wanted to sit down somewhere quiet, but there was nowhere to sit; just wide cracked pavements and traffic racing past.

'Miss Brunton, I'm so sorry. Another of my mistakes.' Toby looked momentarily mortified, but then his face cleared again.

'We need a cocktail,' he said, 'well, I do anyway and I know just the place.'

He put his arm in hers and started to steer her across the road, right into the traffic, which stopped or swerved around them.

'We will go to Brown's. Are you staying at Brown's?'

'No.'

'Then it will be a lovely surprise.'

'I'm not sure—'

'You will be, when we get there,' and raising his arm, Toby hailed a cab.

'I'm afraid I don't know where he is,' Toby confessed, as their taxi rushed along the busy streets, weaving about in a manner that made Evie want to hold on to the window frame. Instead she clasped her velvet purse and frowned out at the traffic.

'Oh, Bernard's in Devon,' she said, not taking her eyes from the window.

'What the deuce is he doing there?' Toby was suddenly furious. 'Forgive me for asking, but how do you know? Did you see him?'

'I met him at Seaton Junction, on my way up.'

Toby groaned. 'So my letter misfired again. If I hadn't written you might still be in Devon and then—'

'I would never have forgiven him,' Evie said.

She was amazed at herself. Was this not the Toby she had once hated almost as much as she had hated Bernard? Where had her generosity come from? Had the pictures in the gallery turned her head?

'I mean, without your second letter,' she added.

'Yes, my first letter was dreadful,' he said sadly, hanging his head. 'It was an uncompromising, pig-headed, fatuous letter, penned with good intentions, but without a thought for the reader.'

Evie winced.

Toby tried again. 'Evie, I wrote you a dreadful letter, I can hardly forgive myself, please allow me to make amends.'

The cab reached Brown's Hotel and pulled up outside. Toby jumped out and opened the door for her. Evie stepped gratefully out onto the pavement, glad to be back on terra firma.

'The thing is – I know you hardly know me, but Bernard and I are very close.' Toby looked at her earnestly. 'And I don't think he'd forgive me,' he continued, leading her into the hotel lobby, 'if I allowed you to escape back to your London hotel without seeing him again.'

Unsure what to say, Evie laughed.

'Good, good!' Toby grinned, seizing on her laugh as a sign of forgiveness.

The hotel lobby was ornate – dark wood everywhere and shining brass and an enormous glass chandelier. The cocktail bar was empty except for a barman polishing glasses. They sat by the window. Evie could see the traffic again: the same frenetic movement but with the sound muted. It was like watching goldfish in a bowl, very fast ones, whizzing round and round in front of the glass. She felt dizzy with tiredness.

'I think I might have tea,' she ventured.

'We can't celebrate with tea, Miss Brunton. Let's have champagne.'

Evie recognised the same bossy tone that Bernard used. London men were impossible. But she couldn't face a battle over the drinks, not today anyway. There had been so many battles to get here, to this beautiful hotel, with its grand interior.

The barman came over.

'A bottle of champagne,' said Toby, 'and some caviar.'

'No caviar for me,' said Evie.

'Then no caviar,' said Toby to the waiter.

Evie felt energised by his climb-down. It was a satisfactory truce. She had wanted tea and he had wanted caviar; they had agreed on champagne. So this was how relationships with men worked: negotiation and compromise, with neither party particularly happy at the end of it, but neither particularly unhappy either.

She smiled at Toby. 'Please call me Evie.'

'Thank you. I will just send Bernard a message, he's bound to be back tonight, especially if he knows you're in town.' Toby went out into the hall.

'I would like to send a telegram,' she heard him say to the receptionist. 'It's to a Mr Cavalier, in Pimlico. Could you put it on my account?'

Evie sat back and closed her eyes. This time the neck in *The Wrong Envelope* flashed before her – a thin neck sporting a horrible mole. She quickly opened them again to find the champagne had arrived, two crystal flutes on a silver tray. She watched the air bubbling up to the surface, creating a golden froth that fizzed against the glass. Now she was alone and quiet she could feel something similar happening in herself. Small bubbles were starting to dance below the surface and, further down, something golden glittered, just out of reach, but getting closer. She could hear the bubbles too, popping in her head – little bursts of excitement. She would have to keep these bubbles to herself, at least until Bernard arrived. It was difficult though, not to feel extremely happy and, when Toby came back, she couldn't stop herself giving him a radiant smile.

***

As soon as he got the telegram, Bernard raced to Brown's. He was so out of breath when he arrived he tripped on the front door step and hurtled into the lobby, creasing up the carpet.

'Sorry!' he smiled at the porter and held up both hands in a gesture of surrender. Then he rushed down the hallway into the cocktail bar.

'Evie!'

One minute she was looking up, startled by his sudden entrance, the next she was in his arms.

'Evie!' he cried. He hugged her tight. 'Evie!'

He started to sob, pulling her closer, pressing her small frame against him, pushing his face into her short blonde bob. Her hat fell off and he could smell London in her hair.

'My God, Evie, I thought I'd lost you. But we're together at last!'

'Together?' She pulled away and looked at him with a mocking seriousness. 'Is that a proposal?'

Bernard immediately fell to his knees on the carpet.

'Will you marry me, Evie?'

'One knee, not two,' hissed Toby.

Bernard changed position so he was just kneeling on the right knee.

'Marry me!'

'Why, are you mad with desire?' Evie laughed, but her eyes filled with tears.

Bernard wobbled slightly. He swapped knees, but the left one was no better.

'Please say yes, Evie!'

'Yes, Bernard, yes! But I'm afraid you'll need parental permission.'

Bernard threw his head back and laughed. 'Don't remind me! Your father more or less said no, your mother had to rescue me!'

'You mean you've already asked them?'

Bernard jumped up, slipped his arm around her waist and started to dance her round the room.

'Wonderful, glorious Mrs Brunton!' he sang as they spun. 'Strong and marvellous Mrs Brunton!'

'What do you mean, what happened?'

'Your mother saved the day!'

Toby stood in the corner, not wanting to watch, not wanting to look away, grinning from ear to ear.

'More champagne!' he cried, as the dancers collapsed giggling into each other. 'And caviar, damn it!'

Tea at Fortnum's

A few days later, Daisy, Lavinia and Cassie met for their weekly tea party at Fortnum's. Cassie had gone for pale shades this time: a white dress coat and an antique cream chemise slip and pearls. Ironically her friends had chosen a much bolder look. Daisy was wearing a black handkerchief hem dress, covered with sparkly fringes; and Lavinia a turquoise beaded flapper dress, covered with tiny crystals. Cassie felt wrong-footed again.

'You'll never guess what!' Daisy's mouth was full of meringue and little bits sprayed over the cake pyramid as she spoke.

'What?' asked Cassie, wearily. Fortnum's was noisy and hot and Daisy's excitement didn't feel the least bit infectious.

'Bernard Cavalier's getting married!'

'No!' Lavinia put down her tea cup with a clatter. 'Who's the lucky girl?'

She said *lucky* with a tinge of irony and the two girls let out tinkly laughs which made the teaspoons rattle. Cassie seemed quiet and Daisy was keen to include her in the joke.

'You remember Bernard, Cassie, you went to his exhibition and I think before that you met him on a train.'

'Oh yes. More tea, anyone?' Cassie lifted the pot and offered it to her two friends, but they waved it away and put their heads together.

'I know very little about her,' said Daisy, 'except that she's from Devon.'

'Devon!' exclaimed Lavinia. 'Is she even slightly modern?'

'Oh very. Apparently, she was his post lady while he stayed there.'

'No! His post lady – what a hoot!'

The ladies laughed again. Cassie was silent.

'Are you acquainted with her, Cassie?' Daisy asked. 'Evie someone?'

'I don't think so.' Cassie looked away and bit hard into a macaroon.

'Anyway, I have to confess I've known for a few days,' said Daisy.

'How come?' asked Lavinia.

'Toby told me.' Daisy's eyes sparkled.

Cassie, who seemed absorbed in something happening at the next table, didn't notice, but Lavinia made a mental note.

'He told me last week and swore me to secrecy, but it's safe to tell you now because it will be in *The Times* tomorrow.'

Cassie bit harder into her macaroon.

'The thing is,' Daisy was thrilled with her information and anxious to share it, 'Toby's offered to host it.'

'Host it?' Lavinia looked puzzled.

'The wedding!'

'Why?' asked Cassie, bluntly.

Daisy leaned forward conspiratorially, 'Well, I mean Bernard couldn't get married in Devon, could he?'

Lavinia shook her head in agreement.

'I didn't like his work much,' said Cassie suddenly.

'Whose work, darling?' asked Daisy.

'Cavalier's.'

'Really? I rather warmed to his new work, I liked his show.'

'When you finally got there.'

'So sorry I was late darling, really I am. I must have just missed you.'

'Well I thought his work was a bit strange. He's an acquired taste.' Cassie glanced at her watch. 'Heavens, is that the time? I must dash.' She smiled weakly at her friends. 'Sorry girls, same time next week?'

'I'll telephone,' said Lavinia.

Cassie smiled again, stood up and slowly made her way across the tea room. Daisy watched her go.

'Swimming through treacle,' she said, half to herself.

'Swimming or drowning?' asked Lavinia.

'Drowning. She took the news of Bernard's engagement very badly. Do you think she knows her?'

'Who?'

'The girl, silly. Evie.'

'If she does it's no excuse, she seemed really miffed. Perhaps she's jealous.'

'Perhaps.'

And have *you* met her?'

'Evie? Not yet. Toby says she's quite a beauty.'

'What a star Toby is these days!' Lavinia exclaimed. 'He used to be rather self-absorbed but suddenly – well, he seems rather sweet.' She glanced at her friend.

Daisy was squashing the meringue crumbs on her plate with her knife, a small smile playing around her mouth.

Post Script

82, Summerhill Road, Saffron Walden, Essex
Monday 25th October 1920

Dear Bernard,

Huge congratulations on your engagement! I saw a picture of you and your fiancée in Country Lives and wanted to write and offer you my very best wishes. I don't have a current address for you so I am sending this care of your gallery, at least I assume it's still your gallery, it would be foolish of them to part company with you after the success of your recent show. (I read all the reviews – marvellous!)

Your fiancée seems absolutely lovely. I can see she's just your type and I believe you will be very happy together. She looks beautiful and charming, but I have a feeling she shares just a little of your impulsiveness! Do let's try and have a reunion, I long to become her friend, and anyway there is someone I would like you both to meet. Oh yes, even Phoebe Carson has a bite on her line and is in the process of reeling in a delightful catch.

So, let's fix a date, in London please – I'm dying for a break from the vicarage.

In the meantime, my hearty congrats and best wishes,

Phoebe

About the Author

Liz teaches English and Creative Writing. She is also an art photographer and her love of images influences her writing. She is married with two children and lives in the Scottish Highlands, by the sea. *The Wrong Envelope* is her first novel.